THUNDER WAGON

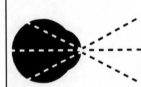

This Large Print Book carries the
Seal of Approval of N.A.V.H.

WIND RIVER SERIES

THUNDER WAGON

JAMES REASONER AND L. J. WASHBURN

THORNDIKE PRESS
A part of Gale, Cengage Learning

GALE
CENGAGE Learning·

Farmington Hills, Mich • San Francisco • New York • Waterville, Maine
Meriden, Conn • Mason, Ohio • Chicago

GALE
CENGAGE Learning·

LIBRARY OF CONGRESS CATALOGING-IN-PUBLICATION DATA

Names: Reasoner, James, author. | Washburn, L. J., author.
Title: Thunder wagon / by James Reasoner and L. J. Washburn.
Description: Waterville, Maine : Thorndike Press, 2016. | Series: Wind river series ;
 #2 | Series: Thorndike Press large print western
Identifiers: LCCN 2016023721| ISBN 9781410490810 (hardcover) | ISBN 1410490815
 (hardcover)
Subjects: LCSH: Large type books. | GSAFD: Western stories.
Classification: LCC PS3568.E2685 T48 2016 | DDC 813/.54—dc23
LC record available at https://lccn.loc.gov/2016023721

Published in 2016 by arrangement with James and Livia Reasoner

Printed in Mexico
2 3 4 5 6 7 21 20 19 18 17

For Link Hullar

1

The only thing certain about a peaceful night in the settlement of Wind River, Wyoming Territory, was that it wouldn't stay that way.

As marshal of the recently established town, Cole Tyler knew that as well as anyone. Which was why he was lounging in the doorway of his office with a frown on his face as he peered up and down Grenville Avenue, the main street. The sun had set a couple of hours earlier, and so far tonight Cole hadn't heard even a single gunshot from any of the town's many saloons. No screams, no angry shouts, no cries of murder or robbery.

"I don't like it," Cole announced.

There was a snort behind him. "Next thing, you'll be sayin' it's too quiet," commented Billy Casebolt, Cole's deputy. "You just ain't got a trustin' nature, Cole. Enjoy things while you can, 'stead of worryin' yourself sick over somethin' that ain't even goin' to happen."

Cole swung around. He was a medium-sized man, but there was nothing ordinary in the easy grace with which he moved, the strength in his broad shoulders, or the alert intelligence in his gray-green eyes. His clean-shaven features bore the deep tan of a man who has spent most of his life outdoors. Thick brown hair that had been hacked off squarely with the Green River knife sheathed on his left hip hung to his shoulders. A five-pointed star, his badge of office, was pinned to his buckskin shirt. Only a few months earlier, he had been a buffalo hunter working for the Union Pacific Railroad, providing meat for the hundreds of men in the UP's work crews who were laying tracks westward. It had been a rugged existence, to be sure, but there were times when he missed it. Back then, he had been responsible mainly for himself — not for a whole blasted town.

"You know how edgy the town's been since those rumors started about the Chinese," Cole said. "I'd sure as hell like to know who's been spreading them around."

Casebolt shrugged his bony shoulders. "Ain't no way of tellin' how things like that get started. But I don't believe it for a second. No, sir."

The deputy was sitting in the chair behind the marshal's desk. He had one run-down boot propped against the desk and was rocking the chair back and forth slightly. Considerably older than Cole, around fifty, Casebolt had been out here on the frontier for a long time and showed it. He was lean, almost gaunt, and his face was brown and seamed like old saddle leather. His thinning hair was iron gray. He wore a woolen work shirt and denim pants over a set of faded red long underwear. A former scout for the army — a job that Cole Tyler had also held at one time — Casebolt claimed to have been just about everywhere west of the Mississip'. . . and he had a story for every place he had visited.

He was just getting warmed up now. "I recollect one time I was down in Santa Fe, and there was a rumor that a whole bunch of Mex troops were on their way up the Rio Grande to take over the town. This was back when the United States and Mexico was still squabblin' over things mighty regularlike. Well, you never seen such. Folks runnin' around all over the place like chickens with their heads cut off. Nobody knew whether to fort up and try to fight off the invasion or cut and run and leave Santa Fe for the

Mexes. 'Course, there wasn't no invasion a'tall. The army ever'body claimed to've seen comin' turned out to be nothin' but a bunch of Mex pilgrims on their way up to the Sangre de Cristos for some sort o' religious ceremony. Talk about a bunch of folks who turned out to look mighty foolish when it was all said and done —"

The sudden crash of gunfire down the street interrupted Casebolt before he could wrap up his story. Startled by the sound, the deputy reared back in the leaning chair, and it almost fell. He had to windmill his arms frantically in order to keep his balance and bring the front legs of the chair back down on the plank floor with a crash.

"What in blazes!" he exclaimed.

Cole didn't bother answering. He was already strapping on the cartridge belt that had been hanging on a nail beside the doorway. The holster attached to the belt held a Colt .44 conversion model. As Cole buckled on the gunbelt he said, "Let's go. That sounded like it might've come from Parker's place."

Casebolt was on his feet. He was already wearing his handgun, a Griswold and Gunnison revolver like the ones carried by some members of the Confederate army during the war that had ended three and a half years earlier. Cole had never asked Casebolt if he'd fought in the Late Unpleasantness; that was behind them now, and the frontier had little patience for old grudges.

Both lawmen hurried out of the marshal's office, which was located in the front room of the Wind River Land Development Company. They turned east and broke into a trot on the boardwalk that bordered Grenville Avenue. The east end of town was where most of the saloons were concentrated, although it was possible to get a drink of whiskey in almost any quarter of the settlement.

The railhead of the Union Pacific had arrived in Wind River a few months earlier to find a settlement already waiting for the railroad. The town was the brainchild of a pair of land developers named Andrew McKay and William Durand; the probable construction of the railroad across this rugged section of southern Wyoming Territory was the very reason for the town's existence. McKay and Durand had intended Wind River to become a center of commerce for the entire Territory, serving not only the railroad but the vast cattle ranches that were being established.

That dream might still come true. Andrew McKay and William Durand were both dead, but McKay's widow, Simone, was carrying on in their place. She had inherited ownership of most of the settlement's real estate, and so far she had demonstrated a canny business sense.

When the first passenger train had pulled into the spanking-new Wind River station, it had brought with it the "hell on wheels," the portable collection of tent saloons, brothels, and gambling dens that moved from railhead to railhead with the progress of the railroad. Since then, more rails had been laid to the west of the settlement, but another railhead had yet to be established. It would be several more months before the Union Pacific's center of operations was transferred. Until then Wind River would continue to be clogged with railroad workers eager for entertainment after their long days of work. The saloons, both the temporary and the permanent, could be counted on to do a booming business.

And with that came trouble, Cole Tyler knew. A few hours of seeming peace didn't change things.

After that initial volley, there had not been any more shots. Angry shouts filled the night air, however, making it easy to locate the source of the disturbance. Just as Cole had thought, the commotion was coming from Hank Parker's big tent saloon.

Parker had decided to remain in Wind River, and the framework of a permanent building was going up on the lot next to his tent. Until the building was finished, however, he would continue doing business in the canvas tent. As Cole and Casebolt approached the entrance flaps two more shots rang out.

Cole palmed out his revolver as he slapped one of the canvas flaps aside and stepped into the saloon. The customers seemed to be divided into two roughly equal groups yelling at each other across the open space between them. Rolling around on the hard-packed ground in that clearing were three men while a fourth man danced around them with a gun in his hand, obviously looking for an opportunity to shoot. The three men on the ground were struggling fiercely, two of them trying to pin down the third. Cole didn't know whose side the man with the gun was on, and he didn't care. He just didn't want any more gunplay.

He stepped up behind the man waving the revolver in the air and brought down a chopping blow with his own gun. The barrel of the Colt crumpled the man's hat and thudded against his skull. He stumbled forward, tripped over the men already on

13

the ground, and went sprawling himself. The gun slipped out of his fingers.

Cole started to fire a couple of shots into the air in hopes of breaking up the fight, but then he remembered how the last time he had done that, Hank Parker had pitched a fit and demanded payment for the bullet holes in his tent. Instead of firing, Cole jammed the gun back in its holster and reached down to grab the collars of two of the men. Muscles bunched in his arms and shoulders under the buckskin shirt as he hauled the startled men to their feet and shoved them in opposite directions. They both tripped and fell again.

That left the other man on the ground; he reached for a knife at his belt, whipping it out with a snarl. Cole's booted foot lashed out, the toe connecting against the man's wrist with a crack. He let go of the knife, clutched his wrist, and howled in pain. Cole stepped back and slid his Colt out of leather again.

"That's it!" he shouted. "This fight is over!" Behind him, Casebolt also had his gun out and was covering the crowd.

Hank Parker came out from behind the bar and shouldered his way through the press of men to confront Cole. "Damn well about time you got here," he snapped.

"What were you waiting for, Marshal? Do you have to see this whole place torn down before you'll do anything?"

Cole kept his features carefully expressionless in the face of Parker's glowering accusations. There was bad blood between them, although circumstances had sometimes forced them to cooperate in the past. "Deputy Casebolt and I got here as fast as we could once we heard the shooting," Cole said coolly. "Doesn't look like there was too much damage."

"Well, there could have been," Parker replied sullenly. "One of these days, this tent's going to get pulled down around my ears while I'm waiting for you two to show up."

Despite his protests, Hank Parker looked capable of handling most kinds of trouble himself. He was tall and burly, with a bald, bullet-shaped head and an impressive spread of shoulders. He had only one arm, the left having been taken off in a blood-swamped field hospital near Shiloh meetinghouse during the war. The pinned-up sleeve did little to detract from the air of power surrounding the big saloonkeeper.

"All right, what started this ruckus?" Cole asked, adding wearily, "And why is it that so many of the fights in this town seem to start here, Parker?"

"That's not my fault, damn it," Parker said. "You don't think I want these bastards tearing up my place, do you?" He gestured curtly at the men sprawled around on the floor. "How do I know what started it? Somebody bumped somebody else and spilled a drink, or somebody said something and somebody else took offense. Bound to have been something like that. Hell, the whole town's so edgy I'm surprised they're not *all* trying to kill each other!"

Cole had already noticed that all four of the combatants looked like railroad workers. It wasn't unusual for members of the predominantly Irish section gangs to clash with cowboys from the ranches in the area; railroad workers and cowhands seemed to have a natural antipathy toward each other. Lately, though, there had been more fights than usual among the Irish themselves, and this was another example of that trend.

One of the men sitting on the ground pointed a finger at another man and said hotly, "This no-good ape said one Chinaman could do the work of four o' me!"

"Well, 'tis true!" shot back the second man. "If the UP brings in a bunch of the yellow heathens, I'll not have to worry about me job. But layabouts like you will, O'Shea!"

16

Cole exchanged a quick glance with Case-bolt. The Chinese rumors again, Cole thought. Ever since they had started, things had gotten more and more tense in Wind River.

Several years earlier, the Union Pacific and its chief rival, the Central Pacific, had begun construction on the proposed trans-continental railroad. The Union Pacific started in Omaha and built westward, their workers recruited primarily from the hordes of Irish immigrants that had come to the United States in the past fifteen years. The Central Pacific originated in Sacramento and came eastward with its rails, most of them laid and spiked into place by gangs of Chinese coolies who, despite their small stature, seemed to have an endless capacity for grueling physical labor. News of the suc-cesses the Chinese had accomplished in crossing the rugged Sierra Nevadas had spread throughout the country.

And now, word in Wind River had it that the Union Pacific was considering hiring Chinese to replace the Irish workers. The resulting tension and hard feelings were to be expected, Cole thought, but that didn't mean he had to like the situation.

"Shut up, all of you," he told the four men who had been fighting. They had continued their argument with words instead of fists and guns and knives, even with Cole and Casebolt standing there. "You're fighting about nothing, just because you're worried about your jobs. Hell, if I was General Dodge, I might fire you just for being so knotheaded!"

General Grenville Dodge — after whom the town's main street was named — was in charge of the Union Pacific's construction, ably assisted by his second-in-command, Jack Casement. Cole had met both men several times and knew them to be honest. The backers of both railroads might be pulling financial shenanigans back east and in California, but out here where the real work was going on, things were pretty straight-forward most of the time. That knowledge led Cole to continue, "If you're so worried about your jobs, why don't you just ask your bosses if you're going to be replaced by Chinese?"

"They'd just lie to us!" a man called from the crowd. "They don't know how to tell the truth! All they care about is gettin' the railroad built as quickly and as cheaply as possible!"

Cole didn't see anything wrong with that, but he didn't aggravate the situation by getting into the argument himself. Anyway, the

Union Pacific wasn't paying his wages anymore. The dealings of the railroad were no longer any of his concern, except as they concerned the town.

"What the railroad does is none of my business," he said loudly, "but what goes on in Wind River is, and there's not going to be any brawling here in town!" He looked at the men on the ground, one of whom was still groggy from the blow with the pistol. "I don't want to have to lock you boys up, but I will if I have to. We may not have a jail here in town yet, but we've got a mighty fine smokehouse that'll do for a hoosegow."

One of the men looked down and muttered, "You don't have to lock us up, Marshal."

Cole turned to Parker and asked, "How much will you need for the damages?"

Parker glanced around, and Cole could tell he was calculating just how much he could get away with demanding. If it was too exorbitant, he would make enemies of most of the men in here tonight. Finally, he decided to tell the truth. "They didn't really bust up anything except one bottle of whiskey. Six bits'll cover it."

"Pass the hat and ante up, boys," Cole told the brawlers. "It'll be a lot cheaper and easier than getting locked up."

Evidently they agreed with him, because a minute later one of the men was on his feet again, dropping coins from his own pocket and those of the others into Parker's outstretched palm. The man said, "We're sorry, Hank. Won't happen again."

"See that it doesn't," Parker growled.

Men were going back to their drinking and talking, and Cole sensed that this crisis — minor though it had been — was over. He holstered his gun and jerked his head at Casebolt, indicating that they should leave.

Casebolt followed Cole outside, and when they had left the smoke-thick air of the tent saloon, the deputy said, "Well, that didn't amount to much."

"It could've been a lot worse if those section hands weren't such piss-poor shots with a short gun," Cole said. "As crowded as Parker's place is, it was just pure luck somebody didn't get hit by one of those stray bullets."

"All I know is I'll be glad when all this business about Chinamen blows over."

"You and me both, Billy."

Cole looked around the street. There were wagons rolling along Grenville Avenue, as well as a few men on horseback, and the boardwalks still earned quite a bit of pedestrian traffic despite the late hour. Wind

River was a busy, crowded town, and it never really shut down each night until well after midnight. Some of the saloons even stayed open twenty-four hours a day, Parker's among them.

"As long as we're out and about, we might as well make the rounds," Cole suggested. "I'll take this side of the street."

Casebolt nodded and moved across to stroll down the opposite boardwalk, testing the doorknobs of businesses that had already closed for the night. Cole performed the same duty on his side of the street. As he neared the solid-looking, three-story edifice known as the Territorial House, Wind River's best hotel, another wagon passed him. Cole barely glanced at the vehicle, paying just enough attention to it to note that a man and a woman sat on the driver's seat while several other figures huddled in the back of the wagon. He stopped short, though, and looked again when he realized there had been something unusual about the people on that wagon.

As it pulled up in front of the Territorial House, light from the hotel's lobby spilled out through the big front windows, falling over the newly arrived wagon and its occupants. The driver hopped down lithely from the seat and turned to help the woman

21

get down. In the light from the hotel, Cole could plainly see the black, pajamalike garb the stranger wore, as well as the little cap on his head and the black hair braided into a pigtail that hung down over the back of his neck. The men who had been riding in the back of the wagon were getting out, too, and Cole could see that they were dressed like the driver and wore their hair the same way.

"Oh, hell," Cole whispered fervently. Despite Billy Casebolt's insistence that the rampant rumors were probably false, there were Chinese in Wind River.

Now, Cole thought in dismay, things were going to get *really* interesting. . . .

2

Ben Jessup heard the dogs barking and the commotion in his corral and knew something was after his stock again. Wolves had come down out of the mountains a couple of weeks earlier and gotten one of his milk cows, and he didn't want that to happen again. Only one of the remaining cows was dependable when it came to producing milk, and with youngsters in the house, milk was a necessity. The baby was still nursing, of course, but the other four children were too big for that.

Jessup rolled over on the thin mattress of straw ticking. His wife, Laverne, stirred restlessly beside him. Jessup sat up, reached over, and patted her reassuringly. He swung his legs out of the bed and winced as his feet touched the planks of the floor. At this altitude, even summer nights were sometimes cold. Tonight certainly was.

A stocky man with graying blond hair, he

stood up and moved carefully across the main room of the log-and-sod cabin. Not much starlight filtered in around the closed shutters and through the few remaining chinks in the walls. Jessup and Laverne had spent long hours plugging the chinks with mud, making the cabin as tight as possible for the winter that would arrive in a few months. Even autumn weather in the high country of Wyoming Territory could be brutal, or so Jessup had been told when he began preparing to move his family out here.

He didn't regret the decision, not for a minute. Life back in Omaha had been stifling. Jessup had never known anything except cramped rooms and a boring existence in a store clerk's apron. Out here a man could walk outside, look proudly at the fields he had planted, the crops he was going to harvest, and know that the air he pulled deep into his lungs smelled of freedom.

Of course, there were minor annoyances, like the wolves that sometimes raided the place and carried off chickens or, in the case of their last visit, pulled down a cow. But Jessup knew how to deal with them. He was already wearing his pants and his long underwear, so all he had to do was find his boots and stomp into them. Then he went to the entrance of the cabin and reached up for the Henry rifle hanging on pegs above the door. He kept it loaded, but the occasions for its use had been few so far in the two months since he and his family had arrived here. A couple of times, he had gone into the foothills with his oldest boy, eight-year-old young Ben, and shot a deer for fresh meat. The only other times the Henry had been fired were when Jessup was chasing off wolves, and he hadn't hit any of the fleeing gray shapes. Still, a few blasts from the rifle were usually enough to spook the wolves and make them run away. Jessup was confident tonight would be the same.

He lifted the latch on the door and pushed it open enough to step out. Pausing before he did so, he looked back over his shoulder and saw his children, nothing but vague shapes in the faint starlight as they slept on their pallets. Jessup didn't have to see them to know them, however. Young Ben there by the wall, with Hank beside him, and on the other side of the room Molly and Sadie. The cradle beside the bed shared by Jessup and Laverne, and the baby, little Matthew, lying there tucked in among the quilts Laverne had made. A smile tugged at Jessup's mouth for a second.

Then he turned and went to see what was

causing the commotion among the stock.

Lon Rogers leaned back in his bunk and gently strummed the strings of a guitar. He had never been much of a hand for playing, could barely pick out a tune on the guitar, in fact, but he liked to strum it while he was singing. He began to hum.

The bunkhouse of the Diamond S ranch, some ten miles northwest of the settlement of Wind River, was filled with the sound of men talking and laughing, punctuated by the slap of cards on a rough-hewn wooden table in the center of the big room as half a dozen punchers played poker. The talking gradually died away as Lon started to sing. Men turned to watch him, and even the card game was momentarily forgotten.

Lon sang of things they all knew: sagebrush, dust on the trail, lonely hours under the stars as they rode night herd. He sang about stampedes and young lives lost and girls left behind, long winters and short summers and hopes that faded too soon. But the words spoke, too, of blue skies and good horses, freedom and friendships that lasted. Some of the songs were old ones, others newly composed on the trail drive from Texas up here to the Wyoming Territory. Lon sang, and the others listened and were quiet.

As he finished a song and strummed the last rough chord on the guitar, a voice said gruffly from the doorway, "Mighty nice singin'. I wish you were as good with a rope and a brandin' iron as you are with that gee-tar, boy."

Lon looked up and saw Kermit Sawyer standing there with a shoulder leaned casually against the door frame. The old cattleman was smiling, and Lon knew the comment about his skill with a rope and a branding iron was more a matter of habit than anything else. Sawyer wasn't one to overpraise his hands — or anybody else, for that matter.

"Thanks, Mr. Sawyer. I'll try to do better at the brandin' next time."

Sawyer nodded. "You do that."

He was a husky man, a little thicker now around the middle than he had been in his youth, but still possessing an air of vigor that belied his years. His thick hair was as white as the snow on the peaks to the north. Time, wind, and sun had tanned and weathered his rugged features. He wore a black shirt and black trousers. Tonight, here at the headquarters of the ranch he had established, he wasn't wearing the pearl-handled revolver he usually carried, which was his only concession to any sort of fanciness. Everything else about Kermit Sawyer was strictly utilitarian.

An oldtime cattleman, Sawyer had left his ranch in Texas to his daughter and son-in-law following the death of his wife and decided to start over in Wyoming. Taking part of the vast herd he had built up over the years, as well as the more fiddle-footed members of his crew, he had started out on the long drive up the Western Trail, forging new trails of his own when the old one ran out. Sawyer had reached his destination only to get involved in the schemes of a crooked individual who had caused a great deal of trouble. That was over now, and the Diamond S was a thriving ranch, here in this high valley watered by a meandering creek.

The whole thing had been good for Sawyer, Lon knew. The haunted look that had been in his eyes for months after his wife's passing was almost gone now, at least most of the time. A new challenge had been exactly what Sawyer needed. And Wyoming was a challenge, no doubt about that.

"Frenchy," Sawyer said now to his foreman, "I want three men to ride up to the north range tomorrow and check out those draws. I got a feelin' some of the cows have been strayin' up in there, and I don't want 'em gettin' caught in that brush."

The foreman, a tall, lean, dark-complected man who hailed from New Orleans, nodded and said, "Sure, Mr. Sawyer. I'll go myself and take a couple of good men with me."

Sawyer grunted in acknowledgment and started to turn away. He paused in the doorway, however, and looked back. "Take Rogers with you," he told Frenchy. "Maybe if there's any cows stuck in those draws, he can sing 'em out."

Lon flushed, not sure whether to feel angry or embarrassed. Sawyer had a way of getting his goat. The old man hadn't even wanted to bring him along on the trip from Texas, Lon knew. But Lon had raised such a ruckus that Sawyer had finally caved in. Lon's widowed mother had cooked and kept house for the Sawyers for years, and she had stayed behind on the ranch in Texas. Lon knew that before the group bound for Wyoming Territory had left, his mother had extracted a promise from Sawyer to look after her son, and Lon had a feeling Sawyer resented that a little.

As far as Lon was concerned, he didn't want any special treatment. He had always carried his own weight, he told himself, and he wasn't going to start doing things different now. Sawyer would get that through his thick skull sooner or later.

"I'll be glad to go with you, Frenchy," Lon said. "If it's all the same to you, though, I reckon I'll leave my guitar here. Don't need it to chouse a few ol' steers out of a gully."

Frenchy glanced from Lon to Sawyer and back again, then grinned. "Whatever you say, kid."

Sawyer nodded curtly and left the bunkhouse. Lon relaxed in his bunk again and placed the guitar on the floor beside him, sliding it under the bunk so that it wouldn't get stepped on during the night. Morning would come early and the day would be a long one, he knew, so he rolled over with his face to the rough plank wall and closed his eyes.

That was when the distant popping sound of gunfire drifted in through the still-open door of the bunkhouse.

Lon rolled back over and sat up sharply. The other hands had heard the gunfire, too, and several of them stood up and started toward the door. Kermit Sawyer appeared there before any of them reached the opening. Grim-faced, the rancher said, "Sounds like trouble at one of those sodbusters' places, down on the flats."

"We goin' to take a look, boss?" asked

Frenchy.

Sawyer hesitated. "Ain't none of our business," he said after a moment. "And I'm sure as hell not anxious to start lookin' out after a bunch of farmers."

Lon stood up. "Those farmers have got families, at least most of 'em," he said.

Sawyer's cold blue eyes snapped over toward the young man. He said, "It was their decision to bring women and kids out here, not mine."

"Yes, sir, I know that —" Lon began, smarting somewhat under Sawyer's implied reprimand.

"Take half a dozen men and ride down there," Sawyer interrupted, looking at Frenchy. "Don't start swappin' lead with anybody if you can help it, though."

Frenchy nodded and reached for his gunbelt, which was coiled on his bunk.

"I'll go with you," Lon said as he stepped forward.

Frenchy looked at him and said dryly, "Somehow that don't surprise me. Don't forget your gun. You're liable to need it."

Somewhere far out there in the night, guns continued to crash.

Ben Jessup tried hard not to sob in fear. He wasn't frightened so much for himself. The hard knot of terror in his stomach was for his family.

He crouched just inside the open shed alongside the corral where his mules and cattle milled around nervously. From time to time he spotted one of the flitting shapes coming closer to the cabin, and when he did he threw a couple of shots at the vague target, knowing he was a lot more likely to miss than to hit anything. With each blast of the rifle, his fear grew. The Henry held fifteen shots, and he had already used eight of them. He didn't have any extra cartridges with him, either.

Jessup's breath came fast and harsh in his throat. He flinched as a gun went off somewhere in the darkness and the slug chewed splinters from the shed wall just above his head. His face stung as the splinters dug into his skin. He blinked and pawed at his eyes with one hand, not sure if any of the splinters had struck him there.

He heard the slap of running footsteps and forced his head back up. One of the raiders was headed straight for the front door of the cabin. Jessup jerked his rifle up to his shoulder, but before he could fire, the door opened a little and a shotgun went off with a dull, heavy roar. Flame geysered from the twin muzzles of the weapon. The man running toward the cabin was caught by the double charge of buckshot and flung backward like a rag doll.

Jessup wanted to shout exultantly. At least one of the bastards wouldn't live to raid again, and he had Laverne to thank for that. The shots had awakened her, and she had been ready with the family's scattergun when the Indian almost reached the house.

So far, Jessup hadn't gotten a good look at the raiders, but he was sure they were Indians. No one else would have any reason to attack this isolated farm.

When he bought the land from the McKay woman, she had assured him that the Indians in the area were peaceful. Shoshone, that was what Simone McKay had called them, Jessup recalled. There were rumored to be Sioux in the area, too, and they weren't so placid, from everything Jessup had heard. But the Sioux were supposed to have recently withdrawn farther north and east, leaving this vicinity to the Shoshone for the most part. And Jessup kept coming back to the fact that the Shoshone were supposed to be honoring the treaties they had signed with the white man's government.

Somebody ought to tell that to those savages running around his farm in the darkness, Jessup thought with a half-hysterical laugh. Maybe they just didn't know they were violating the treaties.

Sure. Jessup was really going to believe *that*. . . .

He had come out of the cabin some fifteen minutes earlier, expecting to see wolves trotting around the corral, and instead he had seen some shadowy shapes that definitely weren't wolves. They had been moving toward the corral gate, and Jessup figured out immediately that they intended to let his stock loose. He had called out, "Hey, there! Get away from that corral!"

And then one of the savages had *shot* at him.

Nobody had ever taken a shot at Jessup in all the years he lived in Omaha, but there was no mistaking the flash of fire and the explosion that split the night and the blood-curdling sound of a bullet whipping through the air within inches of his ear. Instinctively, he had fired back, then ran toward the shed because it was closer than the house. Now he wished he had retreated to the cabin. It would have given him a lot better cover for one thing, and for another he would be in a better position to defend his family.

Faintly, he heard scared crying coming from inside the cabin, and his heart felt like it was going to swell up and explode. Those were *his* kids in there, terrified out of their wits, and he had to do something to protect them. Maybe he could reason with the savages, he thought. They already knew where he was, so calling out to them wouldn't give away anything.

"Hey!" Jessup shouted. "Hey, listen to me! I don't know what you want, but you can have it! You want my stock, you're welcome to it! Just go away and leave us alone! We haven't hurt anybody!"

There was no reply except another shot that made Jessup crouch even lower.

"Please!" he cried. "Take what you want, just don't hurt us!"

It was too late for that, he sensed. One of the raiders had been killed by that shotgun blast, and for all he knew he had winged some more of them. They wouldn't go away until they had avenged the damage that had been done to them. He had heard enough gossip about bloodthirsty war parties of the red savages. They were all doomed, him and Laverne and the kids. . . .

Another figure darted through the starlight. Jessup raised up on his knees and tried to draw a bead on the running man. He squeezed off a shot, feeling the stock of the Henry kick back hard against his shoulder, then worked the lever to jack another shell into the chamber. The figure he had seen had gone to ground, and Jessup had no idea if he'd hit the man or not.

Something scraped in the dirt behind him.

As he started to spin around, warning bells going off in his brain, he knew he had overlooked a threat. They had kept him busy by running around the corral until one of them had a chance to sneak up on him. He let out a shout of fear and rage as he tried to bring the rifle around.

A strong hand came out of the shadows inside the shed, grabbed the barrel of the Henry, and wrenched it aside. At the same time, the raider stepped closer to Jessup and thrust out with his other hand. Jessup saw starlight flicker on the wide blade just before it buried itself in his belly.

He screamed. There wasn't much pain, just a spreading iciness in his middle as the knife was ripped one way, then the other, tearing through his guts. The raider ripped it free so that Jessup's insides could spill out behind it, then brought the blade forward again as Jessup stumbled forward. This time the luckless settler felt the point of the blade penetrate his chest and scrape gratingly on a rib. A white-hot explosion filled his body as the knife sliced into his heart. Jessup thought again of his wife and children, and then died.

It was merciful, in a way, because he didn't have to hear the boom of the shotgun and the rattle of rifle fire and the screams of his family as the raiders burst into the cabin and went about their grisly work. Nor did he smell the smoke or feel the heat of the flames a little later as the cabin burned fiercely, sending a garish red glow high in the night sky.

Frenchy, Lon, and the rest of the Diamond S punchers knew what to expect before they ever reached the farm. They had heard the shots and then seen the fire in the darkness, and Lon's heart was thudding in his chest as he rode into the small yard between the cabin and the shed and the corral. He hoped somebody had been left alive.

But he knew that wasn't likely, and it didn't take long for the cowboys to prove that fear correct.

The fire had died down, leaving what had once been a sturdy cabin nothing but a smoking, smoldering heap of rubble. The flames hadn't spread to the shed and the corral, which was empty; whatever stock had been inside the pole fence had been driven off by the men responsible for this atrocity. A dark shape lay huddled in front of the shed. Frenchy dismounted while the rest of the hands stayed on their horses, rifles held ready for use. The Diamond S foreman turned the man over, grunted, stood up.

"Dead," Frenchy said. "They gutted him good."

There was a horrible smell lingering in the air, something more than woodsmoke. Lon shuddered as he realized how much the smell reminded him of branding time. He called out, "Frenchy . . . in the cabin . . ."

"I expect we'll find the rest of this poor devil's family," Frenchy said. "It'll probably be morning before things cool off enough in there for us to be sure. We can get started on the buryin' then."

One of the other hands spoke up. "Somebody better ride back to the ranch and tell the boss what happened."

Frenchy nodded. "Yeah," he agreed. "And if the Indians have started raidin' around here, I reckon the folks in town need to know." He looked up at the horsemen. "Lon, you feel up to ridin' into Wind River?"

"Sure, Frenchy," Lon answered without hesitation. For one thing, the chore would get him away from that smell.

"Find that marshal and tell him about it. He don't have any jurisdiction out here, but he's about all the law there is in this part of the country right now. I figure he'll want to wire the army and let them know what happened out here, too."

"You think it was them Shoshone who done this, Frenchy?" asked another man.

"Don't know who else it could've been." Frenchy looked at Lon. "Go on now, kid. But keep your eyes and ears open and ride careful. You don't want to run into the bunch what did this."

"No, sir," Lon muttered. "I sure don't."

He turned his horse and heeled it into a trot that carried him rapidly away from the burned-out farm. He knew he could find the trail to Wind River even in the darkness, so that wasn't worrying him.

But as he rode he asked himself what kind of men could slaughter an innocent family like the one back there at that farm. Lon felt cold inside, colder than the night air around him.

And the chill grew as he realized he had no answer to the question he had asked himself.

3

Cole started toward the Chinese as they clustered together on the boardwalk in front of the Territorial House. Before he could reach them, a shout came from across the street.

"Hey! There's a bunch of those damned Chinamen now!"

Cole saw half a dozen men standing on the opposite boardwalk and looking at the newcomers to Wind River. None of them appeared to be very happy, either. Casebolt was a couple of doors down the street on that side, and Cole called to him, "Billy!" When the deputy looked over, Cole gestured toward the group of men. Casebolt started toward them.

The deputy was too late. Already the men were stalking out into the street, heading for the Territorial House. From their clothes, Cole judged them to be railroad workers, which made them among the last people he would have preferred to witness the arrival of the Chinese.

Casebolt stepped down off the boardwalk after them and said, "Here now, hold on, you fellers —"

They ignored him and began shouting curses at the foreigners. Quickly, Cole moved to put himself between the Chinese and the railroad workers. He rested his right hand on the butt of his revolver and raised the left.

"Hold it!" he told the railroad men. "Whatever you boys are thinking about doing, you'd better just move on and forget about it. There's not going to be any trouble here."

The men stopped, but they didn't look any less angry. One of them said, "Stay out of this, Marshal. It ain't any of your business."

"The hell it's not," Cole shot back coldly. "You were planning to jump these people, and don't waste your breath and my time denying it."

Another man pointed at the Chinese, his finger shaking from the fury that gripped him. "Look at 'em!" he demanded. "They're just a bunch of yellow heathens, come here to take the bread out of the mouths of white men! How can you stand there and protect 'em and call yourself a lawman, Tyler?"

Cole forced down the anger welling up inside him. "We don't know how come they're here," he said, trying to sound reasonable, "and anyway, I told you to move along."

Billy Casebolt added from behind the railroad men, "You'd best do what the marshal says, fellers." He had his own gun drawn, and the workers looked uneasily over their shoulders at him. If push came to shove, the two lawmen had them in a cross fire, and they knew it.

Cole could see their anger and the desire to cause trouble fading in their eyes, but before it had a chance to go away completely, a new voice said stridently, "We are not afraid! You will please to move, Marshal. We will fight our own battles."

Surprised, Cole glanced behind him and saw one of the young men who had been riding in the back of the wagon. He had stepped forward, a little apart from the others, and was ignoring the older man plucking at the sleeve of his tunic. His smooth features were set in taut lines, and his dark eyes blazed with emotion.

"Take it easy, son," Cole told him. "It's my job to handle things like —"

He didn't get to finish his sentence. The

young man's hand made a quick move, and steel shone in his grip. He brandished the dagger and exclaimed, "We can take care of ourselves!"

One of the railroad men yelled, "The Chinaman's got a knife! He's tryin' to stab the marshal!"

Cole knew that wasn't true; the young man's dagger was nowhere near him. But that didn't stop the deep-throated shouts of rage that came from several of the railroad men as they charged forward. Cole twisted to the side as he drew his gun, but before he could bring it to bear, one of the men crashed into him, knocking him aside. "I'll save you, Marshal!" the man yelled.

Cole knew better. They were just using the sudden appearance of the knife as an excuse to stampede past him and attack the Chinese. "Stop it, you fools!" he called. Casebolt shouted at them, too, but they ignored him as well.

More knives had appeared in the hands of the young Chinese men. They looked frightened but determined as they moved to protect the older man and woman, drawing themselves into a ring around their elders.

The railroad men were too infuriated by the very presence of the Chinese in Wind River to be thinking too straight — or worrying about knives. After weeks of rumors about how the Chinese were going to come in and take over the jobs of the Union Pacific work crews, nobody was in any mood to stop and think.

Instead, they just attacked.

One of the workers swung a big fist at the young man who had spoken. The Chinese youth ducked under the blow easily and lashed out with the knife. The railroad man let out a howl of pain and jerked back, clutching his arm. Blood welled up between his fingers.

A few feet away on the boardwalk, another one of the Chinese wasn't fast enough to avoid a punch. A railroad man's fist crashed into his face and rocked him back, so that his feet got tangled with those of a couple of his companions. Two of the Chinese lost their balance and went to their knees. A railroad man kicked one of them in the chest and sent him sprawling.

The older man and woman were shouting rapidly and excitedly in their native tongue as the fracas ebbed and flowed around them. Cole didn't understand any of the words, but he could tell how agitated the couple were. He wondered if the young men were their sons. Not that it mattered right now; the important thing was to break up this fight before it got any worse.

Cole had drawn his gun instinctively. Now he shoved it back in its holster and reached out to grab the shoulders of one of the railroad men. He jerked the burly Irishman around and slammed a hard right cross against his jaw. The punch staggered the railroad man but didn't send him down. The man caught his balance, grated a curse, and lunged at Cole, wrapping both arms around him in a bear hug. The momentum of the charge carried both men off the boardwalk and sent them crashing into the dust of the street.

His breath knocked out of him by the fall, Cole gasped for air and at the same time got the heel of one hand underneath his opponent's chin. He forced the man's head back until there was no choice but to release Cole. The marshal rolled away and surged to his feet, his chest still heaving. He was ready when the railroad man started up. A right and a left sent the man tumbling backward again.

On the boardwalk, Billy Casebolt was also struggling with one of the railroad workers. There was a lot more wiry strength in Casebolt than his scrawny frame would indicate. He had his left arm looped around the man's neck from behind and was using his right to drive punches into the side of the man's head. The railroad worker suddenly bent over almost double, however, taking Casebolt with him. The man reached back, grabbed the deputy's shirt, and heaved as hard as he could. Casebolt found himself flying through the air for a dizzying instant before landing with stunning force on the boardwalk. A foot slammed into his side in a vicious kick before he could get out of the way.

Due to the involvement of the lawmen in the battle, the odds had shifted enough so that the young Chinese men were holding their own against the other railroad workers. Another of the Irishmen was bleeding from a knife slash by now, and as they were forced back one of them reached into his pocket and brought out a short-barreled Smith & Wesson revolver.

Cole was turning away from the man he had just knocked out when he saw the lamplight from the hotel shine on the barrel of the pocket pistol. The railroad worker was lifting the gun toward the Chinese men, his face contorted by hate as he prepared to fire. Cole's .44 leaped into his hand and roared first, and the railroad man yelped in pain as the slug burned across his forearm. The Smith & Wesson slipped from his fingers as he stumbled backward and grabbed his bullet-creased arm.

Spotting Casebolt on the boardwalk about to get stomped by another of the railroad men, Cole leveled the revolver and eared back the hammer. "Back off, mister!" he ordered loudly.

"Better do it, Feeney," advised the man Cole had just wounded. His voice was thick with pain. "The son of a bitch creased me, and it was mighty slick shootin'."

"I was aiming to break the bone," Cole told him curtly. "But next time I won't miss."

The man looming over Casebolt slowly lowered his foot and stepped back. He scowled at Cole as he moved over to join the other railroad workers. Cole kept them covered while Casebolt climbed to his feet, punched his hat back into some semblance of its original shape, and settled it on his sparse gray hair. The deputy winced a little every time he moved, and Cole figured he had some bruised ribs, at the very least.

"You all right, Billy?" he asked.

Casebolt nodded. "I will be, soon's we get these here varmints in jail."

"Jail?" one of the men exclaimed. "What the hell for?"

"Disturbing the peace and assaulting an

officer of the law, for starters," Cole said. "Maybe attempted murder. You meant to kill these folks when you jumped them, didn't you?"

"We just wanted to hand 'em a good beatin' so they'd leave these parts and never come back," one of the men replied sullenly. "It ain't fair we have to go to jail just for defendin' our own rights!"

A crowd was beginning to gather, drawn by the gunshot and the preceding commotion. Quite a few of them were railroad men, and mutters of agreement came from them. Cole glanced around but didn't see too many friendly faces. None, in fact. The crowd had the makings of a mob, he sensed, and this disturbance could turn into a full-fledged riot if he wasn't careful. He spotted the men who had been fighting in Hank Parker's tent saloon earlier, and they added their voices to the growing shouts of disapproval.

Cole exchanged a glance with Casebolt, who swallowed hard. The deputy had drawn his gun again, but two guns against thirty or forty angry men wouldn't amount to much. Still, Cole wasn't in the habit of letting anybody buffalo him, even if he *was* outnumbered.

"What's going on out here?"

The new voice cut through the clamor and got everyone's attention immediately because it was female. An attractive woman whose thick dark hair fell to her shoulders strode out of the hotel and looked around at the people gathered on the boardwalk and in the street. She wore a dark blue gown that was elegant in its simplicity. There was a touch of imperiousness in her attitude as she folded her arms, arched a curved eyebrow, and waited for an answer to her question.

"You shouldn't be out here right now, Mrs. McKay," Cole said. Reluctantly, he moved his gaze away from her and back to the railroad workers who had been fighting with the Chinese.

"I heard a shot right in front of my hotel," Simone McKay said. "Naturally I'm going to investigate." There was no fear in her eyes, but perhaps a little uneasiness appeared in them as she surveyed the hostile crowd.

Following the deaths of both her husband and his partner, Simone had inherited everything that had been established by Andrew McKay and William Durand. She owned the hotel, the general store, the newspaper, and practically all of the land on which Wind River was built. Some of the

49

businesses merely rented the buildings where they were housed, while Simone held the notes on other merchants. She was a very rich woman.

But none of that would ever bring back the husband she had lost, Cole knew, and he was aware that Simone was still in mourning for Andrew McKay. With each week that passed, however, he saw more life returning to her eyes, more animation creeping back into her lovely features. One of these days, she was going to be ready to have a man in her life again. Cole hadn't given that time much thought, but in the back of his mind, he knew it was coming.

At the moment he was more concerned with keeping Simone out of the middle of the trouble threatening to break loose. She was in no mood to be kept out, however. When Cole hesitated in answering her question, she turned to Casebolt and demanded, "Well? What about you, Deputy? Can you tell me what's happening out here?"

"Uh . . . well, ma'am, some of these fellers were a mite upset with those Celestial folks there —"

Simone swung toward the Chinese as if noticing them for the first time. "Is one of you named Wang Po?" she asked.

The older man stepped forward. He

clasped his hands together in front of him, bowed slightly, and said in excellent English, "I am called Wang Po. And you are Mrs. McKay?"

"That's right. I wasn't expecting you and your family for another few days. You made good time on your journey."

Cole stared at Simone for a few seconds, then said, "Wait a minute. You know these folks, Mrs. McKay?"

"Of course I do," replied Simone. "I sent for them."

The crowd had fallen silent during the exchange, their curiosity getting the better of their anger. Now one of the men called out, "We thought they came here to work on the railroad."

"Hardly," Simone said, raising her voice a little so that everyone could hear her. "I've hired Wang Po and his family to work here in the hotel."

"They're not going to lay track for the Union Pacific?" Cole asked, as surprised as everyone else. Even though he had been defending the Chinese from the angry railroad workers, he had leaped to the same conclusion about why they were here in Wind River.

"Certainly not. What makes you believe that's why they came here?" Simone wanted

51

to know.

"Well, the Central Pacific uses coolies for work crews," Cole began.

"I beg your pardon, Marshal," Wang Po cut in, "but we are not coolies."

"Of course not," Simone said. "I've hired Wang Po and his wife to be my cooks, and their sons will help out around the hotel. There are plenty of chores that need doing."

Another man in the crowd called out, "Cooks? You expect a Chinaman to cook for *white* folks? Hell, those heathens don't even eat the same things we do!"

Before Simone could answer, Wang Po himself looked at the man who had protested and said, "I cooked in a hash house in San Francisco for several years after my family and I came to this country during the Gold Rush. After that I was the cook for a ranch in the San Joaquin Valley. I can fry up the best steak you've ever eaten, my friend, and my biscuits will melt in your mouth. If you want tortillas and enchiladas, I can do that, too. And my coffee will put hair on your chest." Wang Po regarded the man serenely and added, "That seems to be a commodity you could do with a bit more of."

"What'd he say?" the railroader demanded, but the question was drowned out by laughter from some of the others in the crowd.

Billy Casebolt edged forward. "You know, all this talk reminds me that I ain't had supper yet. You reckon you could whip somethin' up this evenin', Mr. Po?"

"Most assuredly," the Chinese man replied. "That is, if Mrs. McKay here will kindly show me to the hotel's kitchen . . . ?"

"Of course," Simone said warmly. "You and your family come inside. I've had quarters prepared for all of you."

"Wait just a damned minute!" called out one of the men in the crowd as Simone, Casebolt, and the Chinese turned toward the front door of the hotel. As the bystanders looked at him he went on, "If you believe that story, you're nothing but a bunch of damn fools! They came here to work on the railroad. There ain't enough chores around the hotel to keep half a dozen able-bodied men busy!"

Cole had thought of that himself, but he didn't want to lose the progress that had been made toward heading off a riot. He said sharply, "You'd better think about what you're saying, mister. You just called Mrs. McKay a liar."

That charge brought a few angry mutters

53

from the crowd. The railroad men had no particular reason to be fond of Simone, but they subscribed to the same rough code that most men on the frontier followed, and that included respecting women — any and all women, as long as they were decent.

The man who had objected now grimaced. "Hell, I didn't mean to do that. It just don't make sense to me, that's all."

"Mrs. McKay doesn't have to explain herself," Cole snapped. At least, he added silently to himself, she didn't have to explain herself to a bunch of troublemakers in the street. But later on, as soon as he got a chance to talk to her privately, he wanted some answers to his own questions. As the law in Wind River, it was his right to know what was going on in town.

Cole turned to Simone. "Go ahead and take your new help inside, ma'am." He wanted the Chinese off the street and out of sight, where they wouldn't stir up so much commotion.

Simone gave him a quick smile, then led Wang Po and his family into the hotel. Casebolt started to follow, intent on sampling the work of the hotel's new cook, but Cole called him back. "We've still got our rounds to finish up," he reminded the deputy. He had decided not to press charges against the men who had tried to attack the Chinese. With the crowd in a better mood now, he wanted to keep it that way.

"Yeah, I reckon you're right," Casebolt said reluctantly. "Maybe the dinin' room'll still be open time we get finished."

Some of the men in the street were beginning to drift away now. Obviously, there wasn't going to be any more violence, and the lure of the saloons was too strong to be resisted for very long. Cole watched the crowd break up and was glad things hadn't gotten any worse. For a few minutes there, they had been plenty bad enough.

The sudden sound of running hoofbeats made him swing around again. A man on horseback turned a corner down the street and rode toward the marshal's office. Before the rider got there, he spotted the men in front of the hotel and veered his mount in that direction. "Anybody seen the marshal?" he called out.

Cole stepped down off the boardwalk and strode forward to meet the rider, who was hauling his tired horse to a halt. The animal was sweating and its sides were heaving. It had been run hard, and that was usually a sign of trouble.

"I'm right here," Cole said. In the light from the hotel, he recognized the rider as one of the hands from Kermit Sawyer's Diamond S ranch north of town. Cole recalled the young cowboy's name and asked, "What's wrong, Rogers?"

Lon Rogers took off his hat and sleeved sweat and dust from his face. His young features were grim as he said, "There was trouble at one of those farms between here and the ranch, Marshal. Looks like Indians hit the place."

Cole's jaw tightened. "Anybody hurt?" he asked, although he was afraid he already knew the answer.

"The sodbuster was killed, and the cabin was burned down. Frenchy — that's our foreman — he said he figured the rest of the fella's family was inside the cabin." Lon shook his head. "I don't reckon there was anybody left alive, Marshal."

"I'll ride out and take a look anyway," Cole decided. "Did you leave anybody at the farm?"

"Yes, sir, Frenchy and some of the boys are still there. He sent a man back to the ranch to tell Mr. Sawyer what happened, and I came on to town to bring the word. The Shoshones must be going on the warpath."

A startled-looking Casebolt spoke up. "Shoot, they wouldn't do that! I know ol'

Two Ponies, their chief. Him and his people helped me out one time. Saved my life, they did. They're peaceable folks."

"Sometimes things change," Cole said. "You stay here and keep an eye on things in town, Billy. Hate to leave you here alone with everything that's going on, but I better take a look at what happened out at that farm."

"Sure, you go ahead, Marshal. But I can tell you now, the Shoshones ain't to blame."

"We'll see," Cole said as he started toward the livery stable to saddle his horse. He was doubtful, but he hoped Casebolt was right.

With all the tension gripping Wind River over the Chinese situation, the last thing he needed to deal with right now was an Indian uprising.

4

It didn't take long for Cole to saddle up Ulysses, the big golden sorrel he kept stabled at the livery down the street from the hotel and the marshal's office. Lon Rogers's horse was all done in, but at Cole's request, the stable owner allowed the young cowboy to pick out another mount. The next time he was in town, Lon could return the borrowed horse and pick up his own.

Side by side, Cole and Lon rode out of Wind River, angling a little west of north. There was a trail leading to the Diamond S. At first it had been little more than an old game trace, but in the past few months there had been enough traffic over it to widen it and beat down the grass even more. Sawyer's cowboys headed straight for town every time payday rolled around.

"Were you able to hear the shooting when the raiders hit the farm?" Cole asked as the horses trotted across the plains under a brightly starlit night sky.

Lon replied, "We heard it, all right. That's how come Mr. Sawyer sent some of us down there to check it out."

"Could you tell what sort of guns were being fired?"

"Sounded to me like rifles, and that's the best I could do," Lon answered with a shake of his head. "The place is a pretty good ways off from the ranch, you understand, Marshal."

Cole nodded. He knew that quite a few farms were springing up on the rolling prairie between the railroad and the mountains to the north. In the distance, he could see some dark shapes along the horizon that he knew were bluffs and foothills. In some places, those rugged foothills would be considered mountains by themselves, but here in Wyoming Territory, the real mountains were farther north and west.

Since the marshal's office was in the front room of the Wind River Land Development Company, he could hardly fail to be aware of the business Simone McKay was doing. Andrew McKay and William Durand had bought up a great deal of land in this area prior to the arrival of the railroad, and now Simone was selling off some of it to settlers from back east who were anxious to make new starts for themselves and their families here in the vastness of the West. Cole could understand the appeal of that. He had done a great deal of wandering himself, from the Rio Grande down south to the Milk River up in Montana. He had seen the plains and the deserts and the mountains with their snowy peaks and thickly forested flanks. He had stood on a cliff and watched the Pacific Ocean roll in on rocky beaches in Oregon. Even though he had settled down in a town — for the moment — he knew the powerful lure of the frontier as well as any man.

But he had ridden alone for the most part, or with partners just as capable of taking care of themselves as he was. He hadn't brought loved ones, women and children, into a country that for all its beauty and majesty could turn deadly dangerous in the blink of an eye. Simone had the right to sell the land as she saw fit, of course, but Cole had to wonder about the wisdom of establishing a lot of nearly defenseless farms in this area.

It took about an hour to reach the site of the massacre. Lon had covered the ground in less time on his way into town, but there was no hurry now. As the two men rode up to what was left of the farm, Frenchy and the other Diamond S hands stood up from where they had been hunkered on their heels beside the corral, rolling and smoking quirlies to pass the time.

"Howdy, Marshal," Frenchy called out. "Thought you might want to take a look at this. That's why I sent Lon into town."

"Thanks," Cole said as he swung down from the saddle. "That was good thinking. If Indians were responsible for this attack, I ought to notify the army, I reckon."

"Don't know who else it could've been 'cept redskins," Frenchy drawled.

Cole spotted another figure, this one standing closer to the burned-out cabin, hands on hips. The man turned around at the sound of Cole's voice and strode over toward the shed. Cole recognized him as Kermit Sawyer.

"Haven't seen anything like this since the Comanch' were raidin' down home," the Texas cattleman said grimly. "What are you goin' to do to put a stop to this, Tyler?"

Cole felt himself bristling and made an effort to control the instinctive antagonism he felt toward Sawyer. The rancher was arrogant and abrasive and about as mule-headed an individual as Cole had ever run across, but he had to admit that Sawyer had a right to be upset about what had happened here. The man had a ranch, a crew, and a lot of stock to think of.

"Like I was telling your segundo here, I'll wire the army and let them know what happened. That's about all I can do, except for maybe paying a visit to the other farmers around here and warning them to keep their eyes open."

Sawyer snorted contemptuously. "Damn little good that'll do," he said. "Those sodbusters keepin' their eyes open won't accomplish anything except lettin' 'em see the savage that's about to scalp them!"

"This fella here wasn't scalped," Frenchy commented as he pointed toward a dark shape on the ground just under the roof of the shed.

Cole walked over to the corpse and knelt beside it. The man was in the shadow, so Cole couldn't tell much about him, but he could see that Frenchy was right. The farmer still had his hair.

"Somebody took a knife to him," Frenchy went on. "Mighty ugly way to die."

"There aren't any pretty ones," Cole grunted as he straightened from his crouch.

Sawyer stalked over. "Wirin' the army's not enough," he snapped. "I want a stop put to this."

"What do you expect me to do? Go to war against the Shoshone with nobody but one deputy to back me up? Besides, my job is to keep the peace in Wind River, not to fight Indians. I've done enough of that already."

"Yeah, I'd forgotten," Sawyer said sarcastically. "Did some scoutin' for the bluecoats, didn't you, Tyler? Why'd you give it up? Decide you felt sorry for those savages?"

Once again Cole had to swallow an angry retort. "There was more money to be made shooting buffalo for the Union Pacific. Not that it's any of your business, Sawyer."

"I'm makin' it my business," the rancher said, moving a step closer to Cole. "I know all about men like you, Tyler. You're about half-Indian yourself. You live with 'em and rut with their squaws —"

Cole tensed, unable to control his anger any longer. "I don't have to stand here and listen to you run off at the mouth, Sawyer. I'm riding back to town." He turned on his heel and started to walk away.

"Go ahead. We'll handle this ourselves. The Comanch' never could run me off my land down in Texas, and I'll be damned if I let a bunch of pissant redskins like the Shoshone scare me up here!"

Cole looked back sharply at him. "What do you mean by that?"

"I mean if you see a mountain lion standin' on a rock, you're a damn fool if you wait until he jumps to take a shot at him."

Cole turned around and walked up to Sawyer, well aware that he was surrounded by Texas cowboys who would likely charge hell with a bucket of water if they thought the devil was giving their boss any trouble. But he wasn't going to stand by and let Sawyer make a lot of threats that could cause more trouble for everybody in this part of the country.

"You'd best steer clear of the Shoshones, Sawyer," Cole said. "You go attacking a bunch of Indians who may not be guilty of this raid, and you'll have to deal not only with the Shoshones but the army, too. They don't like anybody messing around in their bailiwick."

Sawyer cleared his throat and spat. "I'm about as scared of the army as I am of a bunch of feather-wearin' savages."

"Then you're more addle-brained than I thought."

For a second Cole thought Sawyer was going to reach for that ivory-handled pistol on his hip. Then the rancher barked a short, humorless laugh and said, "Go on back to town, Marshal. Mind your own business. We'll tend to things here, give these folks a proper buryin'."

"You do that. But don't forget, Sawyer —

I'll be around."

Cole turned and walked back to Ulysses, feeling the hard-eyed stares of the cowboys on him. Sawyer's crew was a salty bunch, all right, and if it came down to a fight between them and the Shoshones led by Two Ponies, Cole wasn't sure who he would put his money on. The problem was that the whole thing wouldn't end there. That would just be the beginning. The ending would be anybody's guess.

But Cole was willing to bet that it would involve fire and blood, and a whole lot of innocent folks dying. . . .

Wind River had settled down for the night — at least as much as it ever settled down — by the time Cole got back to town. He put Ulysses in the sorrel's regular stall at the stable without disturbing the owner, who slept in a small room in the back of the barn. Then he headed down the street to the marshal's office.

Billy Casebolt was there, waiting for him and holding down the fort in the meantime. The deputy started to get up from the chair behind the desk, but Cole waved him back into it. "Keep your seat, Billy," he said. "I'm not staying long. I just wanted to find out if any more trouble cropped up while I was gone."

"Not really," Casebolt replied as Cole perched a hip on a corner of the desk. "I figure it's just a matter of time, though. Folks are still talkin' about them Chinamen, and they ain't happy."

"Mrs. McKay explained why Wang Po and his family came here."

Casebolt shook his head dubiously. "Yeah, but I don't reckon there's more'n a few people who believe that explanation. They still think there's more Chinamen on the way to take all the jobs on the Union Pacific."

"Well, I intend to have a talk with Mrs. McKay myself and make sure there's not anything she forgot to mention. I think I'll go on over there tonight."

With a frown, Casebolt drew a watch from his pocket and flipped it open. "Sort of late to go callin' on a lady," he commented.

"Maybe so, but I'm going to take a *pasear* over to her house anyway."

"Before you go, Cole . . . what'd you find out at that farm?"

"Just what that cowboy said," Cole replied bleakly. "There was a dead man lying by the shed, and the cabin was burned down. I reckon the rest of the family was in there.

Sawyer and some of his men were there, and they were going to stay until morning. The ashes ought to be cool enough by then for them to find the bodies and give them a decent burial."

"You see any arrows or lances layin' around, anything like that?"

Cole shook his head. "The dead man I saw was killed with a knife. Rogers said there was a lot of shooting, so I suppose the raiders were armed with rifles." He paused, then asked, "Two Ponies' band has some rifles, don't they?"

"Yeah," Casebolt said grudgingly. "Mostly old trade muskets. They ain't got their hands on many repeaters yet."

"That you know of."

Casebolt shrugged.

"I'm not saying I believe the Shoshones are to blame for those killings," Cole said as he stood up. "But all that farmer's stock was gone, and the cabin was burned down. Those don't sound like things white men would do."

"Some owlhoots like to tear down ever'thing they can get their hands on," Casebolt muttered.

"True enough. But I intend to ride out there again in the morning when there's some light so that I can take a look at the

67

tracks around the place. That is, if Sawyer and his bunch haven't trampled them all out by then."

"I'll go with you," Casebolt volunteered.

"We'll see," Cole told him. "You going to sleep on the cot in the back tonight?"

Casebolt nodded. "Sure."

"I'll see you in the morning, then."

Cole left the office and turned toward the western end of town. He was tired and thought fondly of the bed in the room he rented in the boardinghouse owned by Lawton and Abigail Paine. But sleep could wait. He still wanted some answers from Simone McKay.

Simone lived in a large house at the end of Sweetwater Street, on the western edge of the settlement. The McKay house — mansion was more like it — was at the southern end of the cross street, while William Durand's house was at the northern end. Durand's place was sitting empty at the moment. For a time following her husband's death, Simone had moved into the Territorial House, preferring the imper- sonal atmosphere of the hotel to the house that Andrew McKay had built for her. But now she was living full-time in the mansion again, and Cole could see lights burning in a couple of the upstairs windows as he turned the corner from Grenville Avenue onto Sweetwater Street.

The house was a two-story stone structure with a mansard roof and three gables arrayed along the front, giving it the look of a dwelling that might have been found in New England somewhere, rather than right in the middle of what had been wilderness less than a year earlier. Several cottonwood trees had been planted around the house, but it would take time for them to attain much height. There was a wrought-iron fence around a lawn that was struggling to survive in this rather dry climate. The gate in the fence was open, and Cole went through it and up a walk made of flat stones that led to a wide veranda. A small lamp in a brass wall sconce next to the front door was lit. The door itself was hardwood, ornately carved in places and inlaid with designs of gold in others. Cole grasped a brass bellpull and tugged on it.

The door was thick enough that he couldn't hear the bell ringing inside, but a few moments after he released the pull, the door swung open and a middle-aged woman he knew to be Simone's housekeeper stood there, a disapproving scowl on her heavy-featured face. The glare lessened only a little in intensity as the woman recognized him.

"Oh, it's you, Marshal," she said. "Is there some sort of trouble?"

"Not really, but I need to talk to Mrs. McKay for a few minutes," Cole replied. "Would that be possible?"

The housekeeper's frown deepened. "Miz McKay's already retired for the evenin' —" she began.

A clear voice floated down from upstairs somewhere. "Who is it, Esmeralda?"

The housekeeper turned, and Cole took advantage of the opportunity to step past her into the foyer of the house. "It's Marshal Tyler, Mrs. McKay," he called. "Can I speak with you?"

Simone appeared at the top of a curving staircase, a dark green silk robe belted around her trim waist. She smiled down at Cole and said, "of course, Marshal. I'll be right down. Esmeralda, take Marshal Tyler into the parlor and make him comfortable. Some coffee, perhaps."

"No, thanks," Cole said with a shake of his head as the housekeeper led him into a parlor full of fine furniture, thick rugs, and paintings. A massive fireplace, complete with an oak mantel, dominated one side of the room.

The housekeeper told him to sit down. Cole glanced around and spotted an armchair that didn't look like it was so fragile it would collapse underneath him. The legs of some of the other furniture seemed awfully spindly. The housekeeper asked, "Sure you won't have some coffee?" and he shook his head again. With that, she left the parlor, and Simone McKay swept into the room some thirty seconds later.

She sat down on a small divan across from Cole and asked, "What can I do for you, Marshal?"

"Was there any more trouble about those Chinese folks after you took them in the hotel?" he asked.

"Of course not. Why should there have been trouble?"

Cole shrugged. "A lot of people in town aren't very happy about any Chinese being around here right now."

"You mean because of that ridiculous rumor about the Union Pacific using them to replace the Irish laborers?" Simone shook her head. "I don't believe that will ever happen. And anyway, it has nothing to do with me hiring Wang Po and his family."

"How *did* you come to hire them, if you don't mind my asking?"

"Not at all. I sent word to friends of mine in San Francisco that I wanted to hire the best cook I could find for the hotel here in town, and I was told that was Wang Po. What he referred to as a . . . hash house, I believe was the term he used . . . was actually one of the finest restaurants in San Francisco. At least, it became such after he went to work there."

"I thought he said he was a ranch cook before he came here."

"Well . . . I suppose one could call the place he was working a ranch. Actually, though, it was a retreat of sorts for some very wealthy and influential men in California. Governor Stanford, Mr. Crocker, Mr. Huntington, and Mr. Hopkins have all visited there, among others."

Cole recognized the names of the so-called Big Four, the men behind the Central Pacific Railroad, which was even now building toward the east with the ultimate goal of linking up with the Union Pacific. This fella Wang Po had obviously cooked for some very important men, and Cole wondered how much Simone was paying him to entice him into coming to a place like Wind River.

"Someday the Territorial House will have an equally fine reputation, I'm sure," Simone was saying. "And Wang Po's wife will assist him and be in charge of the hotel laundry. Guests won't have to send their clothes out to be washed anymore."

"Sounds mighty fancy," Cole agreed. "But what about their sons? Those boys are going to want to have something to do besides odd jobs around the hotel."

"You may be right about that, Marshal," Simone admitted. "However, I'm certain they won't go out and seek employment with the Union Pacific. I'll keep an eye on them, you can be sure."

Slowly, Cole nodded and said, "Well, all right. As long as you know what you may be getting into. Having those Chinese around is likely to keep things stirred up in town."

"Even when the railroad workers see that Wang Po's family is no threat to their livelihoods?" Simone sounded like she had a hard time believing that.

"For some of those men, working for the UP, as hard as it is, is the best job they've had since leaving Ireland. It may be the *only* job some of them have had. Whether they've got any reason to worry or not, as long as they *think* they do, there can be trouble."

Simone smiled. "Well, then, I'm certainly glad we have a competent marshal here in Wind River who can keep that trouble under control."

Cole looked at her for a few seconds, then

chuckled. She had sure turned that around on him neatly. "I'll do my best, Mrs. McKay," he said. "But with this Indian trouble maybe starting up —"

"Indian trouble?" she cut in. "What Indian trouble? I haven't heard anything about it."

Cole was a little surprised none of the gossip that had to be going around town had reached her ears. He was sure the news of the raid brought by Lon Rogers was a main topic of conversation in most of the saloons tonight, along with the arrival of the Chinese. He said, "It looks like Indians raided one of the farms north of town earlier tonight. The settler and his family were . . . wiped out."

One of Simone's hands went to her mouth. "Oh, no. Do you know whose farm it was?"

Cole shook his head. "I can tell you about where it was, though."

He did so, and Simone's look of distress grew. "That sounds like the land I sold to Ben Jessup. Dear God." Her voice broke a little. "He and his wife had five children, Cole."

The thought occurred to Cole that if Simone hadn't sold the Jessup family that farm, they wouldn't have been there to be massacred. But pointing out that fact right

now would only make her feel worse, he realized, and it wouldn't do a damn thing for
the murdered sodbuster and his family.
Later on, he would have a talk with her
about it.

He put his hands on the knees of his
denim pants and pushed himself to his feet.
"I'd better be going," he said. "It *is* pretty
late. Sorry I had to disturb you at this hour."

"You're welcome here anytime, Marshal.
You know that. We both have a great interest in the future of Wind River, after all."

Cole looked intently at her for a moment,
wondering if her words meant any more
than that. Probably not, he decided. Her
husband's death was still too recent. He
would have to proceed slowly and cautiously
out of respect for her feelings, if at all.

And maybe he was just imagining things
in the first place, he thought as he nodded
and said good night to her and went out
through the foyer. She was a rich, sophisti-
cated woman, and he was just a novice lawman who had never done much else with
his life except wander around the West. The
feelings he had begun having lately would
be better off forgotten, he told himself.

But that was easier said than done. A
woman like Simone didn't come along very
often, especially not out here on the frontier.

75

Cole shook his head and grinned to himself as he walked back through the night toward the boardinghouse. As if he didn't have enough trouble on his plate already, what with angry railroad workers and proddy Chinese and maybe a full-scale Indian war looming on the horizon. Yep, he told himself, he had enough to worry about right now without mooning over Simone McKay. . . .

5

Michael Hatfield knew it wasn't going to be a particularly good morning as soon as his wife put the plate of eggs down in front of him. The plate rattled loudly against the table, and some of the scrambled eggs fell off the side onto the white linen tablecloth. Michael picked up the pieces of egg as quickly as he could and dropped them back on the plate. Delia wouldn't want a stain on her tablecloth. She was already upset, and something like that might be the last straw.

The sandy-haired young man looked up at his wife as she went back across the kitchen to the stove. To him, Delia had never looked more beautiful, even though she thought she had gotten positively huge with child. With a sigh of frustration, she pushed back some of the red hair that had fallen over her face as she began transferring strips of bacon from the frying pan to another platter.

According to Dr. Judson Kent, Delia ought to deliver the child she was carrying in approximately one more month, Michael recalled. Delia had visited Dr. Kent a few days earlier, and the British physician who had come to Wind River to practice had assured her that the pregnancy was proceeding quite satisfactorily. That assurance, however, did little to ease Delia's mind, Michael knew. She was still frightened, still afraid that something would go wrong when her time came.

"Eggs!"

The demand came from Gretchen, Michael and Delia's daughter, who was closing in on three years old now and talking more than ever. Some days, in fact, Michael felt positively sorry for Delia because she had to stay home and listen to Gretchen while he at least got to leave the house and go to work.

With a smile, Michael turned to the pretty blond youngster and said, "Certainly, you can have some eggs, Gretchen. But what do you say first?"

"Bacon with 'em!"

Michael shook his head patiently. "That's not exactly what I meant."

"Oh." Abruptly, Gretchen's lower lip came out and she frowned. Pouting was something else she had gotten very good at recently, Michael mused. He waited, and she finally said, "Please." She didn't sound happy about it, though.

"That's better." He took a wooden spoon and pushed some of the eggs from his plate onto hers. "Mama will have the bacon over here in a minute."

From the stove, Delia said acidly, "Yes, that's all Mama is good for, isn't it?"

Michael sighed. A simple comment, that was all it had been. But these days, that was all it took to make Delia angry. Sometimes even less than that.

Not that she didn't have a right to be upset, he thought as he sipped some of his coffee and began eating the eggs. She had not been pleased with the idea of moving out here to Wyoming Territory from their home in Cincinnati, and her worries had only increased when she found out she was going to have another baby. Then there had been that business with that outlaw called Strawhorn, and Delia had come perilously close to losing her life.

But all that was over now, and indeed, for a time Delia had seemed happier, more content in her life and confident in Michael's ability to take care of her and their family. No longer, though.

Surely it had to be the impending birth of the baby that had her so edgy. Once the child was here, she would be too filled with love for it — and too busy taking care of it, to be honest — to spend her days moping around and wishing she was back in Cincinnati. That was Michael's hope, anyway.

"Here," Delia said curtly as she placed the platter of bacon on the table. It rattled almost as loudly as the plate of eggs had.

"Aren't you going to eat?" Michael asked as she turned away from the table.

"Not now. I don't feel very well." She wouldn't look at him. Instead she closed her eyes, raised a hand, and rubbed at her forehead as if she was trying to massage away the pain.

Michael pushed his chair back slightly. "Is there anything I can do to help?"

"No! No, there's not. Go ahead and eat. You have to get to the paper." Delia turned around and looked at the table. "Gretchen! Eat your food, don't play with it."

Michael sighed again, picked up a slice of bacon, and took a bite. It was good, very good. Delia left the kitchen, and Michael looked at Gretchen, who was pouting again after the rebuke from her mother. "You can have all the bacon you want," he told the little girl. "Just eat."

Today, he was even more glad than usual that he had a newspaper to get out.

"There you are, Marshal," Rose Foster said as she put the plateful of ham steaks, flapjacks, and fried eggs in front of Cole Tyler. She placed a second plate, similarly loaded with food, in front of Billy Casebolt. The lanky deputy practically licked his lips in anticipation as he looked at his breakfast.

Cole reached for his fork. "Thanks, Rose," he told the proprietor of the Wind River Café. "Looks mighty good."

She nodded in acknowledgment of the compliment and went back through the door leading to the kitchen, where the wizened old railroad cook, Monty Riordan, labored over the big stove. Cole had been acquainted with Riordan for several years and knew the fare the old man prepared would be simple but good.

As Cole and Casebolt ate their breakfasts Rose reappeared, her arms laden with trays she carried out to the tables that filled the main room of the café. Casebolt glanced over his shoulder at her and commented in a low voice, "Miss Rose looks mighty pretty this mornin'."

Cole grunted, swallowed a mouthful of food, and reached for his coffee cup. "I reckon so," he said, without looking around. He was hungry, and he was concentrating on his meal. Besides, he knew Rose Foster was pretty, had known so ever since he had seen her for the first time.

She had reddish-gold hair worn in thick curls that framed an attractive, fair-skinned face. Her eyes were a deep shade of green, almost startlingly so. Cole judged her to be in her middle twenties, with a bountiful figure that was revealed to her advantage even in the simple cotton dresses she seemed to favor. Rose was a hard worker, too, Cole knew; she was in the café from well before dawn each morning until long after dark. But her efforts, along with Monty Riordan's cooking, had made a success of the business. The café had more steady customers than any other eatery in Wind River. Cole frequently took his meals there even though he could have eaten in the dining room at the Paines' boardinghouse.

Maybe he would have to start eating more often at the Territorial House, he thought now, since Simone McKay had hired that Chinese cook from California. If Wang Po's grub was as good as Simone claimed, Cole figured he ought to at least give it a chance.

That was assuming Wang Po and his family stayed here in Wind River once they realized just how many of the town's citizens were lined up against them.

Even now, Cole could hear angry, low-voiced conversations in the room behind him. He picked up expressions like "yellow heathens" and "low-down Chinamen" and "run 'em back where they came from." That was only one of two dominant themes around town this morning, however. The other concerned how the army ought to come in and "exterminate all the red-skinned vermin they can find!"

Cole cut off a thick bite of flapjacks with his fork and used it to sop up some of the grease from the ham and fried eggs. As he ate he listened to the little moans and groans coming from Casebolt, and after a few minutes he said, "You sound like you're in pain over there, Billy."

"No, sir," replied Casebolt. "This here food is just pure-dee good, that's all. And I've always been one to appreciate good vittles."

That was true. Cole had seen his deputy pack away prodigious amounts of food, but Casebolt never seemed to gain any weight. He remained his normal gaunt self.

The front door of the café opened, and a tall, bearded man in a black suit and bowler hat came in. He hung the bowler on the hat rack by the door and came over to the counter, slipping onto an empty stool next to Cole. "Ah, good morning to you, Marshal, and to you, Deputy Casebolt," Dr. Judson Kent greeted the two lawmen.

"Mornin', Doc," said Casebolt. "You're out and about sort o' early."

"A physician keeps odd hours, much like a guardian of the law, as I'm certain you gentlemen are aware." Kent had an air of dignity about him, despite the genteel shabbiness of his dark suit. His beard was streaked with gray, and his brown eyes were intelligent but somewhat weary. He went on, "I've been treating a man at my office who was injured rather badly in some sort of altercation last night."

"What happened?" Cole asked. "I hadn't heard about any more trouble."

"Evidently this fellow didn't report his bad luck to you, Marshal. He was set upon as he left one of the saloons late last night — or early this morning, I should say — and robbed by several men who assaulted him. One of the thieves had a knife."

"The feller was stabbed?" Casebolt asked.

"Not exactly. His ear was cut off."

"His ear!" exclaimed Cole.

"Yes, indeed. Rather gruesome, I must say. Not only that, but the thieves took the ear with them, as a trophy, perhaps."

Casebolt shook his head. "I never heard of such. What're folks comin' to?"

"I tended to the injury as best I could, of course. I think the wound will heal . . . although the poor man will never look quite the same."

Rose had come up behind the counter as Kent was telling about the bizarre case, and now she shuddered and said, "That's terrible! Why didn't the man report the crime to the marshal?"

Kent shook his head. "I couldn't say, but when I suggested that he do just that, the fellow claimed that Marshal Tyler here wouldn't care."

Cole frowned. "That's not true. I try to help out anybody who's in trouble around here. What was this gent's name?"

"Shaughnessy, I believe he said."

Casebolt frowned. "One of the fellas we got in that fracas with last night was named Shaughnessy, wasn't he?"

Cole nodded, remembering the brief fight when the Irish railroad workers had attacked the newly arrived Chinese. "That's right. I guess he figured he was lucky he didn't wind up in jail on account of that little dustup and that it would be all right with me if he got his ear cut off. He was wrong, though, and when I run into him again, I intend to tell him so."

"He was going back to work, despite my advice that he should take a day or two and rest," Kent said. "You may not see him in town again for a while, Marshal. I'm certain he was on the work train when it pulled out a short time ago." The doctor rubbed his palms together. "Enough of this talk, lads. I'm quite hungry, Miss Foster, and I'll have whatever Mr. Riordan has a sufficiency of on his stove this morning."

Rose smiled. "Ham and eggs and flap-jacks, coming up," she said.

"You won't be disappointed, Doc," Case-bolt said.

As he finished off his meal Cole thought about the story Dr. Kent had told. Wind River was pretty much a wide-open town, and there were all sorts of shady, dangerous characters around. But this business of not only robbing somebody but cutting off his ear as well . . . that was just downright strange, and Cole didn't like it, not one bit.

He and Casebolt swallowed the last of their food, drained their coffee cups, and then Cole paid Rose for both meals. As they were on their way to the door, it opened and another familiar figure stepped into the café. Lon Rogers, the young cowboy from the Diamond S, stopped and nodded to Cole. "Mornin', Marshal," he said.

Cole was a little surprised to see him. "I thought you were staying out at that farm with the others, Rogers," he said.

"Mr. Sawyer sent me and Frenchy into town to pick up a few things at the general store," Lon explained. "Him and the other boys stayed out there to handle the burying." Lon's voice dropped as he continued, "Just between us, Marshal, that was all right with me. I didn't much hanker to see what was in that burned-out cabin."

"Can't blame you for that," Cole muttered. He nodded to Lon and moved on out of the café, Casebolt trailing him.

Lon went straight to the counter and smiled broadly at Rose. "Good morning, Miss Foster," he said as he tugged off his hat. "You're looking mighty pretty this morning."

"Why, thank you," she said, then frowned a little. "Do I know you, cowboy?"

"I'm Lon Rogers." He looked surprised and maybe even a little hurt. "I ride for the Diamond S. I stop by here for a meal every time I get a chance to come to town. You got mighty fine food, ma'am."

"Well, thank you. Have a seat, Lon. What can I get for you?"

"A stack of hotcakes would be nice, and plenty of coffee. Better bring enough for my friend Frenchy, too. He'll be over here soon's he finishes picking up an order at the store." Lon had taken the stool vacated by Cole Tyler, which put him next to Dr. Kent. He looked over at the British medico and added, "Howdy, Doc."

"Good morning," Kent said. "I heard about the message you carried into town last night, young man. Quite a grisly business, eh?"

"Yes, sir," Lon replied with a sigh. "I don't know what's going to happen if the Shoshone really are going on the warpath."

"Plenty of work for me, I expect," Kent said dryly, "and unfortunately even more work for the undertaker."

Editing the *Wind River Sentinel* was more than just a job to Michael Hatfield, and newspaper work was much more than just a profession. It was in his blood, it was what he did, and he looked forward to each day's tasks with renewed anticipation that had nothing to do with his desire to avoid his wife's erratic moods.

This morning he was even more excited than usual, because he had stopped to pass the time of day with several people during the walk from his house to the newspaper office, and he knew some important things were going on in Wind River. As he approached the café he saw Cole Tyler and Billy Casebolt emerge from the front door and felt his pulse quicken. Now he could get the facts of the cases from the best source of all.

"Marshal Tyler!" Michael called, lifting a hand in greeting. "Could I talk to you for a minute?"

Cole hesitated, then nodded. "Sure, Michael, I reckon so. Billy, you can go on to the office and make sure nobody's looking for us. When I get through with Michael here, I'll be riding out on that errand we talked about earlier."

"You bet, Marshal." Casebolt nodded and moved off down the boardwalk, his gait that of a man made of sticks and held together with twine.

Cole turned back to Michael. "What is it you want to know?"

"I've been hearing some gossip around town this morning about some Indian trouble north of here, as well as a near riot last night right here in Wind River. Can you give me the details, Marshal?"

Cole regarded the young editor coolly. "I

didn't know gossip was your stock in trade now."

Michael flushed, feeling angry and embarrassed at the same time. After sharing some dangers with the marshal, he knew Cole respected him a little more than when they had first met. But he still seemed to regard him as something of an adversary, especially when Michael was just trying to do his job.

"Sometimes there's some truth in the wildest gossip," Michael said. "As a newspaperman, it's my responsibility to sift out the facts and report them."

"I suppose so. But I've got enough to handle right now without having folks get all worried and upset about something that may not even be true."

He was going to have to ask some direct questions, Michael sensed. That was the only way he would have even a chance of getting direct answers. "Did the Shoshones attack a farm north of town and kill the family living there?"

"Somebody did," Cole said. "I don't know if it was the Shoshones or not."

"Are you going to try to find out?"

Cole nodded. "I'm riding out there this morning to take a look around."

"What do you expect to find?"

Cole's eyes narrowed, and he said, "A man

who expects to find something usually does, even when it's not there. I plan to just keep my eyes open and see whatever it is I see."

"What about that riot?"

"There wasn't any riot," Cole said firmly. "And there's nothing unusual about a bunch of liquored-up railroad workers causing a commotion. That's all that happened."

"I heard there were some Chinese coolies involved."

"I wouldn't call 'em coolies. But if you want to know more about that, go talk to your boss. She's responsible for them being here in Wind River, not me."

Michael tried not to look as surprised as he felt. "Are you talking about Mrs. McKay?" he asked.

"She still owns the newspaper, doesn't she?"

"Of course. I —"

Cole pushed past him, not particularly rudely, but firmly, obviously not willing to devote any more time to this conversation. "I've got to get busy. Sorry, Michael."

Michael turned and watched him go down the street, then realized that Cole was heading for the livery stable. He remembered what Cole had said about riding out to that farm where the massacre had taken place. That was probably his destination now. For a second, Michael considered hurrying after him and asking if he could come along, but he was afraid Cole would refuse. Besides, Michael told himself, he had work to do at the office.

And, if the truth were told, he didn't really want to see what was left of that settler's family after the Indians had gotten through with them. The bodies might have been buried already, but they might not have been, too. Michael had seen violence since coming west, more violence than he had ever wanted to witness, but looking at dead people still made him sick to his stomach. He was going to have to toughen himself up if he was going to be a good newspaperman, he supposed.

Besides, there was the matter of the Chinese strangers to look into. Marshal Tyler had told him to ask Mrs. McKay about them. What connection could Simone McKay have with some Chinese coolies? Michael wondered. Maybe he would take a detour and go out to the McKay house before he went to the office.

Once thought of, the decision was made, and Michael turned toward Sweetwater Street. The idea of interviewing Mrs. McKay, his own employer, was a little intimidating, but Michael told himself not to worry.

He was just doing his job, after all.

6

Cole allowed Ulysses to really stretch out this morning. The big horse loved to run, loved it more than anything else in the world. The wind of the stallion's passage blew Cole's hair out behind him and tugged at the broad-brimmed brown hat that hung on his back from its chin strap. Like Ulysses, he enjoyed the speed, the smooth play of the horse's muscles underneath him. Horse and rider became almost one being when Ulysses galloped like this. Cole could almost let himself believe they were alone in the world, racing along over rolling prairie beneath a high, clear blue sky. Nothing but the two of them, and the speed, and the wind and the sun in his face . . .

And then reality intruded harshly, in the form of a burned-out cabin that was still smoking a little in places.

As he rode up to what was left of the Jessup place, Cole saw that the Diamond S horses were unsaddled and in the corral. Sawyer and his punchers were standing a little ways off from the ruins of the cabin, near the garden that Ben Jessup had started. Six mounds of freshly turned earth were before them, and several of the cowboys were leaning on the shovels that had been used to dig the graves.

Cole swung down from the saddle, looped the sorrel's reins over the corral fence, and walked over to the others. Sawyer turned, his black hat tightly gripped in his knobby hands. He gave Cole a grim nod and said, "You got here too late for the buryin', Marshal. Found the other bodies inside the cabin, just like I figured we would."

"They were all dead?" Cole asked.

"What the hell do you think?" Sawyer snapped. "We put the baby in with its mama. Seemed fittin'." There was an edgy tone to Sawyer's voice, as if he expected Cole to challenge the decision.

Instead, Cole nodded in agreement. "Say anything over 'em?"

"I've buried folks before. I know what needs to be done."

Cole nodded again and changed the subject. "Have you or any of your boys looked around the place?"

"For tracks, you mean?"

95

"That's what I was thinking about."

Sawyer clapped his hat on his head and grunted, "Come on. I'll show you what we found."

For all of Cole's dislike of Sawyer, he had to admit the man was an experienced frontiersman. Sawyer never would have survived as long as he had down in that wild country in Texas without an equal mix of sand and savvy. Sawyer led Cole over to a jumble of horse tracks on the far side of the shed from where the cabin had stood.

"Looks to me like they rode up over here, then one of 'em held the horses while the others tried to slip up on the house," Sawyer said as he gestured at the tracks. "Somethin' roused that sodbuster and he came out to see what was goin' on. Probably the dogs were raisin' a ruckus. We found a couple of 'em, shot to ribbons."

Cole hunkered down on his heels and studied the hoofprints for a long moment, then glanced up at Sawyer. "Unshod," he said.

"Yeah, how about that?" Sawyer didn't sound surprised. "Look at the footprints. Nobody wearin' boots or shoes made those. Those are moccasin prints."

Cole had to agree with him. He straightened and said, "I wish we'd found some arrows or something else with markings on it. That way we could tell which band was responsible for this."

"The Sioux have been raidin' off to the north and the east, from what I've heard," Sawyer said. "Now, maybe they've come back to these parts and maybe they haven't. But I know for damn sure that the Shoshones are still around here. That's where I'd start lookin', was I you."

As usual, the Texan was free with his advice, whether it was asked for or not, Cole thought. He said, "I already figured I'd send Deputy Casebolt out to talk to Two Ponies. Billy's friends with the Shoshones, and if anybody can find out what's going on around here, he can."

Sawyer stared at him for a moment, then said dubiously, "You're goin' to let that old man question those savages? Hell, they're liable to send him back to you with a war lance stuck clear through him!"

"I don't think so," Cole replied, knowing that he sounded stubborn but not giving a damn, either.

Sawyer snorted. "You just don't want to believe the Shoshones are to blame for these killin's."

"I'm not going to blame anybody until I know some more."

"What about the army? When are you going to wire them?"

"I'll get around to it," Cole said.

Sawyer stuck a blunt finger at him, and Cole had to make an effort not to grab it and break it with a sharp twist. "You best remember one thing, Tyler," the cattleman warned. "You ain't the only one who knows how to use a telegraph. I can send a wire, too."

Cole stiffened. "You go to meddling in official business and you'll regret it," he said.

The Diamond S punchers had all moved over to stand behind their boss, and Cole was aware of the hostile stares they were directing toward him. As seemed always to be the case when he and Sawyer were going at it nose to nose, the odds were heavily against Cole. But he wasn't going to let that make him back down. Sawyer was going to have to get used to the fact that he didn't run everything around here, the way he likely had in Texas.

"This raid was too damned close to my ranch for comfort," Sawyer grated. "I'll do whatever I have to to protect the Diamond S. You just remember that, Tyler."

Cole jerked his head in a nod. "I don't reckon you'll let me forget it," he said.

Sawyer swung around and strode stiffly

toward the corral. "Come on, boys," he called over his shoulder. "We're goin' home."

Cole waited while Sawyer and the other men saddled up and rode out, then he stepped up into his own leather and pointed Ulysses toward Wind River. There was nothing more he could do here.

Now that Sawyer was gone, Cole calmed down a little and reflected on the things he had said to the cattleman. Being in charge of things, having all these responsibilities, was still new to Cole. For most of his life, he hadn't been responsible for anything or anybody except himself. That was a hard, lonely existence most of the time, but being a part of something like Wind River had hardships of its own. He had to spend too blasted much time *thinking* about whether or not a course of action was the right one, rather than just letting his instincts take over. There was more riding on his decisions now than just his own survival. It was quite a chore, but it was one he had pledged to do, at least for a while.

And Cole Tyler had always believed that a man did what he said he would do, or died trying. . . .

Michael Hatfield swallowed hard as he

stood in front of the gate of Simone Mc-Kay's estate. He had been in the big house several times previously, but although the day was bright with sunshine, the place seemed somehow ominous to him.

That was ridiculous, he told himself sternly. He and Mrs. McKay had gotten along well, right from the start. After her husband's death, she had told Michael how she was depending on him to help her keep the newspaper going, and so far he didn't think he had let her down. The *Sentinel* was doing well; practically everyone in town read it, and a few paid advertisements were starting to appear in it. Michael had no doubt the paper was going to be a success, and he didn't think he was being immodest when he credited part of that success to himself.

But still he dreaded asking Simone about the Chinese. Marshal Tyler had indicated that she knew the facts, however, and Michael had to have those facts if he was going to write a truthful story about the matter. He took a deep breath, gathered his courage, and strode up the walk to the veranda of the mansion.

The housekeeper, Esmeralda, answered the summons of the bellpull. "Oh, 'tis you," she said when she saw who the visitor was. She wore the same sour expression Michael had seen on her face every other time he had come here. He wasn't sure how Simone put up with the woman.

"I need to speak to Mrs. McKay," he said, trying to make his tone sound official, as if he would tolerate no argument.

"Well, you can't," Esmeralda snapped.

Michael sighed. "If you'll just tell her I'm here —"

"Can't do that, either. The missus ain't here."

"Oh." Michael blinked. "Where is she?"

"Down at the hotel'd be my guess. Said she had to see to somethin' or other about them Chinamen, and that's where they stayed last night." Esmeralda sniffed. "Although why the missus'd be kind enough — or foolish enough — to let those heathen Chinee sleep under the same roof with white folks —"

"Thank you, Esmeralda," Michael said quickly, cutting in before the woman could get really wound up and launch into a tirade. "I'll go down there and see if I can find her."

"You do that," the housekeeper said curtly as she shut the door, leaving Michael standing on the veranda.

He took another deep breath. He felt a bit foolish now. Here he had gone and girded up his loins, so to speak, and Mrs. McKay wasn't even home.

That was all right. He would feel more at ease talking to her in the hotel after all, he realized. He walked back out to Sweetwater Street and headed for Grenville Avenue.

By this time of the morning, the town was quite busy. Men and women moved along the boardwalks, intent on the errands that had brought them out. There were several wagons parked in front of the huge general store. Other vehicles — farm wagons, buckboards, buggies, canvas-covered Conestogas — rolled along the street. Men on horseback moved along Grenville Avenue as well. A few dogs lazed in the morning sun, and children ducked in and out of the alleys, laughing and playing. As yet there was no school in Wind River, and that was something the town would have to see to soon, Michael thought as he watched the youngsters playing. The only education available was whatever the children could get at home, and often that didn't amount to much. The leaders of the community were going to have to look into hiring a real teacher before too much longer. Michael wanted his children to be able to attend an actual school when they got older.

That was a matter to bring up with Mrs.

McKay, since she was the most influential citizen in town, but not today, Michael decided. He wanted to concentrate on finding out about those Chinese. He reached the Territorial House and went into the lobby. The clerk behind the desk looked up and greeted him with a nod.

"Good morning," Michael said. "Is Mrs. McKay here?"

The clerk inclined his pomaded head toward the dining room. "I believe she's out in the kitchen."

"Thanks," Michael said. He walked through the dining room, where over half the tables were occupied by patrons, and through a door that led to the kitchen. As he stepped through the opening, air laden with the delicious smells of cooking washed over him.

There were three cast-iron ovens in the kitchens, further evidence of how Andrew McKay and William Durand had spared little expense in making sure their new town was a shining example of civilization, even before the Union Pacific arrived. It must have cost a lot of money to have those heavy ovens freighted out from St. Louis, Michael thought. He had never been in the hotel kitchen before. It was a surprisingly busy place as waitresses moved in and out, several young men worked around a couple of long tables, and a middle-aged Chinese man watched over everything with his arms folded on his chest and a placid expression on his round face. The young men working in the kitchen were Chinese as well, Michael noted, and now he was beginning to understand why Cole had told him to talk to Simone McKay.

The Chinese who had come into Wind River the night before weren't coolies at all, Michael realized now. They were cooks.

Simone was talking to the older Chinese man, who nodded as she spoke. She noticed Michael and smiled, then beckoned him over.

"Good morning, Michael," she greeted him. "I want you to meet Wang Po. He's going to be in charge of the kitchen here at the hotel. Wang Po, this is Michael Hatfield, the editor of our local newspaper."

The Chinese man put his hands together in front of him and bowed slightly. "I am honored to meet you, Mr. Hatfield," he said in excellent English.

"Uh, same here," Michael said.

"Were you looking for me, Michael?" asked Simone.

Michael hesitated. He didn't want to admit that he had come to ask her about the Chinese, not right here in front of Wang Po and the others. He said, "I, uh, just wanted to let you know that I'll have this week's edition of the paper ready to come out tomorrow, right on schedule."

Simone smiled slightly. "I never doubted that. While you're here, though, let me tell you a little about our newest citizens, Wang Po and his family."

She must have read his mind, Michael thought, and he was grateful to her for her perceptiveness. She proceeded to answer his questions without him even having to ask them, explaining how she had hired Wang Po from his job in California and how he had previously cooked in one of the finest restaurants in San Francisco.

"My wife and I came to this country to search for gold," Wang Po put in, "but instead we found riches in the form of our sons and the friends we have made."

"From what I've heard, not all of your people were so fortunate," Michael said.

Wang Po nodded solemnly. "This is true. Many suffered during the time known as the Gold Rush. Now there is the building of the Central Pacific railroad to provide jobs for many of my countrymen, but it is hard, dangerous work. I am thankful my sons do not have to do these things." He beamed with obvious pride at the young men scurrying around the kitchen tables, preparing plates of food for the hotel's diners.

"Was there anything else you wanted, Michael?" Simone asked.

"No, I suppose I had better get on to the office. I'll be seeing you, Mr. Wang."

The Chinese man smiled and bowed slightly again, obviously pleased that Michael knew the correct way to address him.

Michael felt relieved as he left the hotel. Now he could write a story for tomorrow's edition of the *Sentinel* that would tell the truth about the Chinese newcomers. Maybe that would help prevent any more trouble and put a stop to the rumors about how the Chinese were coming in to take over the work on the Union Pacific.

A grin appeared on Michael's face. It looked like this day was going to work out all right after all.

It was late morning before Cole reached Wind River again. On the trail, he had passed Lon Rogers and Frenchy, who were on their way back to the Diamond S after their errand in town. The saddlebags of both men were packed with supplies they had picked up at the general store, and they each lifted a hand to wave at Cole as they passed. They probably wouldn't have been so friendly if they had seen him arguing with their boss earlier, he thought when the two cowboys were out of sight.

He came into town on the main trail, swung right onto Grenville Avenue, and headed for the livery stable, intending to drop Ulysses off before going on to the office. He hadn't reached the barn when he heard the sharp crackle of gunfire behind him.

Cole hauled the sorrel around and searched for the source of the trouble. There had been three shots, but they hadn't seemed to be directed at him. People were shouting and running toward the cluster of tent saloons at the eastern end of town, the "hell on wheels" that had arrived with the railhead. Suddenly Cole spotted a man stumbling out of one of the tents. There was a gun in his hand, and as Cole heeled Ulysses into a run, the man turned around shakily and fired back into the tent.

Leaning forward in the saddle, Cole weaved expertly around wagons and buggies and other horsebackers as he galloped toward the man with the gun. The man was earing back the hammer of his weapon for another shot when Cole reached him. Cole left the saddle in a dive that sent him crashing into the gunman. Both of them went down.

Cole landed on top, as he had planned. The impact knocked the breath out of the other man and made him drop the gun. Planting his knees on the man's chest, Cole palmed out his own Colt and growled, "That'll be enough shooting! What's going on here?"

A voice behind Cole shouted, "Don't let him up, Marshal! He's crazy! Tried to kill us all!"

Cole glanced back over his shoulder, saw a man in a gray-striped suit and dark vest emerge from the tent. The man had black, curly hair and a thick mustache, and there was a smear of blood on his right cheek underneath his eye. He put a hand to the injury, which looked like a bullet crease, and winced.

"What's this all about, Langdon?" demanded Cole. He recognized the man with the mustache as Abner Langdon, the owner of this particular tent saloon.

Langdon pointed at the man Cole had knocked down and said, "Nichols there tried to get rough with one of my girls. He was already upset because he'd lost some money at the poker table, and when he started bothering the girl and Bert told him he'd have to leave, he pulled his gun and started shooting up the place."

A burly, fair-haired man appeared at Langdon's shoulder. "That's right, Marshal," he called. "That's what happened. You better lock up that son of a bitch."

The man Cole was holding down — Nichols, Langdon had called him — abruptly let out a moan. He hadn't struggled since Cole had tackled him, and now as Cole looked more closely at him, he saw the dark stain on the man's midsection. Nichols's eyes were closed, and he didn't look like much of a threat anymore. Cole holstered his gun and moved into a crouch beside the man.

"He's been shot," Cole said grimly as he pulled aside Nichols's shirt and saw the bullet hole in his belly. "Somebody fetch Dr. Kent."

One of the bystanders started down the street at a run, heading for the physician's office. Cole looked at Langdon again and went on, "Who shot him?"

The fair-haired man called Bert spoke up. "I did," he declared belligerently. "What the hell was I supposed to do, stand there and let him gun down me and the boss without even fighting back?"

Cole straightened and moved over to the two men. He held out a hand. "Let me see your gun."

Bert took a Starr four-barrel pepperbox from his pocket and handed it to Cole, who sniffed the barrels. The gun had been fired recently, all right.

"Only shot him once," Bert said. "That was all it took. He was a pretty wild shot even before he was hit."

Cole nodded, recalling the shaky way Nichols had aimed at the tent. He looked down at the wounded man again just as Dr. Judson Kent came bustling up and knelt beside Nichols.

It took Kent only a glance to determine what Cole could also see for himself. "This man is badly hurt," the doctor said. "I need some men to take him down to my office as quickly as possible. Carefully, though," he added as several men stepped forward to lift Nichols's unconscious form.

Cole caught Kent's arm as the doctor started to follow his patient. "I'll be down there in a few minutes," he said. Kent nodded and hurried on down the street.

"What about my gun?" Bert asked. "Aren't you going to give it back?"

"Not just yet," Cole replied. "Not until I've talked to some of the people who saw this ruckus start."

Bert's face, which was naturally florid, flushed even more as he started to step forward toward Cole. Abner Langdon moved smoothly between his employee and the lawman and said, "That's fine, Marshal. I'm sure anyone you talk to will tell you that it happened just as we said. But you go right ahead. Bert and I know you're just doing your job, don't we, Bert?"

"Yeah, I guess so," Bert said grudgingly. He didn't like giving up his gun, even for a little while.

Plenty of the saloon's customers had come out of the tent behind Langdon and Bert, and it took Cole only a few minutes to question them and determine that the two men had been telling the truth. He handed the pepperbox back to Bert, who accepted it with the same lack of grace with which he had given it up.

"You'd better try to keep things under control a little better in your place," Cole advised Langdon. "Right now Wind River's still pretty wide open, but one of these days folks are going to demand that all these killings stop."

Langdon shrugged. "It's not my fault if people can't handle their drinking and their tempers, Marshal. But we'll try to avoid such situations in the future."

"See that you do," Cole snapped. He headed down the street toward Kent's office as Langdon, Bert, and their customers went back into the tent saloon.

Cole heaved a sigh as he walked along. It wasn't like this was the first saloon killing he'd run into since taking the job of marshal. There were plenty of saloons in town, and they drew customers from all of this part of the country, since Wind River was the only real settlement between Rawlins and the Snake River, farther to the west. Nobody was ever going to mistake the motley mix of railroaders, cowboys, trappers, gamblers, and outlaws for a bunch of Sunday-school psalm singers, either. Men like that were accustomed to settling their own differences, and settling them sudden and violentlike. Cole knew that. But it was still his job to keep the streets of the settlement as safe as he could.

The sheet was already drawn up over the face of the man on Kent's examining table when Cole entered the doctor's office. Kent had taken off his coat and was drying his hands on a towel, probably after washing off some blood. He shook his head as Cole looked an unspoken question at him.

"The fellow never had a chance," Kent

said. "But you seemed to know that as well as I, even without any medical training."

"I've seen men gut-shot before." Cole nodded. "Sometimes it takes 'em longer than that to die, but they generally wind up dead."

"Are you going to arrest that man Bert?"

Cole shook his head. "Nichols pulled his gun and fired the first shot."

Kent put his towel down. "One of the disadvantages of being the first outpost of civilization in a wilderness, I suppose, is that it attracts all sorts of violent men."

"It'll change one of these days," Cole said.

"Yes, but will any of us still be alive to see that day?" Kent asked with a slight smile.

That was a question Cole couldn't answer.

7

Former brigadier general John Stephen
Casement was only five feet four inches tall,
but he seemed taller than that to the hundreds of Union Pacific workers who followed his orders. As the construction chief
of the UP, Jack Casement was in charge of
the actual details of laying the tracks, as well
as the surveying and grading work that had
to be done miles in advance of the steel rails
themselves. Grenville Dodge might be the
brains of the project, but Casement was its
heart and soul. He might turn up anywhere
along the fledgling line, ready to bark
orders, spot problems before they became
catastrophes, and generally keep things
moving.

Today the stocky Casement was riding on
horseback several miles ahead of the work
train, along with a couple of his assistants.
The roadbed through this stretch had
already been laid out and graded, of course,

and Casement had sent a crew out here earlier in the day to make sure the bed was still ready for the rails. Sometimes a storm could wash out part of the route, or a wandering herd of buffalo might chop up the roadbed so badly with their hooves that it would have to be graded again before the real work could proceed. Casement wanted to make sure nothing was going to interfere with the progress of his railroad.

The scouts hadn't reported back yet, however, and as the day advanced toward noon Casement had begun to worry. Taking a couple of men armed with Spencer carbines with him, he had ridden out here to take a look for himself.

A lot of this prairie appeared flat at first glance, but that was deceptive. There was a rolling nature to the plains that concealed ridges and gullies and long slopes. Casement and his assistants were nearing the top of one such slope when they heard the faint popping sound of distant gunfire.

"Hold it!" Casement called sharply, habitually lifting a hand in the military signal to halt.

The shooting continued, somewhere on the other side of the ridge ahead of the three riders. Casement's assistants nervously lifted the carbines they carried across their saddles.

"What do you think, Jack?" one of the men asked after a moment.

"Sounds like our boys are in trouble, all right." Casement leaned forward in the saddle, chewed the unlit stub of a cigar in his mouth for a few seconds, then said, "Let's go. We won't ride right in until we know what's going on, though."

The men with him exchanged a look that said they would have preferred hotfooting it back to the work train, where there were plenty of rifles and men to use them, but they both knew better than to argue with Casement. They fell in behind the construction boss as he nudged his horse into motion again.

The three riders reined in at the top of the rise. They had been following the road-bed, and the graded path was easy to see as it traced its way down the far side of the slope and across a wide valley. Dust hung in the air about two miles to the west. Casement pulled out his field glasses and lifted them to his eyes. Frowning, he studied the scene. He could make out some moving figures on horseback, but the distance was too great for him to tell anything else about them. They seemed to be galloping around a small cluster of rocks about a hundred yards north of the roadbed. The shooting was more sporadic now, and as Casement watched, the riders closed in on the rocks. There were a few more shots and some milling around, then the men on horseback galloped away, crossing the roadbed and veering off to the south. Casement watched their progress until they vanished over a distant ridge.

"It doesn't look good," he growled to the men with him. "I'd say somebody ambushed our scouts and pinned them down in some rocks. The fight's over now, though."

"What about our men?" asked one of the assistants.

"Let's go find out. I don't imagine it'll be a very pretty sight, though."

Cautiously, Casement rode forward, the other two men trailing him with their rifles ready. By the time they reached the rocks, buzzards had begun to wheel high overhead in the blue sky, confirming what Casement suspected.

They found the five scouts sprawled among the rocks. The men had been shot and scalped. Mercifully, none of them had been left alive. One of Casement's assistants turned away and heaved, while the other couldn't even bring himself to look at the corpses. Casement regarded them with the steely detachment of a veteran soldier, however. Only the anger glittering in his eyes showed how deeply he was affected by this atrocity.

Casement turned his horse and stared off to the south, where the marauders had disappeared. "That's Shoshone country," he grunted. "They hadn't given us any trouble . . . until now."

"What are we going to do, Jack?" asked the man who hadn't gotten sick. He was looking around nervously, jerking his head from side to side as if he expected a band of murderous savages to appear at any moment out of thin air.

"We'll ride back to the work train and alert everyone there," Casement said. "Then I'm heading for the telegraph station at Wind River. The army's got to know about this."

"You think they'll send some troops?"

Casement rolled the cigar from one side of his mouth to the other. "Damn right they will. The country's got a lot riding on the completion of the transcontinental railroad. If the army has to put down an Indian uprising or two along the way, then so be it."

He kicked his horse into a run and headed

east without looking back to see if the others were following him. Somebody was threatening to slow up his work, and Jack Casement wasn't going to stand for that!

Cole met Billy Casebolt on the way to the marshal's office after he had left Ulysses at the stable. "I heard some shootin' a while ago," the deputy explained, "but I had my hands full and couldn't come see about it until now."

"Somebody tried to shoot up that tent saloon owned by Abner Langdon. Langdon's bouncer shot the fella. Killed him."

Casebolt shook his head. "Damn. Folks go for their guns mighty quicklike around here. Anybody else hurt?"

"No, we were lucky this time — just one dead man." Cole started back to the office with Casebolt beside him and asked, "You said you had your hands full?"

Casebolt's frown deepened. "Yeah, and it was a mite strange, too. You recollect what Doc Kent was tellin' us at the café this mornin' about that feller with his ear cut off?"

"Sure. I'm not likely to forget about that."

"Well, it happened again."

Cole stopped and turned to stare at his deputy. "What did you say, Billy?"

119

"A gent come down to the office with his head all bandaged up and said he'd been jumped early this mornin' whilst he was leavin' Miss Lucy's place. Couple of fellers knocked him down, stole his money, and sliced his right ear clean off."

"Did he get a good look at them?" asked Cole.

"Didn't get any sort of a look at all," Casebolt answered mournfully. "It wasn't dawn yet and was still pretty dark."

Cole rubbed his jaw. "Wonder why Dr. Kent didn't say anything about this one?"

"Oh, the feller didn't go to Doc Kent. He staggered back into Miss Lucy's, and she patched up his head for him. He said she done a good enough job for him and that he didn't want no real doctor like Doc Kent. Said he'd rather have a whore takin' care of him than a sawbones any day."

"I reckon that's his right." Cole hesitated a second, then asked, "Was he one of the men who were mixed up in that fracas last night?"

Casebolt nodded solemnly. "Sure was. He didn't much like comin' to the marshal's office to report what happened to him, neither. But whoever robbed him and cut him up got off with his daddy's watch, and he wanted us to know about it in case we turned it up. I told him we'd keep our eyes open but that we couldn't promise nothin'."

"Did he stay in town?"

"Couldn't say for sure. He said somethin' about goin' on up the line with a handcar full of supplies later on this mornin'. Could be it's left by now."

Cole thought that was probably the case. His frown deepened as he turned over in his mind everything Casebolt had told him. This attack was a duplicate of the one Dr. Kent had reported, and it had to have been carried out by the same criminals. The robberies themselves weren't that unusual; it was a rare night in Wind River when *somebody* didn't get robbed. But this business of cutting an ear off the victims . . . that was definitely out of the ordinary.

Cole wanted to do some poking around in this matter, but it would have to wait. There were more pressing problems than somebody with a knife and a penchant for cutting off ears. He said to Casebolt, "You'd better go get some lunch, then I've got a job for you. I want you to ride out and see if you can find Two Ponies' band."

Casebolt looked at him intently. "What'd you find out yonder at that farm?"

"Some prints of unshod horses," Cole said, "and some moccasin tracks, too. It sure looks like Indians were responsible for the raid."

"Any arrows or anythin' else like that?"

Cole shook his head. "I thought of the same thing. Without some markings to go by, we can't be sure the Shoshones are to blame. I thought you'd have a better chance than anybody else to find out the truth, Billy, since you've spent some time with Two Ponies and his people." Cole added, "Of course, if the Shoshones *are* on the warpath, I could be sending you into some mighty bad trouble."

"I'll take my chances," Casebolt declared without hesitation. "I trust ol' Two Ponies 'bout as much as I do any redskin out here. He's a good man, and his people have always been friendly to me."

"Sawyer's pushing me to call in the army," Cole said quietly. "I don't want to do that until I've got some proof. That could start a war quicker than anything else."

"You're right about that, Marshal. May take me a day or two, but I reckon I can scare up Two Ponies and find out the truth."

"Thanks, Billy."

"You'll be all right here in town till I get back? Folks're still mighty touchy 'bout them Chinamen."

"They'll get over that," Cole said confidently, hoping he was right. Casebolt's comment reminded him that he had intended to have a talk with Simone McKay. There just hadn't been time so far. Events had kept him hopping.

Casebolt headed for the café to get some lunch before he set out on his mission, and Cole went on to the marshal's office. As usual, the land office that was also located in the building was doing a brisk business. Several immigrant wagons were pulled up in the street in front, and Cole saw wives and children waiting eagerly while their menfolks settled deals with the clerks who worked for Simone. Cole was torn between welcoming them to the area and telling them they'd be a hell of a lot smarter to go back where they had come from. So he did neither and just pushed past an overall-clad farmer who was shaking hands in the doorway with one of Simone's assistants. When the clerk stepped back inside, Cole called out to him, "Do you expect Mrs. McKay to be in anytime today?"

"She usually stops by sometime during the afternoon, Marshal," the man replied. "I would think you'd have noticed that by now."

"If I'm in the office when she does come by, tell her I want to see her," Cole snapped, annoyed by the clerk's attitude. Of course, he *had* known that Simone usually checked on the land office during the afternoon hours, but with everything else that was going on right now, it had slipped his mind. Breaking up fights and hauling drunks to the smokehouse to sleep it off were relatively simple, although sometimes dangerous, tasks; dealing with Chinamen and Indians and proddy Texans and folks who got their ears cut off by mysterious attackers was entirely different.

Casebolt stopped by the office about an hour later to tell Cole he was leaving. Cole wished the deputy well and stepped out on the boardwalk to watch Casebolt ride out of town. He went back to the desk and sat down. Not ten more minutes had passed when Simone McKay appeared in the doorway.

"You wanted to see me, Marshal Tyler?"

Cole stood up hurriedly. Simone had that effect on men, he supposed. A fella just naturally jumped to his feet when she was around. That was because she was undeniably every inch a lady.

Today she was wearing a dark green skirt and jacket, with a ruffled shirt of a lighter green under the jacket. A hat with a feather dyed the same shade of green as the shirt was perched on her dark hair. The first time he had seen her close up, she had been in his hotel room, asking him to take the job of marshal. Cole had thought then that she was one of the most beautiful women he had ever seen. Now that he had spent quite a bit more time around her, she struck him as even more attractive than he had first thought. Simone McKay was like a fabulous gem, beautiful in its own right but even more so because of its scarcity. Cole would have been willing to bet there was no one like her nearer than San Francisco.

He realized he was standing there gawking. "Please, come in and sit down," he said hurriedly, moving around the desk to hold one of the ladder-back chairs for her. "Sorry I don't have a more comfortable seat."

"This is fine, thank you," she said as she settled into the chair with a rustle of fabric. "What can I do for you?"

"I just wanted to know how that Chinese fella you hired is working out." Cole went behind the desk again and sat down in his own chair.

Simone smiled at him. "Well, it's a bit early to tell. Wang Po and his family only began working for me this morning. But we not only had a full dining room for breakfast, we had townspeople waiting for a table at lunch. I suppose the word is getting around quickly that the food at the Territorial House has improved."

"I reckon so," Cole said. "Wang Po's boys are helping him out in the kitchen, are they?"

"Yes, they are. I think there will be plenty for them to do, Marshal, so you can stop worrying about them disrupting work on the Union Pacific."

Cole held up his hands, palms toward her. "I wasn't the one who was worried about that," he said. "But I was afraid having some Chinese around after all those rumors was really going to stir up some trouble. Things ought to quiet down now." It would be a relief, he thought, if one of his problems went away, and this one seemed to be the most likely.

"Of course," Simone went on, "I have to supervise things fairly closely. These people can't be entrusted with too much responsibility."

Cole nodded, a little puzzled by the comment but not wanting to show it. He had never heard Simone refer to any group as "these people" before.

He didn't have an opportunity to follow that line of thought very far, because in the next moment he heard shouting outside in the street. The commotion was coming closer, and Cole stood up and muttered, "Excuse me," to Simone. He moved to the window so that he could see what was going on. It sounded like more trouble, and that was one sound he didn't like these days.

Striding down the boardwalk toward the marshal's office was a short but impressive figure followed by a group of townspeople and railroad workers. Cole recognized Jack Casement, the construction boss of the Union Pacific. He seemed to be bound straight for the marshal's office, and from the look on his face, he wasn't happy, not by a long shot.

Cole turned away from the window as Casement passed in front of the glass, and a second later the front door of the building banged open. Casement appeared in the doorway. "Marshal," he said briskly, "there's trouble."

Cole wanted to tell him that this came as no surprise at all. Instead, he asked, "What's wrong, Mr. Casement?"

"Indians slaughtered five of my men this morning," Casement said bluntly, drawing a gasp of horror from Simone. "They were shot and scalped about ten miles west of town, and the savages rode off to the south.

Toward Shoshone country, if I need to remind you."

Cole didn't need the reminder. "Billy," he said softly to himself.

If Jack Casement was right, Cole might have sent his deputy right into the heart of danger.

He shook off that apprehension and said, "I'm sorry to hear about this, Mr. Casement. What do you want me to do about it?"

"I'm not asking you to do a damned thing. I'm just notifying you of my actions as a courtesy, since you constitute the authorities around here, Tyler. For now at least."

Cole stiffened. "What do you mean by that?" he demanded.

Casement's teeth clenched on the unlit cigar in his mouth. "I mean that soon there'll be somebody else here to handle this problem," he said. "I've wired the army, and a troop of cavalry is being dispatched immediately from Fort Laramie." The former general grinned humorlessly. "Just wait until those horse soldiers get here. We'll see some action then, by God!"

8

Cole stared at Casement for a moment, not sure he had heard him correctly. He said, "You've already sent for the army?"

"That's right," Casement snapped. "They'll be here in about three days. Until then I'm putting extra guards on the work trains just in case those red devils try to attack again. Once the cavalry arrives, it won't take long for them to be run to ground. We can't afford to be delayed. Every mile of track the Central Pacific lays and we don't means less money for the UP."

Casement was taking an awful lot for granted, Cole thought. He was leaping to conclusions to blame the Shoshones for the deaths of his men. The finger of guilt *did* seem to point to the Indians, though. Cole had to admit that much.

"A couple of my men and I witnessed the end of the battle," Casement went on. "We weren't close enough to help, however." He

129

took the cigar out of his mouth and pointed at Cole with it. "Forgive me for speaking bluntly, Marshal, but you should have already wired the army yourself. I'm told by the stationmaster here that a band of savages attacked a farm north of town last night and wiped out a family of settlers."

"That's what it looks like," Cole said slowly. "I don't have any proof that's what happened."

Casement just stared at him contemptuously and put the cigar back in his mouth.

Cole understood the way the construction boss felt. Time was, he'd been a man of direct action himself — and it hadn't been that awful long ago. But he had gotten in trouble more than once for jumping into something before taking the time to ponder on it. If this marshal's job had taught him anything so far, it was that things often weren't as clear-cut as they seemed.

"Like I said, I was just doing you the courtesy of notifying you," Casement said curtly. "I've got to get back to my people." With a brisk nod, he turned and walked out of the office.

Simone looked at Cole with a worried frown on her face — which, Cole noticed, didn't seem to make her any less pretty. "This is terrible," she said. "Do you really think the Shoshones are going to go on a rampage, Cole?"

"I'm not sure what to think anymore," he told her honestly. "But I sent Billy out to find Two Ponies and talk to him, and I'm starting to wonder if that was a bad mistake."

Billy Casebolt had left town only a couple of hours earlier, Cole recalled, and if he himself rode out now, he might be able to catch up to his deputy and call off the mission. That would leave Wind River temporarily without a lawman, and this was a situation Cole tried to avoid.

Some more shouting from outside made him postpone the decision. He stepped to the window and looked out, saw Jack Casement surrounded by a dozen or more angry, red-faced railroad workers. Casement was jawing back at them, the cigar clenched in his teeth bobbing up and down furiously.

"What now?" Cole muttered as he turned away from the window. To Simone, he said, "You'd best go on back to the land office, ma'am. Looks like there might be some trouble outside, and I'd better tend to it."

She stood up as he moved past her, reaching out to lay a hand on his arm. Cole felt the warmth of her touch even through the sleeve of his buckskin shirt. "Be careful,

Marshal," Simone said. "I don't know what the town would do without you."

He would have rather heard her saying that she didn't know what *she* would do without him, but Cole was willing to take what he could get. He gave her a tight smile. "Don't worry, Mrs. McKay. I figure I'll be around for a while yet."

While Simone went down the hall to the office of the land development company, Cole stepped out through the foyer and onto the boardwalk. The shouts coming from the men surrounding Casement were even louder now, and Cole heard the words "damned Chinamen" more than once.

Cole grimaced. He had hoped the problem with the Chinese was over, but obviously these men hadn't heard — or didn't believe — that Wang Po and his family were in Wind River strictly to work for Simone at the Territorial House. The railroad men were still worried that their jobs were in jeopardy.

"I'm telling you, I don't know what the hell you're talking about!" Casement barked back at the men. "I don't have anything to do with any Chinamen!"

"He's lying!" yelled one of the workers. "I know damned well the UP's goin' to hire hundreds of those heathens to take our place!"

"Where did you hear that scurrilous lie?" Casement demanded, but the question was drowned out by more shouts.

More men were joining the crowd all the time, swelling its ranks until it was practically a mob. Not all of them were railroad workers, either, Cole noted. Some were hard cases and drifters eager for any sort of excitement, even if it didn't concern them at all. Unless he moved to break this up, Cole thought, it could turn ugly in a hurry.

The railroaders were more courageous in a group than they might have dared to be otherwise. One man prodded Casement in the chest with a stubby finger and thundered, "If it's coolies ye'll be wantin' to hire, Jack Casement, go ye right ahead! We'll not work for ye any longer! Just see how much track ye get laid with the likes o' them. From this moment forward, we're on strike!"

"Strike! Strike! Strike!" The crowd took up the chant, leaving Casement looking furious and befuddled at the same time. The press of men around him jolted him back and forth, and since most of the workers were taller than Casement, Cole had trouble keeping sight of him. It was time to pull

Casement out of this mess before things got really bad.

"Break it up! Break it up, damn it!" Cole bellowed as he forced his way into the crowd, shouldering some of the men aside and taking hold of others to shove them out of his way. He drew some angry looks, but no one struck out at him. Cole Tyler had already started to develop a reputation as a tough lawman, and some of these men who remembered him from his days with the Union Pacific knew he was a dangerous man to cross.

As Cole reached Casement's side he became aware that someone else was forcing his way through the mob from the other direction. The newcomer was barreling men aside even more efficiently than Cole had. He was tall, with massive shoulders and arms, and his legs were like the trunks of young trees. The man wore a leather apron, and his round face was red from the heat of his forge. Cole was glad to see Jeremiah Newton, Wind River's blacksmith and part-time preacher. Jeremiah was a good friend, and in the absence of Billy Casebolt, he was the next best thing to an official deputy.

"Move back!" Jeremiah thundered with the voice that called down hellfire and brimstone every Sunday morning at services. "Stand fast, Brother Tyler! I'm here to help you."

"And I'm glad of it, Jeremiah," Cole told the blacksmith. He placed himself on one side of Casement while Jeremiah planted his feet solidly on the other side.

"Blast it, the day I can't handle my own men —" Casement began over the continued chanting of the mob.

"Nobody's getting hurt in my town if I can help it," Cole cut in. He took hold of Casement's arm. "Come on."

Together, he and Jeremiah bulled their way through the press of angry men and reached the boardwalk with Casement still between them. Cole stepped up onto the planks, followed by the railroad boss and the burly blacksmith. He swung around to face the shouting mob.

Amazingly, nobody had thrown a punch or pulled a gun yet, and Cole wanted to keep it that way. He lifted his hands for quiet, but the crowd kept yelling. It took Jeremiah Newton shouting "Be silent!" in a voice like an earthquake to shut them up.

In the grudging silence that fell, Cole glared at the mob and began, "I don't know exactly what's going on here —"

"We're on strike, that's what going on!" called one of the men. Some of the others echoed the cry of "Strike!"

"It's none of my business how you handle things with the Union Pacific," Cole went on in a loud voice, "but there's not going to be any more trouble here in Wind River! You boys go on back to your barracks and cool off, blast it!"

"We'll not go back to those hellholes!" protested the man who had first called for a strike, referring to the railroad cars that had been outfitted as barracks for the workers. The accommodations were pretty spartan, Cole knew from experience, but he wouldn't go so far as to describe the cars as hellholes. The mob's spokesman went on, "We're not workin' for the UP anymore, and we'll not have anything to do with the connivin' rascals!"

Casement bellowed, "You can't go on strike, you damned Hibernian! You agreed to do the job, and you've got to keep your word!"

"The hell we do!" more than one man shouted back at him.

This situation was rapidly getting worse, Cole thought wearily. He said to the blacksmith, "Jeremiah, take Mr. Casement into my office and keep him there until things quiet down."

"You can't do that!" Casement objected.

"I've got things to do —"

"It's for your own good," Cole told him, "and besides, if you force me to, I'll arrest you for provoking a riot. Now get him out of here, Jeremiah."

Casement still protested, but Jeremiah had hold of his arm, and trying to pull out of that grip was like fighting an avalanche. There was no holding back such power. Jeremiah led Casement across the boardwalk and into the marshal's office while a few members of the mob yelled insults.

"So ye've taken the side of the UP, have ye, Marshal?" the group's spokesman demanded.

"I haven't taken anybody's side," Cole snapped. "But I'm not going to let any harm come to Casement from a mob. The way I see it, you men don't have to worry about the Chinese —"

More shouting overwhelmed his words at the mere mention of the Chinese, and he had to wait for it to quiet down before he could continue, "There's only one Chinese family here in Wind River, and they're working in the hotel. They don't have anything to do with the railroad."

"It's a lie!" somebody called from the back of the crowd. "They're just the first! There'll be more of them, hundreds of 'em! You just wait and see!"

Cole tried again. "I have Mrs. McKay's word —"

"She's workin' with the Union Pacific!" This was a different voice, but it also came from the back of the crowd. "Her husband was thick as thieves with the railroad, and we all know it!"

Cole couldn't deny that. While not having any direct interest in the railroad, Andrew McKay and William Durand had had spies within the Union Pacific, and a complex network of bribery and chicanery had tied the two men to the railroad. To these workers who feared for their jobs, it was at least conceivable that Simone McKay could now be in cahoots with the Union Pacific to bring in Chinese laborers.

"If you want to strike, go ahead and do it!" Cole said in frustration. "But if you cause any trouble here in Wind River, you'll answer to me, and you've got my word on that!"

He stood there glaring stubbornly at the crowd until it began to break up. Most of the men headed for the saloons, and that didn't bode well for what might happen later. Once they got liquored up, there was no telling what they might do. Cole knew he needed to get Jack Casement out of town and back to the work train as quickly as possible. At least out there Casement would be surrounded by workers who were still loyal.

Cole hoped that was the case, anyway. If this strike spread to the rest of the railroaders, there was no telling what might happen. To his surprise, he found that he was now almost glad the army was on its way.

If things kept going to hell around here the way they had the past two days, he was liable to need all the help he could get. . . .

Delia Hatfield looked up as the sound of angry shouts drifted in through the open window of Dr. Kent's office. She pushed back her red hair, and a frown creased her forehead. "Do you hear that, Doctor?" she asked.

"Yes, indeed I do," Kent replied, "but I'm not going to concern myself with it right now. I already have a patient."

"You shouldn't worry about me," Delia told him. "Someone might be hurt. You might be needed."

"If I am, they'll fetch me." Kent lowered the window and then turned back to Delia. "Tell me, how have you been feeling?"

"Oh . . . all right, I suppose."

"No unusual pains since your last visit?"

"Not that I remember." Delia suddenly

caught her breath as a pang of fear shot through her. "There's not anything wrong with the baby, is there?"

Kent smiled and shook his head. "Not that I know of. It was a routine question, my dear. Every medical indication is that your condition is proceeding quite normally and naturally. I suspect that within a few weeks you and Michael will be the proud parents of another healthy, happy child."

Delia knew she should have been relieved to hear such good results from her latest examination by the physician. But even with Judson Kent's encouragement, she was unable to shake the dark mood that had gripped her tightly for most of the past month.

"What if there's some sort of . . . problem when the baby's born?" she asked.

"Then we'll deal with it when the time comes," Kent said quietly but firmly. "I do hope you're not worrying yourself sick over this pregnancy, Delia. You're a very healthy young woman, and there has been absolutely no sign of any ill effects whatever from your, ah, adventure."

"You mean from when I was taken prisoner and nearly killed by that outlaw?" Delia asked bitterly. "It was just luck that nothing happened."

"Well, there, you see," Kent said. "Providence itself is obviously watching over you, so there's no need for you to worry, is there?"

She realized that no matter what she said, he was going to twist it and put some sort of bright, optimistic face on it. A part of her brain told her that was better than automatically seeing the worst in everything, but these days she didn't seem to be capable of doing anything else.

She wished she knew what was going on down the street. If there was some sort of trouble, Michael would probably be right in the thick of it. He liked to claim that he was just doing his job whenever he plunged into some dangerous situation, but Delia knew better. He *liked* it. He liked the danger and the fact that he was actually on the frontier, on the very edge of an untamed wilderness full of wild animals and bloodthirsty savages and cruel, ruthless desperadoes —

"Delia. Mrs. Hatfield."

She became aware that Dr. Kent was talking to her again. She looked up and said, "I'm sorry, Doctor. What were you saying?"

"At the risk of repeating myself, I was advising you not to concern yourself with imagined terrors." Kent held out his hands to help her down from the examining table.

"Now, I want you to go home, enjoy your husband and your daughter, and come back to see me next week."

Delia summoned up a smile, even though it was a weak one. "All right."

Kent reached for his coat, which was draped over the same rack that supported the skeleton he called Reginald, shrugged into the garment, then picked up his bowler and his medical bag. "I'll walk with you part of the way," he said. "I have to stop by and see Mrs. Raymond."

"Estelle Raymond?"

"That's right. She's expecting, too, you know."

Delia was aware of this. She knew Estelle Raymond, but not very well, just enough to nod politely when they met on the street. Estelle was married to Harvey Raymond, the manager of the general store. Delia probably knew Harvey better than she did Estelle, since she often shopped at the big emporium.

"How is she doing?" Delia asked Kent, telling herself she would be better off thinking about someone else rather than concentrating on her own problems all the time.

Kent hesitated before answering. He frowned, stroked his beard lightly, and finally said, "I'm not sure I should mention

142

this to you in your current frame of mind, but I'm afraid Mrs. Raymond's pregnancy is not proceeding as well as your own. She's considerably older than you, you know, and not as well built for childbearing."

Delia felt herself blushing at the doctor's frank comments. She supposed that a medical man like Kent became accustomed to being blunt about such things as childbearing. She asked, "Is there anything I can do to help her?"

"Oh, no," Kent replied with a shake of his head. "I'm certain she'll be fine. I just have to keep a closer eye on her than I do on a healthy young specimen such as yourself." He offered her his arm and led her out of the office.

Whatever the earlier commotion down the street had been, it was gone now. Delia saw a small knot of men still standing in the street in front of the marshal's office, talking and gesturing angrily. She looked around, trying to see if Michael was anywhere in sight. She didn't spot him and felt a sudden surge of worry. If he was all right, he would have been there so that he could write a story for the paper about whatever the trouble had been.

"I think instead of going home I'll walk down to the newspaper office," Delia said to the doctor. "If you think that would be all right, that is."

"I think that's a splendid idea," said Kent. "And it's on my route to Mrs. Raymond's house, so I can accompany you the entire way. Nothing like a stroll in the summer sun with an attractive woman on one's arm, eh?"

Delia found a genuine smile on her face, one of the few such expressions in recent days. "You're a charmer, aren't you, Dr. Kent?"

"I try, my dear lady, I try."

They walked west along Grenville Avenue, past the big general store. The *Sentinel* offices were a block farther along the street. When they reached the door, Dr. Kent tipped his hat to Delia, told her once again not to worry too much, and ambled on down the boardwalk. Delia turned to the door and opened it, allowing the acrid, all-too-familiar odor of printer's ink to strike her nostrils. She repressed a shudder and went inside.

Michael was sitting at a tall, inclined desk, taking bits of type from trays and setting them in place in the frame that would make up a page of the newspaper when it was printed. He was frowning in concentration and didn't even notice Delia when she first came in. That gave her a moment to study her husband. He had ink smeared on his face, as usual, and his hair was tangled from his habit of running his fingers through it. But Delia felt warmth spreading through her as she realized he was still the most handsome man she had ever seen.

"Michael," she said softly.

He was alone in the office at the moment. Delia didn't know where his assistants were and didn't care. All that mattered to her was the sudden glow of happiness in Michael's eyes as he looked up and saw her. He stood up and hurried over to her. "Are you all right?" he asked as he put his hands on her shoulders. "Where's Gretchen?"

"Mrs. Paine is looking after her. I've been to Dr. Kent's."

Michael's eyes widened. "Is something wrong?"

"Not at all. Everything is all right, Michael. I just . . . I just wanted to see you, to have you hold me for a minute."

"Well . . . sure. I'll be glad to do that." He folded her into his embrace, and she leaned her head against his chest.

Delia couldn't have explained it, but she suddenly felt better. Maybe all her worries *had* been for nothing. . . .

9

Nothing catastrophic happened the rest of the day, and Cole supposed he should have been glad of that. The striking railroad workers didn't cause any sort of ruckus, although they put away enough whiskey in the saloons to float a Mississippi riverboat. Jack Casement and his lieutenants headed back to the work train on the same handcar that had brought them into town. Nobody got an ear cut off — at least as far as Cole knew — and nobody stormed the hotel in order to tar and feather Wang Po and his wife and sons. Afternoon turned into evening and evening into night, and as Cole stood on the boardwalk in front of his office and watched quiet settle over the town, he heaved a sigh of relief.

Of course, there was no telling what tomorrow might bring. . . .

For one thing, Cole was still worried about Billy Casebolt. After some long, hard thinking, Cole had decided not to ride after him. Everything was just too unsettled here in Wind River to leave the town without a real lawman. And Casebolt was a seasoned veteran of the frontier. Even thinking that Two Ponies and the rest of the Shoshones were his friends, Casebolt wouldn't just openly ride into their camp without taking a look around first. If the Shoshones were preparing for war, Casebolt would likely be able to tell it from a distance, and then he would hotfoot it back here to the settlement as fast as he could. That was what Cole hoped, anyway.

Judson Kent came strolling along the boardwalk. He paused to nod to Cole. "Good evening, Marshal."

"Howdy," Cole said. "Anybody else come to see you with a chopped-off ear?"

Kent chuckled and shook his head. "Not so far."

Cole told him about the incident outside of Miss Lucy's that Casebolt had reported to him, and the doctor's jovial expression turned into a frown. "I say, that's rather strange, don't you think?" he asked when Cole was finished.

"I haven't been able to figure it out," Cole replied. "Let me know if you see any other injuries like that, will you?"

"Certainly."

The doctor moved on down the board-walk, and Cole went inside the office. There was a cot in a back room where he would sleep tonight so that he would be handy if anybody came looking for the law. He generally took turns with Casebolt, but tonight the deputy was gone. Casebolt was somewhere out there in the darkness, and Cole hoped that wherever he was, he was all right. He had come to depend on the old-timer.

Give Casebolt some credit, Cole told himself. Billy had survived for a long time out here in this rugged land. He could take care of himself.

Casebolt would have swallowed, but he was afraid the movement of his Adam's apple would be enough to make the point of the war lance that was pressed against his throat prick the skin.

The warrior standing over him was just a darker shape against the black night sky. The Indian said something in the Shoshone tongue, his voice harsh and guttural. Casebolt couldn't make out all the words. He savvied a little Shoshone, but not when it was rattled out so quicklike. There was nothing he could do but remain silent and hope this didn't make the warrior angry enough to thrust the war lance down through his captive's throat.

The Shoshone switched to English, but he didn't sound any friendlier. "What do you do here, white man?" he demanded. The fella's tone convinced Casebolt that if he didn't get an answer soon, he was going to lose his patience.

Carefully, Casebolt said, "If you'll take that pigsticker away from my neck, I can tell you a whole heap easier, ol' hoss."

"I am not called Horse. I am Climbs on Rocks." The point of the lance moved away from Casebolt's neck, but only a couple of inches.

Still, that was enough to make Casebolt feel considerably better. He said, "Pleased to meet you, Climbs on Rocks. My name's Billy Casebolt. You reckon I could sit up?"

"Tell me first why you are here on Shoshone land."

"I'm a friend of Two Ponies. I come out here to pay him a visit."

Casebolt couldn't see the Indian's face, but he figured Climbs on Rocks was thinking about what he had said. If this warrior was part of Two Ponies' band, and if the strange white man was telling the truth, then Climbs on Rocks wouldn't want to of-fend the chief by killing one of his friends. Casebolt hoped Climbs on Rocks was going to give him the benefit of that doubt.

The warrior stepped back a few paces, but kept the lance leveled and ready for instant use. "Sit up, Billy Casebolt," he commanded.

Casebolt did so gratefully. He lifted a hand and touched his throat. The skin wasn't broken. Climbs on Rocks obviously had a deft touch with a war lance.

The deputy was a mite annoyed with the Indian, but he was downright mad at himself. Time was, even an Apache would have had to be lucky to sneak up on Billy Casebolt without being heard. He should have heard a Shoshone coming a mile away, even if he *was* asleep.

He figured he was some fifteen miles west of Wind River. He had ridden all afternoon after leaving town, without spotting a single Indian. Looking for the Shoshone if they didn't want to be found was a pretty futile pastime in this rugged landscape; Casebolt had figured *they* would find *him,* and then he would ask to be taken to the camp of his old friend Two Ponies.

Well, somebody had found him, all right, after he had made camp and turned in for the night, but Climbs on Rocks didn't seem as friendly as most Shoshones normally were. Not near as friendly, in fact. As much as Casebolt didn't want to believe it, maybe the Shoshones *had* decided to turn hostile to the whites.

If that was the case, he was in mighty big trouble.

No point in giving up just yet, though. He said, "Can you take me to Two Ponies, Climbs on Rocks?"

"Why should I do this thing?" asked the warrior.

"I got to talk to him. It's mighty important. There's bad medicine back where I come from, and folks are sayin' it's the fault of the Shoshone."

Climbs on Rocks grunted contemptuously. "The Shoshone have nothing to do with any white man's trouble."

"Now, that's just what I thought, too. But I got to talk to Two Ponies about it anyway."

Climbs on Rocks backed off a little more. "Get up," he said. "I will take you to Two Ponies. And if you are lying, Billy Casebolt, you will wish you had never come here."

Casebolt relaxed a little. He hoped Two Ponies would welcome him. The Shoshone chief and his people had saved Casebolt's life when he was badly wounded, and he had spent several pleasant days in their camp recovering from the injury. Since that time, he had visited them on a couple of other occasions.

He reached for his hat, clapped it on his head, and stood up. A few yards away, coals glowed faintly in the ashes of the small fire he had built earlier to warm his supper. "How'd you spot me?" he asked Climbs on Rocks as he hefted his saddle. "Did you see my fire?"

"I saw fire and smelled smoke and knew some foolish white man was abroad in the land," Climbs on Rocks answered. "I was right. If the Sioux had seen you, they would have killed you without asking any questions."

"The Sioux ain't around these parts anymore, or so I'm told."

"And you would wager your life on this?"

Casebolt grunted as he settled the saddle on his horse's back and started fastening the cinches. "You're right," he admitted. "Guess I'm gettin' careless in my old age."

"A careless man does not get much older."

Casebolt would have thanked him to keep his redskin philosophy to himself, had he not known that Climbs on Rocks was right. And that knowledge rankled. Maybe he really *was* getting too old. Maybe he ought to find himself a porch and a rocking chair somewhere and just sit down to wait out the time he had left. It would be a lonely existence, Casebolt thought, since he had never settled down and didn't have any grandkids to cluster around his feet and listen to all his stories about the old days. He sighed. That rocking chair would just have to wait.

Anyway, there was a good chance he'd never make it. Men like him usually wound up in unmarked graves somewhere underneath the big western sky.

Once the horse was saddled and his bedroll snugged in place, Casebolt turned back around to pick up the gunbelt he had left coiled on the ground, only to find that Climbs on Rocks already had it slung over his shoulder. The Shoshone warrior strode over and pulled the Henry rifle from its sheath on the saddle, too. "You will need no weapons where you are going," he told Casebolt.

"Feel a mite nekkid without 'em," Casebolt groused as he swung up into the saddle. "Well, what're you waitin' for? Let's go."

Climbs on Rocks faded off into the shadows somewhere and returned a moment later leading a pony. He mounted with a lithe motion, still carrying the war lance. Casebolt heard the head of the weapon hiss through the air as Climbs on Rocks gestured with it. "Ride," the Indian ordered flatly.

Casebolt heeled his horse into motion. It was a dark night, the moon only a thin slice of silver in the sky, but between its feeble illumination and the starlight, it was bright enough for Casebolt to see where he was going. He heard Climbs on Rocks riding right behind him. "Which direction you want me to head?" Casebolt asked.

"Keep going the way you are going," the Shoshone told him. "I will tell you when to turn."

Grumbling to himself, Casebolt rode on into the night.

A couple of hours wheeled past, and Casebolt was getting mighty tired. He hadn't gotten much sleep before Climbs on Rocks woke him up by poking that lance against his throat. He needed his rest. But Climbs on Rocks just kept prodding him on, steering him through some canyons and around a couple of mesas. This was a different area from where Two Ponies' camp had been located before, but that came as no surprise to Casebolt. The Shoshones were hunters, and folks who lived that kind of life tended to move around quite a bit.

"How much farther you reckon we got to go?" Casebolt asked after a while longer.

"We keep this up, we're goin' to wind up in Oregon."

"I think we will stop before we go that far," Climbs on Rocks said, and for the first time, Casebolt thought he heard a hint of humor in the warrior's voice.

A few minutes later, as the two riders topped a rise, the Shoshone said, "We are here."

Casebolt could barely make out the cluster of tepees in the narrow valley in front of him. There was a dark, winding line across the landscape that he recognized as thicker vegetation along a small creek. The tepees were on the other side of the little stream. The barking of dogs came faintly to Casebolt's ears. He rode slowly down the gentle slope, Climbs on Rocks following behind him.

The dogs got louder and more aggressive as the riders approached, splashing across the creek and running around the legs of the horses to nip at the feet of the riders. The mounts shied, and the Indian pony kicked out at the bothersome dogs. Climbs on Rocks reversed his lance and smacked the handle across the flanks of one of the capering creatures, drawing a yip of pain and sending it scurrying away. The warrior snapped a command in Shoshone, making

155

some of the other dogs cringe.

By this time the commotion had attracted the attention of the village. Casebolt saw a wedge of light as the entrance flap of a tepee was pulled open, letting the glow from the fire inside spill out into the darkness. A voice called a question, and Climbs on Rocks answered. He and Casebolt rode across the creek and into the cluster of lodges. A man strode from the one with the open flap and asked, "Billy Casebolt? Is that you?"

Casebolt felt a surge of relief as he recognized Two Ponies' voice. "Yep, it's me, all right," he told the Shoshone chief. "Good to see you again, Two Ponies."

"Get down and come into my lodge." Two Ponies looked past Casebolt at Climbs on Rocks and added something in Shoshone. He sounded annoyed.

Climbs on Rocks replied in the same tongue, and Casebolt could tell that the warrior was trying to explain why he had jumped the deputy from Wind River. Two Ponies cut into the explanation with a curt sentence or two, then his tone softened slightly as he concluded by telling Climbs on Rocks to go get some sleep. Casebolt could follow that much of the conversation, at least.

Several more Shoshones had come from their tepees to see what was going on, and at a command from Two Ponies, one of them took the reins of Casebolt's horse and said to the deputy, "I will care for your animal."

"Why, thank you kindly," Casebolt said. "He's come quite a ways today."

As the warrior led the horse away Two Ponies said to Casebolt, "Come inside. We will smoke the pipe of friendship."

Casebolt's worries had eased considerably since his arrival at the Shoshone camp. Everything seemed peaceful here. None of the men he had seen had been painted for war, and the atmosphere in the camp was one of peace. Despite the touchiness exhibited by Climbs on Rocks, the Shoshones just didn't act like people who had brutally wiped out a family of settlers the night before.

Two Ponies wore a buckskin shirt and leggings, and a single eagle feather stuck up at the back of his head. His hair was still dark and thick but beginning to be streaked with gray. As he and Casebolt entered the tepee he gestured for his guest to sit to the right of the fire in the center of the living space. A soft buffalo robe was spread there, and Casebolt sank down on it gratefully. Two

Ponies went around the fire in the other direction and sat down to Casebolt's right. There were four women in the tepee, too, ranging in age from an adolescent girl to an elderly squaw with a face so wrinkled that her features were barely visible. The other two women were perhaps thirty. Both of them were quite handsome, and Casebolt knew they were Two Ponies' wives. The girl was his daughter, the old woman his mother. All of them were acquainted with Casebolt from his previous visits, but they kept silent and didn't greet him. Such was not their place.

Two Ponies crossed his legs and slipped off the moccasins on his feet. Casebolt followed the tradition, removing his own boots but leaving his socks on as Two Ponies prepared the pipe for smoking. It was an exquisite piece of carving work, with decorative feathers and strips of fur tied to it. Two Ponies packed the bowl with tobacco from a small rawhide bag, then lit it with a glowing twig from the fire. When the tobacco was burning well, he blew smoke to the four winds and then passed the pipe to Casebolt.

These rituals could be a mite tiresome, Casebolt thought, but he knew better than to try to bypass them. As he and Two Ponies smoked, the chief inquired as to his health, then told him what had occurred with the Shoshone since his last visit. Two Ponies concluded by saying, "I am sorry it was Climbs on Rocks who found you tonight, Billy Casebolt. He is the brother of my second wife and was not with our band when last you honored us with a visit."

"Oh, that's all right, Two Ponies," Casebolt said. "I reckoned it was somethin' like that. He seemed a mite edgy, though. Is there trouble among the Shoshone?"

Two Ponies sighed. "Only the trouble we have seen coming ever since the Thunder Wagon began rolling over the plains and into our hunting grounds. The Shoshone have no quarrel with the whites, but there are so many of them . . . and more come all the time now. We have sat on our horses and watched as the men built the iron road, and in our hearts we have known what would happen."

Like most Indians, the Shoshones had at first regarded the railroad as something of a curiosity. When the Thunder Wagons — the locomotives — began arriving, the smoke and noise had spooked some of the watchers, who were convinced the things were alive and were some sort of flame-belching monsters. In some tribes, such as the Sioux and the Pawnee, the curiosity had rapidly turned to hostility as the Indians tried to halt what they considered encroachment on their territory. Casebolt knew the Shoshones had never taken that attitude. They maintained a sort of aloof neutrality, keeping an eye on the progress of the railroad without interfering with it. Such a stance had to be difficult for many of them, Casebolt realized, especially warriors such as Two Ponies, who were intelligent enough to know what the coming of the Thunder Wagon would mean to his people in the long run. Some of them, like Climbs on Rocks, were doubtless getting a little fed up with the white men and their never-ending advance.

"We've got some trouble, too," Casebolt solemnly told Two Ponies. "A farm belonging to a family of settlers was attacked last night. The whole family was killed, even the little'uns, and the cabin was burned down." He paused for a second, then went on, "Some folks say the Shoshones are to blame."

Two Ponies' strong-featured face hardened. "This is not true!" he declared. "My people have harmed no one. It must have been the Sioux, or some other tribe."

"All I'm doin' is tellin' you what I've

heard, Chief," Casebolt said. "Marshal Tyler rode out to that farm and said the raiders were ridin' unshod horses and wearin' moccasins."

"That does not make them Shoshone," Two Ponies said stiffly.

"That's sure enough true. But the Sioux ain't around here much anymore; most of 'em have moved over east a ways. And we're too far south for Blackfoot or Crow, 'less'n they're raidin' a long way from their home ground." Casebolt shrugged. "Folks who don't know you like I do just naturally figure the Shoshones must've done it."

Two Ponies shook his head. "I know nothing of this. I have always been a friend to the white man, even though I know what his coming will one day mean to my people."

"You don't have to remind me of that. You sure saved my bacon that time, and we've been pards ever since. That's why Marshal Tyler sent me out here to talk to you and see if maybe you could tell me what's goin' on around here."

"I have told you what I know, Billy Casebolt — nothing."

Casebolt sighed. "There's some folks want the army called in."

He saw anger glitter in the chief's dark

eyes. "We have heard about the bluecoats you call the army. We have heard what happened at the place called Sand Creek. If the bluecoats come here, they will not find women and children waiting to be slaughtered. They will find warriors who will greet them with blood and death!"

Casebolt grimaced and held up his hands. "Now just hold on, Two Ponies," he said. "Nobody's said anything about slaughterin' women and kids!" He felt sweat pop out on his forehead, and it wasn't because it was hot inside the tepee. "The marshal hasn't sent for the army. He doesn't want to. If I've got your word that the Shoshones didn't have anything to do with attackin' that farm, why, I can just ride back to Wind River and tell that to Marshal Tyler. Then he can try to find out who *is* responsible."

Two Ponies looked a little mollified. "You tell this to Marshal Tyler. The Shoshone are still friends to the white man — even though it might be better for us if we were not. But we do not want the bluecoats coming here."

"I'll sure tell him," Casebolt promised.

The chief's severe expression eased. "Tonight, you will stay here as our guest. We have missed your stories, Billy Casebolt. None of our warriors tells such exciting tales." Two Ponies smiled slightly. "Perhaps none of them have enough . . . imagination."

Casebolt frowned. "You sayin' you think I make up all the yarns I spin? Why, there ain't a word of any of my stories that ain't the gospel truth! You take that time me and Jim Bridger was cornered by the biggest damn mountain lion you ever did see. I swear, he was pert' near as tall as a mountain, and when he swished his tail, he knocked over a bunch of pine trees and cleared out a whole basin. Where he walked, his pawprints left holes in the ground so deep that boilin' water shot up out of the earth, and when he let out a roar it'd shake a feller right out of his boots. . . ."

Casebolt felt a little better as he continued spinning the tall tale. Now that he knew the Shoshones weren't responsible for the massacre at the Jessup farm, that would be welcome news back in Wind River.

But the trouble had only been postponed, not settled, because the most important question of all still remained.

If the Shoshones hadn't wiped out that family of sodbusters, then who had?

10

Lon Rogers reined in and cuffed his hat back on his light brown hair. A frown creased his forehead as he looked out over the small valley in front of him. This was a side valley that ran off the main one where the Diamond S was located, and cattle frequently strayed up into it. Finding the strays and pushing them back out into the main valley was a time-consuming chore, and since the headquarters of the ranch was a good ten or twelve miles to the south, Kermit Sawyer had ordered his men to build a cabin up here so the hands whose responsibility it was to keep these side canyons cleaned out would have a place to stay.

Beside Lon, Frenchy had also reined in, and he was frowning, too, as he said, "What do you make of that?"

The cabin was about two hundred yards in front of them, just inside the mouth of the smaller canyon. There was a corral behind the cabin, but it was empty at the moment. No smoke curled from the stone chimney of the building, which had a deserted air about it.

"Jess and Smalley are supposed to be up here," Lon said, stating what he and Frenchy already knew. Sawyer had sent them up here with some extra supplies for the two punchers, after all.

"Yeah," Frenchy grunted, hitching his pinto into a cautious walk toward the cabin. "Could be they're up that little canyon somewhere, chousin' out some cows that wandered up there. But there's something about this setup that bothers me, Lon. Don't know what it is, yet, but it's there."

Lon felt the same way. Despite his youth, he had spent his life on one frontier or another, and he had developed some of the same instincts that an older hand like Frenchy possessed. He walked his horse forward alongside the foreman, and as they drew closer to the cabin Lon realized what was wrong. He lifted a hand to point, but Frenchy had seen it, too.

"Door's open," Frenchy said. "Jess and Smalley wouldn't have gone off and left it like that. There's still some bears around here, not to mention other sorts of varmints, and those boys wouldn't want any critters wanderin' into the cabin."

"Look at that!" Lon exclaimed abruptly, indicating some tracks on the ground ahead of them. Both he and Frenchy reined in sharply so their horses' hooves wouldn't obliterate any of the sign.

"Somebody moved some cows and hosses through here, headin' away from the cabin and out into the main valley," Frenchy mused. "Then they headed south. I'm a mite surprised we didn't run into 'em. It's a big country, however."

Lon asked worriedly, "What's going on here, Frenchy? Jess and Smalley didn't leave those tracks."

"Nope, I don't reckon they did." The foreman swung down from his saddle and squatted on his heels, still holding his reins as he studied the marks on the ground. After a moment he said grimly, "Looks like there were only a couple of shod horses — and a handful of unshod ones."

Lon felt a chill go through him at those words. He knew what they meant. "We'd better get on to that cabin," he suggested anxiously.

"Yeah." Frenchy mounted up and heeled his horse into a brisk trot. "Probably too late to do any good, but we got to try."

The two riders broke into a gallop, heedless now of any tracks they might disturb. They had seen enough to have a pretty good idea of what had happened here. As they approached the cabin both men pulled rifles from saddle boots.

"Stay on your hoss," Frenchy called to Lon as they hauled their mounts to a halt in front of the cabin. "I'm goin' in first."

Lon wanted to be with the foreman, but he knew better than to go against a direct order from Frenchy. He sat tensely in his saddle as Frenchy ducked through the open doorway of the small, crudely built log cabin.

There were no shots. Frenchy emerged a few minutes later with his lean face set in hard, angry lines. "Shot and scalped, both of 'em," he said. "Killed in their bunks. Looked like they never had a chance, damn it."

Lon's stomach clenched and he felt sick. "What do we do now?"

"Bury Jess and Smalley, then light a shuck for home. Mr. Sawyer's got to know about this as soon as possible."

"You think Indians did it?"

Frenchy looked at him. "Don't know who else could've. It was a small war party, judgin' from those tracks, but big enough.

They killed Jess and Smalley, stole the remuda from the corral, and pushed the hosses and a bunch of cattle south. Likely swung around the town and went right back to their camp. Damn 'em!"

"But Frenchy," Lon began, "we don't know —"

"We know two friends of ours are dead, men I rode night herd with, many a time. And we know one more thing." Angrily, he reached in his saddlebags and pulled out a folding shovel to scrape a grave out of the hard ground. "Somebody's goin' to pay for this!"

Cole was in the Wind River Café having his lunch when the door was thrust open hurriedly and a man burst into the place. "Is the marshal here?" the man asked excitedly.

Cole swiveled around on his stool. "Right here," he called. He recognized the man looking for him as Stan Brewster, one of the ticket clerks from the Union Pacific depot. "What's wrong, Stan?"

"You'd best get over to the station, Marshal," Brewster replied, panting slightly as if he had been running around town looking for Cole — which was evidently what he had done. He continued, "I think there's about to be some bad trouble."

168

Cole wanted to know what sort of trouble, but he figured he could find out quicker by heading for the depot rather than sitting there asking questions of the winded clerk. Digging a couple of coins out of his pocket, Cole tossed them on the counter, eyed his unfinished bowl of chili regretfully, and said, "So long, Rose," to the pretty, redheaded proprietor of the café.

The depot was only three and a half blocks from the café. Cole's legs carried him quickly toward the big wood-and-stone building that served as the centerpiece of the settlement. Stan Brewster trotted along behind him, still breathing hard. Before Cole had covered even half the distance to the station, he heard angry shouts coming from that direction. He suppressed a sigh of weariness. What in blazes was happening now?

The night had been hectic, with even more saloon fights than usual. Everyone was on edge, and the slightest provocation had caused fists to start flying. Cole had been forced to press Jeremiah Newton into service as a temporary, unofficial deputy to keep the fracases broken up. He hadn't slept, except for a few catnaps during lulls in the commotion, and he was bone-tired this morning. Luckily, things had quieted down a little since the sun came up, and Cole had hoped they would stay that way at least until Billy Casebolt got back. Casebolt was another worry. Cole was anxiously awaiting his deputy's return so that he would know Casebolt was all right.

Cole tossed a question over his shoulder at Brewster. "What's going on down here?"

"A bunch of those striking workers showed up a little while ago," the clerk answered breathlessly. "They said they'd heard General Dodge and Jack Casement sent for men to make them go back to work."

Cole halted and looked around. "Hired guns, you mean?"

"Well, sort of, I guess," Brewster said, his voice betraying his nervousness. "Not gunmen, necessarily, but men who know how to use fists and clubs."

"Damn it," Cole said, softly but fervently. "When are these strong-arm men supposed to get here?"

"The train from Rawlins is due any minute. Those strikers say they came to the station to meet it and run the UP's hard cases back where they came from."

Once again, the trouble had escalated when Cole thought that such a thing wasn't possible. And the utterly ridiculous part about it was that the whole thing had started because of some stupid, groundless rumors. There were no Chinese coolies on their way to take the place of the Irish workers, but the way everybody was stirred up now, nobody was listening to reason anymore.

Cole heard the faint, keening sound of a locomotive's whistle drifting into town from the east. The men gathered at the depot must have heard it, too, because the shouts from that direction grew louder and more angry. With his face set in grim lines, Cole started toward the station again, this time moving at a quick trot.

He pushed through the doors of the building and saw that not only was the platform full of men, but the crowd had also spilled into the lobby. Every face was contorted with anger, and many of the men were gripping makeshift clubs. Cole saw several workers he recognized from his own time with the Union Pacific, but as their hostile gazes turned toward him he knew that none of them regarded him as a friend anymore. The badge pinned to his buckskin shirt had changed all that.

Another familiar face caught Cole's eye as he paused just inside the lobby. Abner Langdon stood to one side, an anxious expression on his florid face. Over the shouting of the mob, Cole asked the saloon-keeper, "What are you doing here, Langdon?"

"I followed these boys down here to try to talk some sense into them," Langdon replied. "Most of 'em were in my place when they got so riled up."

"What happened?"

Langdon shook his head. "I'm not sure. They heard somewhere that the UP sent for men to make them go back to work. A lot of 'em had been drinking all night already, and that news went through them like a house afire. They were headed down here to the depot almost before I knew what was going on, and they stirred up all the men in the other saloons along the way."

Cole had already figured out that there were more men here than could have fit into Langdon's tent. But Langdon was right about the way news spread in Wind River these days. All it took was a rumor — a *hint* of a rumor — and half the people in town seemed ready to raise hell and shove a chunk under the corner.

Cole turned to Stan Brewster, who had followed him into the building. "You've got a shotgun in the express office." It was more of a statement than a question.

"Well, sure," Brewster began, "but —"

"Get it," Cole cut in. "Bring it to me."

Brewster blinked and hesitated, then hurried across the lobby and behind the ticket counter to a door that led into the freight office. Cole followed, aware that many of the striking workers were watching him, waiting to see what he was going to do. He didn't want them getting between him and Brewster when the clerk emerged from the office with the scattergun. A glance over Cole's shoulder showed him no sign of Abner Langdon. Now that the marshal was on hand, the saloon owner had done the smart thing and gotten out while the getting was good.

Brewster came out of the freight office as Cole reached the ticket counter. Angry mutters came from the assembled railroad workers at the sight of the shotgun in the clerk's hands. Cole reached over the counter and took it, then swung the double barrels toward the men clustered around the doors to the platform. Some of them had started to move toward him, but the twin muzzles of the greener stopped them. There were few things in the world more intimidating close up than the yawning black bores of a double-barreled shotgun.

"Everybody quiet down!" Cole shouted as the whistle of the approaching locomotive sounded again, considerably closer this time.

"This is none of your business, Marshal!" one of the men called back at him. "This is between us and the Union damned Pacific!"

"We've had this argument before," Cole said, his voice loud enough to carry to the men out on the platform. "I'm not going to allow any riots in my town. You boys go on and get out of here before the train comes in."

"We got a right to be here!" another man yelled. "This depot wouldn't even be here if it wasn't for us!"

The man had a point, Cole thought to himself, but he wasn't about to concede it aloud. Instead he said, "You can leave peacefullike and go about your business, or you can go to jail. Up to you."

He heard the sound of the other door into the lobby opening behind him, but he didn't want to take his eyes off the men on the far side of the room. He had made a mistake by not bringing Jeremiah with him to cover his back, Cole realized, but it was too late to do anything about it . . . except hope that whoever was behind him wasn't an enemy.

That was a futile hope, he discovered an instant later, as a man in the crowd yelled,

"Get him!" and there was a rush of footsteps behind him.

He twisted halfway around and saw several men charging toward him. They must have slipped off the platform and circled the building to come in the front door, Cole thought. He should have anticipated that move. As he swung the scattergun toward his attackers his finger tensed on the double trigger, then eased off at the last second. He didn't want to cut these men down with a load of buckshot. They weren't outlaws; they were just men honestly afraid that they would lose their jobs.

But that didn't make them any less dangerous.

Swiftly, Cole reversed the shotgun and chopped at the man nearest him with the butt of the weapon. The shotgun's stock cracked into the man's jaw and sent him sprawling backward under the feet of his companions. A couple of them got their feet tangled up and fell heavily. That didn't account for all of them, however, and one of the men still on his feet swung a club at Cole's head.

Cole ducked under the blow and drove the barrels of the greener into the man's midsection, doubling him over with a grunt of pain. Cole whipped the shotgun around again and smacked the stock against the side of the man's head. Before he was able to do anything else, a heavy weight landed on his back, and a voice howled in his ear, "I got him! Gimme a hand here!"

Cole stumbled forward as the man on his back drove a punch against his skull above the right ear. He let go of the shotgun with his right hand, reached up, and grabbed hold of the man's hair. Bending forward and hauling with all his strength, Cole sent the man flying off his back to crash down on the floor of the depot.

There were men all around him as he straightened, too many men for him to fight. He tried to angle the barrels of the greener toward the ceiling, hoping to fire the shotgun into the air, knowing the blast would at least make them pull back momentarily. But hands grabbed the barrels and wrenched them down. A club slammed into the back of Cole's shoulders from behind, staggering him. He couldn't keep his hold on the weapon. It was torn away from him as the train whistle blew again, very close now, and the rumble of the locomotive shook the station with its intensity as it rolled past the platform, slowing to a stop.

Through the open doors to the platform, Cole caught a glimpse of angry men charging the passenger cars. They were met by more men who jumped off the train wielding clubs. Obviously, they had been ready for trouble. The platform became a chaotic sea of slashing clubs, swinging fists, and furious shouts.

Then the part of the mob that had surrounded Cole closed in on him even more, cutting off his view. Blows pummeled him back and forth. He reached for his Colt, but it was gone. Someone kicked the back of his left knee, knocking that leg out from under him. His balance deserted him and he would have fallen if not for the press of men around him, holding him up as they crashed fists into his body. Cole fought back as best he could, relishing the impact that rolled up his arm as his fist crashed into the middle of a man's face, pulping his nose. Blood spurted hotly across Cole's knuckles, and he reveled in that brief sensation, too. He wasn't thinking anymore, just fighting berserkly, his lips pulled back in a grimace and his breath panting harshly between clenched teeth.

Cole was able to stay on his feet for a few minutes, but then the sheer weight of numbers was too much for him. He went down, and boots began to thud into him as the striking railroad workers kicked him viciously. A part of his brain knew that he was likely to die here and now, stomped to death in a damned train station. It was not a death he would have picked for himself.

Vaguely, he heard something that sounded like a bugle being blown. Yes, that was exactly what it was, he decided. He had ridden with enough cavalry patrols as a civilian scout to recognize the sound of a bugle, even half-conscious as he was. There was a ripple of gunfire, then Cole realized nobody was kicking him anymore. In fact, as he drew great heaving breaths of air into his bruised and battered body, he saw that the men around him had drawn back, giving him some room not only to breathe but to push himself up on hands and knees.

A strong hand gripped his upper arm. "Let me help you, Marshal," an unfamiliar voice said. Cole was lifted to his feet, seemingly with ease. The hand let go of his arm and he swayed for a second, then caught himself.

He found himself facing a tall, well-built man in the uniform of an army major. The officer had a strong jaw, high cheekbones, and crisp black hair underneath his dark blue hat. He asked briskly, "Are you all right, Marshal?"

Cole lifted his left hand and used the back

of it to wipe blood off his mouth. "Reckon I will be," he replied, his lips and tongue thick from the beating he had suffered. "Thanks, Major."

"Major Thomas Burdette," the officer introduced himself. "I'm glad we arrived when we did. It appears that things have gotten rather out of hand here in Wind River."

There was a certain smugness in Major Burdette's tone that rubbed Cole the wrong way, but he had to admit that without the cavalry's intervention, he would have likely been trampled into an ugly smear on the floorboards by now. Cole glanced around and saw half a dozen troopers armed with Spencer carbines ranged around the depot lobby, covering the rioters. At least a dozen more soldiers were on the platform, maintaining order out there. Major Burdette had drawn his saber, and it was still in his left hand, ready for use if need be. That necessity seemed to have evaporated.

"I'm not sure what's going on here," Burdette went on. "When we rode in, one of the townspeople told us there was a riot here in the train station and that you were in trouble, Marshal. Perhaps you could explain . . . ?"

Cole jerked his bloody chin toward the

men filling the lobby. "Some of these gents used to work for the Union Pacific, until they went on strike. The others work for the UP now, and they came to convince the others to go back to their jobs." That left out the reasons behind the trouble, but it was enough for the moment, Cole figured.

"I see," Burdette said. "Do you want any of these men arrested?"

Cole thought about it for a few seconds, then shook his head. "I want 'em to go on about their business," he said, loudly enough for them all to hear. "There's been enough trouble today."

"Very well." Burdette turned to his noncom, a burly, sandy-haired sergeant who stood nearby with the flap of his holster unsnapped. "Sergeant Mullins, disperse this crowd."

"Yes, sir," the sergeant replied, then turned to the erstwhile rioters and bellowed, "You heard the major! Get out o' here while you got the chance!"

The striking railroad workers began drifting out of the depot, muttering and grumbling all the way. The men who had come in on the train gathered on the platform, no doubt waiting for orders from the man in charge of their mission here.

"I think you should have a doctor take a

look at you, Marshal," Burdette said as he sheathed his saber and fell in alongside Cole and both of them started for the street door. "I have a medical officer if there's not a physician here in town."

"We've got a doctor, a good one," Cole replied curtly. "But I'm all right, Major. I've been in enough fracases to know when I need a sawbones and when I don't."

Burdette shrugged slightly. "Suit yourself. You're certainly not under my command."

"I wasn't expecting you for another day or two," Cole said as they walked the short block to Grenville Avenue and turned onto the boardwalk along the main street.

"We were on patrol when a rider from Fort Laramie reached us with new orders. That cut down the time it took for us to arrive." The major walked with his hands clasped behind his back and his spine ramrod straight. "I suppose you can tell us more about why we were summoned?"

"That's what I figure to do," Cole grunted. "Come on down to my office with me, and I'll give you the whole story."

"Just the background will be sufficient. I'm fully aware of the purpose of our basic mission here."

Cole glanced over at the officer. "And what would *that* be?" he asked.

Burdette looked a little surprised. "Why, to eradicate the threat of an uprising by the Shoshone and ensure the peaceful progress of the Union Pacific, of course, by any means necessary."

"Including the eradication of the Shoshone?" Cole felt a surge of anger that he tried to control.

Burdette looked at him blandly and repeated, "By any means necessary."

Well, Cole thought, he had been wrong yet again.

It looked like things could *always* get worse.

11

Cole and Major Burdette reached the building that housed the land development company, and the cavalry officer cast an amused glance at the handmade sign with the legend WIND RIVVER MARSHELS OFFICE burned into it. The sign hung from the roof over the boardwalk and was the work of Billy Casebolt. Burdette quirked an eyebrow and asked dryly, "I take it this is our destination?"

Cole controlled his temper with an effort, his dislike for Burdette growing. He said, "This is my office. Come on inside. There's coffee on the stove — well, sorry, there's not, come to think of it. My deputy usually puts it on to boil, and he's out of town right now."

"That's quite all right," Burdette said. He followed Cole through the door and then into the spartanly furnished front room. "We had coffee this morning before we broke camp and rode on into town."

Without being asked, the major took off his gauntlets, tucked them behind the broad black belt around his lean waist, then removed his hat and sat down in the chair in front of Cole's desk. Cole went behind the desk and sat down gratefully. That fight had taken quite a bit out of him.

"Well, now," Burdette said, "tell me about this Indian trouble. I understand a settler's farm near here was raided and the entire family massacred by the Shoshone?"

"We don't know that," Cole replied.

"The settler and his family *weren't* killed?" Burdette did that annoying thing with his eyebrow again.

"They're dead, all right," snapped Cole. "But I don't know who killed them."

"Were there any tracks to be found? Surely the raiders left *some* sign."

"There were tracks," Cole admitted. "Unshod ponies."

"And footprints?"

"Wearing moccasins." Cole wasn't sure why his answers were so grudging. He ought to be happy to cooperate with the cavalry, he told himself. Maybe it was just the instinctive antagonism he felt toward Major Burdette. He had run into officers like Burdette before, back when he was working for the army. All spit 'n polish and thought they knew everything, even if they were fresh from the East and didn't know sic 'em about the frontier.

Burdette spread his hands. "Well, there," he said with a smile, "who else could the killers have been except Indians?"

"Doesn't mean they were Shoshone. There are other tribes of Indians. Used to be plenty of Sioux around here, and they've hated the railroad right from the start."

"To the best of the army's knowledge, there are no Sioux in this vicinity at the present time," Burdette said. "They've moved to the east." His voice stiffened. "That's where I should be right now, in fact, where I could do some real good. Instead I was sent here to clean up a minor threat from some ragtag band of savages."

"It wasn't a minor threat to Ben Jessup and his family," Cole said, struggling to hold a tight rein on his emotions. "They're just as dead, no matter who killed them."

Burdette waved a hand. "Of course. That's not what I meant. And orders are orders, after all. I'll run down those Shoshone, and unless they can convince me that they intend to honor our treaties with them in the future, they will be forced to comply."

Cole didn't ask Burdette how he intended

to force the Shoshones to do anything. It had been his experience that it was damned near impossible to *force* somebody to do something. You could force them not to do something, you could show them it was in their best interests to follow a certain course, but most of the time when you got right down to it, forcing somebody to do something usually meant killing them for not doing it.

"Do you know who's responsible for you being here?" Cole asked the major.

"I understand that former general John Casement of the Union Pacific sent the wire to Fort Laramie requesting military assistance."

"And do you know why Casement sent that telegram?"

"Some of his workers were shot and scalped by hostiles, I believe."

"That's what Casement thinks."

"And you have reason to doubt his conclusions?" Burdette asked.

For a moment Cole didn't answer. Then he shook his head. "Not really. Only what my guts tell me."

Burdette smiled thinly. "No offense, Marshal, but that's hardly conclusive proof of anything."

"Neither are some unshod pony tracks."

"Those tracks indicate a high likelihood of Indian involvement, and the only Indians around here are the Shoshone." Burdette sighed. "Really, Marshal, I'm afraid we're not getting anywhere. I merely asked for some information, and you're trying to argue me out of what should be quite obvious. The Shoshone have risen." He leaned back and crossed his arms. "And I intend to put them down again."

Cole scraped his chair back, stalked over to the window, and peered out unseeingly at Grenville Avenue for a long moment. Finally, he turned and said, "I don't reckon you'd give me a little time."

"Time for what?" Burdette asked.

"I sent my deputy out to talk to Two Ponies, the Shoshone chief. He's not back yet."

"You sent one man on a dangerous mission like that?" Burdette was clearly surprised and disapproving.

"Billy's friends with the Shoshones, especially Two Ponies. He'll get to the truth if anybody can."

"How long has he been gone?"

"He rode out yesterday afternoon," Cole said.

"Not quite twenty-four hours . . . You might as well face it, Marshal, your deputy's scalp is probably adorning the lodge of some Shoshone war chief by now, unless it's still hanging from the savage's belt."

"I don't think so," Cole said stubbornly. "I think Billy's going to get to the bottom of this, and I don't believe the Shoshones are behind it."

Burdette stood up and faced Cole squarely. "I'm sorry, Marshal, but what you believe or don't believe is a matter of no concern to me. My orders say to investigate this uprising and deal with it. That is what I intend to do." He clapped his hat back on his head.

"What exactly do you mean by that?" Cole demanded.

"I intend to ride out of Wind River first thing tomorrow morning with my patrol. I'd leave this afternoon, but the men have had a long ride, and their mounts need rest. After we leave, I intend to find the hostiles and punish them for what they've done."

"Punish them?" Cole repeated. "I thought you were supposed to make them honor the treaties."

"What better way to do that than to impress upon them the futility of opposing the United States Army?" Without waiting for Cole to answer, Burdette nodded his head and turned toward the door. "Good day, Marshal. Let me know if you have any more trouble with civil disturbances."

The arrogant comment was enough to finally push Cole over the edge. He stepped around the desk quickly and reached out to grasp Burdette's arm. "Just wait one damned minute!"

Burdette stiffened, and his left hand went to his saber. "I'll thank you to let go of me, Tyler," he snapped. "I don't take kindly to being grabbed, especially by civilians."

"And I don't take kindly to stiff-necked army greenhorns coming in here and telling me what they're going to do and what they're not going to do," Cole shot back. "You just want to go out and kill a few Shoshones, whether they've done anything or not, so that your commanding officer will send you against the Sioux. You figure that's where the glory is!"

"Let go of me," Burdette grated.

Cole released the major's arm and stepped back. "Don't get the idea I like touching somebody like you, Burdette." He snorted. "Hell, when you get down to it, you're nothing but an errand boy for the Union Pacific."

"How dare you —" Burdette blazed.

Cole cut in, "Well, that so-called civil disturbance you rode in on is going to be a lot more trouble for the UP than the Shoshones! In case you didn't notice, Major, that was one hell of a riot, and it was all because most of the track layers around here have gone on strike. They've got some crazy idea in their heads that Chinese coolies are going to come in and take over their jobs. You'd accomplish more by getting to the bottom of that than you would chasing the Shoshones around."

Burdette shook his head stubbornly. "My orders don't say anything about this matter. I'm to deal with the Indian threat, and that's all."

Cole sighed in frustration. Trying to talk sense to Burdette was like arguing with a pine tree.

Boot heels rattled on the boardwalk outside. Cole looked over in time to see Kermit Sawyer pass by the window and then turn in at the door. The Texan appeared in the doorway of the office a second later and glared at Cole before turning his attention to the major. Sawyer seemed surprised to see an army officer.

"So," grunted Sawyer, "you took my advice and finally got around to callin' in the army, eh?"

"You've got that wrong, as usual, Sawyer," Cole said.

Burdette looked steadily at Sawyer. "Who

might you be, sir?"

"Kermit Sawyer, late of the Colorado River country down in Texas, now owner of the Diamond S spread north of here," the cattleman replied. "I reckon you're here to put a stop to all the thievin' and killin' those damned redskins have been doin'."

Before Burdette could reply, Cole asked, "Has something else happened, Sawyer?"

"Damn right it has. Two of my hands were killed, and some of my stock was run off. The killers were ridin' unshod horses."

Burdette threw a triumphant glance at Cole, then said to Sawyer, "You say this happened north of town, Mr. Sawyer?"

"That's right. I can show you the place. You can pick up the bastards' tracks there, probably follow 'em right back to their camp. Likely my cattle will have been butchered by the time you catch up to 'em, but I don't care about that near as much as I do makin' those savages pay for killin' my hands."

"I can assure you, sir, we'll do our best to recover your stolen property, as well as meting out justice to the killers of your employees."

Cole watched them, his disgust growing. Sawyer and Burdette were two of a kind, all right, despite the differences in their backgrounds. Both of them were eager to jump to conclusions — and those conclusions revolved around hunting down the Shoshones.

"Sorry to break up your party, gents," Cole said, "but you said you and your men weren't pulling out until tomorrow, Major, and I expect my deputy will be back before then. He can tell us what Two Ponies has to say."

Sawyer snorted contemptuously, and Burdette turned his smug expression on Cole. "Under the circumstances, Marshal, I believe the troop will leave this afternoon after all. I want to investigate the incident on Mr. Sawyer's ranch." He paused, then added, "And I fail to see why you think the word of a savage would carry any weight with the United States Army, even if this deputy of yours does return shortly."

Cole's face was bleak as he shook his head. "You're making a mistake, Major."

"No, Marshal. I'm following orders." Burdette turned back to the Texan. "Come along, Mr. Sawyer. I want to hear more about this atrocity."

They started out the door, Sawyer saying as they departed, "You and your troop can make camp at the Diamond S tonight, Major. I'd be glad to put you up."

"Thank you, Mr. Sawyer. We can study those tracks and start following them as soon as it's light tomorrow morning."

Cole sank down behind his desk and sighed. Control of this situation had well and truly slipped away from him now — if he had ever really had control of it in the first place, which he was starting to doubt.

The sound of a new voice in the corridor outside made him look up sharply. "Hello, Mr. Sawyer," Cole heard Simone McKay say.

"Howdy, ma'am," Sawyer replied. "I'd like you to meet Major Burdette. Major, this is Mrs. McKay."

Cole was on his feet again by that time, moving quickly around the desk to the door so that he could see into the short hallway opening onto the boardwalk. Simone, wearing a dark blue dress and hat, had just entered the building and was smiling at the cavalry officer, who had gallantly doffed his hat. "It's an honor and a privilege to make your acquaintance, ma'am," he said as he took Simone's hand.

At least Burdette was just shaking her hand, Cole thought. He halfway expected the officer to bend over and kiss it like some sort of fancy-ass European. Simone seemed just as impressed as she would have been had Burdette done such a thing, though. Her smile grew wider as she looked at the handsome young officer.

"What brings you to Wind River, Major Burdette?" she asked.

"Duty, ma'am. My troop and I are here to pacify the Indians that have started to give trouble in this area."

"Oh." Simone glanced over Burdette's shoulder at Cole, who was glowering in the doorway of the marshal's office. "I wasn't aware you had sent for the army, Marshal Tyler."

"I didn't," Cole said flatly. "Jack Casement wired Fort Laramie. I think it's a mistake."

Burdette chuckled. "No offense, Mrs. McKay, but Marshal Tyler here seems to think that the Shoshone are some sort of peace-loving psalm singers."

"I never said that," Cole snapped. "I wouldn't cross 'em unless I had to — especially if I wasn't sure there was a good reason for doing it."

"Those hands of mine they slaughtered are reason enough," Sawyer said.

Simone frowned. "There have been more killings?"

"Two of my men were murdered, and I had some cows and horses stolen," the

Texan told her. "There ain't no doubt the Shoshones were responsible."

"There's doubt," Cole said stubbornly. "I sent Billy Casebolt out to talk to Two Ponies, Mrs. McKay, but he's not back yet."

Simone looked at Burdette. "Deputy Casebolt does know those Indians better than anyone else around here, Major. Perhaps you would be wise to wait until he returns and gives the marshal his report."

"I'm sorry, ma'am, but I've got to follow my orders," said Burdette. "And they say to deal with this Indian problem as I see fit. My men and I are riding out to Mr. Sawyer's ranch, and we'll pick up the trail of the raiders there."

"Well, that seems to make sense, too." Once more Simone smiled at the officer. "Good luck on your mission, Major."

"Thank you, ma'am."

"If you have a chance later, please stop by the Territorial House. I own it, you know, and I'd like to have you as my guest for dinner in our dining room."

"Thank you again, ma'am." Burdette smiled warmly at her in return. "I'd like that."

Cole gritted his teeth, wondering why Simone was playing up so to this addlepated young fool. But it was none of his business whom she had dinner with, or whom she smiled at, he reminded himself. He sure as hell didn't have any claim on her.

"We'd best be movin' along," Sawyer said, and Burdette nodded in agreement as he replaced his hat on his head. He tugged on the brim as he nodded politely to Simone, then she moved aside to let the two men step out onto the boardwalk.

As Sawyer and Burdette strode down the street Simone turned to Cole. "Having the cavalry here should solve our problems, shouldn't it?"

"I wouldn't count on it," Cole said curtly.

"I heard there was some trouble earlier." She moved a couple of steps closer to him. "You've been hurt. I hadn't noticed the bruises until now."

That's because you were too busy mooning over Burdette, Cole thought, but instead of saying it, he just shrugged his shoulders. "The Union Pacific sent for some strong-arm men to try to force the strikers to go back to work," he explained. "Those hotheaded Irishmen were waiting for the train when it pulled in. There was quite a fracas."

"And you were caught right in the middle of it," Simone guessed. "Were you hurt badly?"

"I'll be all right," Cole replied, brushing

off her question. Truth to tell, he hurt all over, his muscles aching and throbbing from the beating he had taken.

"At least you were able to keep things from getting out of hand."

Cole hesitated, then said, "The army did that. Burdette and his troop rode in while the ruckus was going on." The admission tasted bitter in his mouth.

"Oh. Well, I'm sure you were doing your best, Marshal."

"Yeah. Too bad that's not good enough anymore." Cole nodded briskly to her. "Good day to you, Mrs. McKay."

He turned and went back into his office before Simone could say anything else, knowing that he was being rather rude to her but no longer caring, at least not right now.

Something was wrong as all hell about this whole mess. Cole could sense it, but damned if he could put his finger on what it was.

And while he tried to figure it out, things just kept spiraling downward. It was like trying to dig a hole in quicksand — the harder he tried to get out, the lower he sank.

Maybe Billy Casebolt would throw him a rope. Right now it was about the only hope he had left.

12

Delia Hatfield had learned how to ignore her daughter Gretchen's babbling, at least for the most part. Delia's maternal instincts told her when to pay attention, when Gretchen might be saying something important. But at the moment, as Delia got ready to put a pan of corn bread in the oven, Gretchen was going on about some spotted dog she had seen earlier in the day, and Delia was letting the child's words go in one ear and out the other.

At least things were a bit more peaceful now between her and Michael, Delia thought. Her visit to the newspaper office the day before had buoyed her spirits for some reason. Perhaps seeing Michael in his element . . . seeing him where he was the happiest . . . had convinced her to be more tolerant of his passion for the newspaper. After all, a man had a right to do what made him happy — within reason, of course.

She bent over to open the door of the oven, then picked up the pan from her kitchen counter. Suddenly a sharp pain shot through her body, and she gasped from surprise as much as from discomfort. The pain grew rapidly, however, completely replacing the surprise. Delia bent down again, and the pan slipped from her hands and clattered to the floor.

"Mama?" Gretchen said, forgetting about the spotted dog in her worry. "Mama sick?"

Delia sank to her knees, biting her lip to keep from crying out at the pain gripping her. "Y-yes, Gretchen," she managed to choke out. "Mama is . . . very sick. Can you . . . can you go find . . . Papa?"

Gretchen came over to her and extended a hand, but the little girl stopped short of actually touching her mother. Her face was filled with fear. "Find Papa?" she echoed tentatively.

"Yes . . . p-please. Go on . . . now . . . dear."

Slowly, Gretchen backed away, her blue eyes wide. She didn't stop until she bumped up against the back door of the house. Hesitantly, she reached up to touch the latch.

"Th-that's it," Delia encouraged her. "Go on, Gretchen." Another thought occurred

199

to her. Michael might not be at the newspaper office. He could have gone somewhere else to report on some news. She added, "If you can't . . . can't find Papa . . . then fetch Dr. Kent. Can you do that, Gretchen?"

Wordlessly, the child nodded, her face solemn as well as frightened.

"Th-thank you . . . G-Gretchen . . ."

Sweat had popped out on Delia's face, beading and rolling down her forehead and her cheeks. A pulse throbbed in her temple, and she felt hot for some reason, even though the late-summer day wasn't particularly warm. At the same time, her fingers were trembling as if she was chilled.

With maddening slowness, Gretchen made up her mind to carry out her mother's commands. She reached up again, unlatched the door, and swung it open. For a long moment she stood there in the doorway, watching Delia with that scared, solemn expression.

Then she turned and broke into a run, vanishing from Delia's sight.

Delia closed her eyes and tried to push the pain out of her mind. She tried thinking about the baby, but that only made it worse, because she was desperately afraid there was something wrong with the child she was carrying. That was the only explanation for the agony she was suffering. Something was wrong with the baby, she sobbed wordlessly, and she was going to lose it and maybe die herself and leave Michael and Gretchen all alone. . . .

A fresh wave of pain, worse than any that had come before, and accompanied this time by nausea, washed through her. Delia felt herself swaying on her knees, then she slumped forward despite her best efforts to stay upright. She managed to turn herself to the side, so that her shoulder struck the floor first, rather than her swollen belly. Panting rapidly, she tried to hang on to consciousness, but it was slipping away from her and she knew it.

Vaguely, she was aware that she was not in labor. She had experienced that when Gretchen was born, and this was different, terrifyingly different. She was sure, too, that her water had not broken. But she was still convinced that the pain came from the baby, that something had gone horribly awry in her body.

She offered up a silent prayer for the unborn child, for Michael and Gretchen, for herself. Then, with a shudder, she surrendered to the blackness that rose up to claim her.

■ ■ ■ ■

"Papa!"

The frightened cry made Michael Hatfield wrench his head up from the freshly printed sheet he was studying proudly. The press was still working, its clatter and clank filling the little building where the newspaper office was housed, as Michael's assistants turned the big cranks attached to the apparatus. Gretchen's scream cut cleanly through the noise, however.

Michael whirled around and tossed the sheet of newsprint aside. Gretchen came stumbling through the front door of the office, and Michael ran through the gate in the railing that divided the room to sweep her up in his arms. She was alone and crying big tears that rolled down her face as she sobbed.

"What is it?" Michael asked urgently. "What's wrong, Gretchen?"

"M-Mama!" she sobbed. "Mama sick!"

An icy feeling of dread shot through Michael. For weeks now, Delia had seemed convinced that something was wrong. Perhaps her intuition had been correct all along. "What happened to her?" he asked Gretchen, trying to keep his voice steady.

He didn't want the little girl to see how frightened he really was. That would only scare Gretchen worse.

"Mama fall down," she said, sniffling. "Mama cry."

Michael looked around desperately, not sure what he was looking for. Answers, maybe. Something to tell him what to do. He drew a deep, ragged breath.

"Hello, Michael," a new voice said from the doorway. "I just stopped by to pick up a copy of this week's paper as it comes off the pre— oh, my God, what's wrong?"

Simone McKay stood there, a worried expression on her attractive face. Michael practically ran over to her and thrust the squirming Gretchen into her arms.

"Something's wrong with Delia!" he said frantically. "Can you watch Gretchen for me while I fetch Dr. Kent?"

Simone tightened her grip on Gretchen. "I'll do better than that. I'll get word to Judson. You go on home as quickly as you can, Michael."

He nodded jerkily. That was a better idea, he thought. He started out the door at a run, then caught the jamb and pulled himself back. "The press run is going fine," he told Simone.

"Don't worry about the paper!" she

203

scolded. "Just go home!"

Michael nodded again and dashed out the door, his shoes pounding against the boardwalk as he ran.

He provided quite a spectacle for the townspeople, sprinting down the street like that toward his house. But he didn't care. All he wanted to do was reach Delia's side and help her, before it was too late.

Too late. The words echoed ominously in his head. If anything happened to Delia — or the baby — or both of them — he would never forgive himself. She had never wanted to move out here in the first place, and she hadn't wanted to stay once they had seen what life was like here in Wind River. Ruthless outlaws, savage Indians, brawling railroad workers, wild cowboys . . . Delia was right. This was no place to be bringing up a family.

Self-recrimination wasn't going to do any good now, Michael told himself. He blanked all the thoughts out of his mind and concentrated on getting to his house as fast as he could.

Almost out of control, he careened around a corner onto the side street where he and Delia lived. He saw the house up ahead. It looked perfectly normal, nothing fancy, just a nice little house. Michael bounded onto the porch and slammed the door open. "Delia!" he shouted. "Delia, where are you?"

He should have asked Gretchen, he thought, but it hadn't occurred to him at the time, so surprised had he been by his daughter's unexpected arrival at the newspaper office. He thought about the time of day it was. Delia would have likely been preparing supper for him. He ran past the parlor and down the hall to the kitchen.

She was there, slumped in a motionless heap on the floor. Michael fell to his knees beside her, crying out, "Delia! Oh, Lord, Delia!" He grasped her shoulders and turned her so that he could see her face. Her features were pale and washed out, contorted with the pain that had gripped her.

But she was breathing, he realized with a surge of relief as he saw the faint up-and-down motion of her chest. As he leaned closer to her he could hear the air going in and out of her. Her mouth was open, and her breathing was harsh and strained.

He felt her forehead. She was feverish, her skin very warm to his touch. Not knowing what else to do, Michael opened the throat of her dress, hoping that might make her breathe easier, as he said, "Please be all right, Delia! Please be all right."

The table was within reach. He took hold of a corner of the linen tablecloth and yanked it off the table, spilling the sugar bowl in the process. Michael laid the cloth over her and tucked it around her, not knowing if he was doing the right thing or not.

Was the baby coming? he wondered. He knew little about how a woman gave birth. When Gretchen had been born, he and the other menfolks in the family had been banished from the house in Cincinnati. The doctor had been the only male allowed anywhere near the new mother. All Michael really knew about birthing babies was how to grin from ear to ear when somebody came and told him he had a fine, spanking-new daughter and that mother and child were doing fine.

That skill didn't do him, or Delia, one damned bit of good now.

He took a deep breath, then another, forcing himself to calm down a little. He wasn't completely ignorant, he reminded himself. Delia had told him some things about the process, if only he could remember what she had said. There had been something about pains that came and went, and something else about . . . water breaking, was that it? That didn't make any sense.

If Delia was still in pain through her unconsciousness, it seemed to be fairly consistent. She wasn't writhing or moaning. Feeling awkward and stupid, Michael slipped his hand underneath the tablecloth and felt her dress around her lower body. There was no dampness as far as he could tell. Maybe she wasn't having the baby now.

But if she wasn't, what had caused her to pass out like this, in such obvious pain that Gretchen had been terrified?

The sound of footsteps in the front room made him lift his head hopefully, and the next instant a British-accented voice called urgently, "Michael! Where are you, lad?"

"In here, Dr. Kent!" Michael shouted back to the physician. "In the kitchen!"

Kent hurried down the hall and into the room, followed by Simone McKay. As the doctor knelt on the other side of Delia, he said briskly, "Please move back and give me some room, Michael. Don't worry about Delia. I'll do my very best for her."

Michael knew that, but it was still difficult to leave Delia's side. Simone put a hand on his shoulder, gently urging him back, and after a moment he straightened from his crouch and let her steer him over to the wall next to the oven, where the fire was still burning. Michael felt the heat coming from the squat, black, cast-iron oven.

"I'm sure she'll be all right, Michael," Simone told him. "There's no finer doctor west of the Mississippi than Judson Kent."

"I know," Michael said, wiping a trembling hand across his face. "I . . . I just wish I knew what was wrong." Something else occurred to him, and he looked at Simone and asked, "Where's Gretchen?"

"After I sent someone to fetch Dr. Kent, I took her to Abigail Paine's house," Simone explained. "Abigail said she would be happy to look after Gretchen for as long as you need her to."

Michael nodded shakily and said, "Thanks. That was a good idea." Abigail Paine, who ran the nearby boardinghouse with her husband, Lawton, had a brood of her own children, and she had frequently kept Gretchen for Michael and Delia in the past. The little girl always enjoyed staying with the Paine youngsters.

That was one worry off Michael's mind, at least. Now he could concentrate on Delia. Dr. Kent had felt her forehead, probed her stomach, and now had his stethoscope out and was listening to Delia's heartbeat. Michael couldn't tell anything from the physician's expression, which seemed to be a bearded mask at the moment. Kent lowered the tablecloth Michael had spread over Delia and placed his hand on the unconscious young woman's abdomen, low down on the right side. He pressed firmly, and Delia stirred and let out a groan of pain.

"What are you doing to her?" Michael asked in a ragged voice.

"Trying to determine what's wrong," Kent replied evenly.

"It's the baby, isn't it? Something's wrong with the baby?"

Kent shook his head. "I don't believe so. Did Delia complain of any pains earlier in the day?"

Michael frowned in thought. "Not while I was around. Oh, she said this morning that her stomach didn't feel very good, but that's pretty much normal when a woman's in the family way, isn't it?"

Kent looked intently at Michael. "She told me yesterday that the so-called morning sickness hadn't afflicted her in several months. Isn't that correct?"

"Well . . . come to think of it . . . I guess you're right, Doctor. You mean those pains she was having earlier were caused by something else?"

"It certainly seems that way to me. I believe, Michael, that your wife has suffered an acute attack of appendicitis."

"What?" Simone asked.

"Appendicitis. An inflammation of a small, vestigial organ attached to the lower intestine. It will have to be removed as soon as possible."

"My God!" Michael exclaimed. "You mean you're going to have to operate on her?"

Kent stood up, his face grim now. "Immediately. Delia will have to be taken to my office. I could fetch my instruments and do the procedure here, but it would be much better if she was moved."

"It won't hurt her worse to move her?"

"I won't lie to you, Michael," Kent said. "She'll be in great pain, but she has already lost consciousness. The advantages outweigh the risks." He moved toward the hall. "I'll find some men to carry her, then go on down to the office to get ready."

"I'll carry her," Michael declared, stepping determinedly toward Delia.

Kent moved smoothly in front of him. "I'd rather you didn't," he said. "We don't want to run the risk of dropping her, to put it bluntly. That could make things a great deal worse."

For a couple of seconds, Michael looked as if he wanted to shove the medico out of his way. Then he sighed and nodded. "You're right. Go ahead, Doctor. But if there's anything I can do . . ."

"Certainly there is," Kent told him briskly. "You can pray, my boy. And I suggest you do so."

It was late afternoon when Billy Casebolt tied his pinto to the hitch rail in front of the marshal's office. Cole had been watching for him, hoping that nothing had happened that would delay the deputy's return to Wind River, and he met Casebolt on the boardwalk.

"You all right, Billy?" Cole asked.

Casebolt thumbed back his hat. "Well, sure. Why wouldn't I be?"

"Did you find Two Ponies?"

"Yep. Or I reckon I should say, he found me. Well, to tell the truth, it was his brother-in-law, a feller called Climbs on Rocks, who first run across me, but he took me right to the Shoshones' camp."

"Did Two Ponies know anything about that raid on the Jessup farm?"

Casebolt snorted. " 'Course not. I didn't figger him and his band had anything to do with that. It just ain't like 'em."

"What about some railroad workers who were killed and scalped along the roadbed west of here? Or two of Sawyer's cowboys who were done in the same way when some of his stock was stolen?"

Casebolt gaped at Cole, obviously shocked by the news. "When in blazes did all that happen?" he demanded.

"Jack Casement of the UP found his workers yesterday morning and got to town later in the day to report it. Sawyer rode in earlier today. Just so happened the cavalry was already in town when he got here."

"Cavalry?" Casebolt repeated.

Cole nodded. "A whole troop under the command of a major named Burdette. You know him?"

Casebolt thought it over, then shook his head. "Don't recollect the name from when I was scoutin' for the army."

"Neither did I. He struck me as being fairly new to the West. Maybe not fresh out of West Point, but you can tell he hasn't been out here long." Cole shook his head. "For one thing, he seems to think there's some sort of glory to be had from fighting Indians. Wants to be over east of here tangling with the Sioux, instead of hunting down the Shoshones. He'll do that if he has to, though, in order to get his superiors to notice him."

"Holy jumpin' toad frogs!" Casebolt

exclaimed. "You don't mean this here Major Burdette's goin' after Two Ponies' bunch, do you?"

"That's what it looks like," Cole replied grimly. "He and his troopers have ridden out to the Diamond S with Sawyer. They plan to pick up the tracks of whoever killed Sawyer's hands and stole his cows."

"Well, I can damn sure tell you it wasn't Two Ponies nor none of his people. I was with 'em last night, and they wasn't nowheres near the Diamond S."

"The whole band was there?" asked Cole. "There weren't any hunting parties out, or anything like that?"

Casebolt shook his head. "They did some drummin' and dancin' after I got there, sort of to celebrate me visitin', I reckon, and I saw all of 'em. Unless Two Ponies' band has grown a whole heap durin' the past couple of months, there ain't no way any of 'em could be off raidin'."

Cole nodded, feeling the urgency growing inside him. If Burdette had just been willing to wait before he went charging off after so-called hostiles . . . !

"Sorry to do this to you, Billy, after the long ride you've had the past couple of days, but you'd best get your saddle on a fresh horse."

"We're goin' after them bluebellies?"

"Damn right," Cole snapped. "Maybe we can catch up with them in time for Burdette to hear your story. Once he has, he'll have to admit that Two Ponies and his people are innocent." Cole rubbed his jaw wearily. "Although that major's stiff-necked and hardheaded enough, he might not pay any attention to what you've got to say. But he's still got to know the truth."

"Well, what're we waitin' for?" Casebolt said. "Let's get after 'em 'fore it's too late!"

13

Dusk was settling over Wind River. Michael Hatfield sat in the front room of the house that served Dr. Judson Kent as both office and home. He was staring at the faintly patterned wallpaper on the opposite wall without really seeing it. All he could see in his mind's eye was the face of his wife, accusing him as she fought for her life — and the life of the child within her — on the operating table behind the closed door of the next room.

Jeremiah Newton laid a huge hand on Michael's shoulder. "Would you like to pray, Michael?" the big blacksmith rumbled.

"We've already prayed, Jeremiah," Michael answered hollowly.

"More prayer cannot do any harm."

"You go ahead," Michael said. "And thank you, Jeremiah, for coming over here to stay with me."

"When I heard about your wife's misfortune, I knew I had to come. We all need someone to stand beside us in times of trouble. The Lord is always there, of course, but sometimes it helps to have a fellowman to help bear the load."

Michael nodded as Jeremiah began to intone a prayer. He found himself wondering if it would do any good. Could *anything* do any good now? Dr. Kent had been in there with Delia for well over an hour. Michael wanted desperately to know what was going on on the other side of that door, but at the same time he shrank away from the thought. The idea of seeing Delia, his Delia, laid open like . . . like some sort of butchered animal, while the doctor poked and prodded and cut inside her —

Michael shuddered all the way to the core of his being and tried to force his brain away from those thoughts. He considered instead the things that had been happening in Wind River today. He had certainly neglected his job as the editor of the *Sentinel.* There was news in the making, important news.

The cavalry had been in town, Michael knew that much. Late the previous day, he had been able to get a last-minute story in this week's edition about the killing of the Union Pacific scouts along the roadbed west of town. He knew Jack Casement, the railroad's construction boss, had sent a wire to Fort Laramie requesting that troops be sent. How could the cavalry have gotten here so quickly, though?

And why had the troopers and their major then turned around and ridden out with Kermit Sawyer a little while later? Michael had interviewed the crusty old Texas cattleman in the past, and he knew Sawyer's tendency to stir up trouble. Had Indians raided the Diamond S?

A little earlier, the rapid beat of hooves outside had made Michael look up just in time to see Cole Tyler and Billy Casebolt riding out of town in a hurry. Why had the marshal and his deputy headed out of Wind River hell-bent for leather?

On any other day, Michael would have been trying to find the answers to those questions so that he could get the story in the next edition of the *Sentinel.* If the news was important enough, he could even put out an extra. He had never done that before.

The only news he was interested in today, however, was what Judson Kent would have to tell him when the doctor finally emerged from the other room. Michael put his elbows on his knees, clasped his hands together, and rested his chin on them, hoping that time would come soon.

A door opened, making Michael's head jerk up, but it wasn't the one he wanted to see open. Instead it was the front door, and Simone came in, an anxious expression on her face. "Any news?" she asked.

Jeremiah shook his head. "The doctor's still in there with her, but Michael and I are praying for her."

"So have I been," Simone said as she moved across the room to sit down in an empty chair beside Michael. She patted his hand and went on, "I'm sure Delia will be just fine. You'll see."

"I don't know if I'll ever see her alive again," he choked out.

"Of course you will!" Simone insisted. "I tell you, Delia will be perfectly fine. She's stronger than you give her credit for, Michael. When we were both being held prisoner, I never saw her give in to her fears. All she worried about was her family. She'll be all right."

Michael nodded. He ran a hand over his face and gave a slight shake of his head, trying to clear the cobwebs of grief and fear out of his brain. "How's Gretchen?" he asked.

"I stopped by the Paines' on the way over here," Simone said. "She's doing fine, Michael, you don't have to worry about her.

She's concerned about Delia, of course, and still a little scared. That's natural, considering what she saw."

"I reckon so. I was sure scared — I still am — and Gretchen's just a little girl."

Simone patted his hand again. "I'm sure Dr. Kent will be finished soon, and then you'll see that everything's going to be all right."

As if he had been listening on the other side of the door for the right moment, Kent opened it and stepped through. His sleeves were rolled up, and he was wiping his hands on a cloth. Michael shot to his feet, and Simone and Jeremiah hurriedly stood up, too. Michael asked breathlessly, "How . . . how is she?"

Kent looked tired and drawn, and his grim expression sent a wave of panic crashing through Michael. In the next instant, though, the physician said quietly, "She'll be fine, Michael. She's resting now, and I don't think you have anything to worry about at the moment."

Michael felt as if every muscle in his body went limp with relief, and he had to catch himself to keep from falling. Jeremiah's strong hand on his arm steadied him. "Thank God," Michael said hoarsely. "And thank you, Doctor."

"I must admit it was a bit touch and go there for a while. The advanced state of Delia's, ah, condition caused me a spot of trouble. Nothing I couldn't deal with, though. The appendix is out and will no longer cause her any trouble." Kent tossed the cloth on his desk. "I put it in a jar of alcohol. Would you like to see it?"

Michael shook his head emphatically. "I'd rather see Delia."

"She's sleeping, as I told you. I had to give her a bit of ether so that she could cope with the pain of the surgery. Didn't much like to, considering her condition, but I deemed it worth the risk." Kent began rolling his sleeves back down. "You can sit with her for a moment. Just don't disturb her."

"I won't," Michael promised. He stepped through the door and caught his breath at the sight of his wife lying on the table, her face pale and her eyes closed. If not for the barely perceptible motion of the sheet that was drawn up over her chest, he might have thought that she was —

No, Michael told himself sternly. There was no reason to think such things anymore. She was going to be all right. Dr. Kent had said so.

Michael moved forward quietly and gently laid the tips of his fingers on Delia's cheek, letting them rest there as he stared down at her and thought about how much he loved her. Tears rolled down his own cheeks, but he didn't feel them. . . .

In the other room, Simone quietly asked Dr. Kent, "What about the baby?"

Kent picked up the coat of his dusty black suit and shrugged into it. "As far as I can tell, the child is fine. Delia has taken good care of herself during this pregnancy, and that certainly helped matters." He chuckled. "It may not sound much like the cool, rational thinking of a doctor, a man of science, if you will, but it seems to me this child has someone or something looking out after it. First there was the episode with that outlaw, and no harm came of that. Now this appendicitis attack, and it appears the child is still all right. If one can live a charmed life even before birth, this baby seems to be doing so."

"The Lord's watching out for the little one, that's what it is, Doc," Jeremiah put in, smiling and nodding.

Kent returned the smile. "I certainly won't argue that point with you, Mr. Newton." He turned to Simone. "Michael is lucky to have an understanding employer to stand beside him in such a time of distress."

"I hope I'm more than his employer,"

Simone said. "Michael is a friend. He stuck by me after Andrew's death, and he's kept the paper running almost without a hitch. He deserves all the help he can get right now." She lifted the small purse she held in her hands. "That's why I want to pay you for your services, Judson."

"For this operation, you mean?"

Simone nodded.

Kent considered for a moment, then said, "Tell me, did you mean it when you told Michael that I was the finest doctor west of the Mississippi?"

"Of course I meant it."

"Then I shall consider that partial payment, my dear Mrs. McKay. A compliment from a beautiful woman is without price, after all."

Simone smiled. "Why, Dr. Kent, are you flirting with me?" she asked.

He snorted, tugged at his beard, and looked away. "I'm much too tired for that," he said after a moment. "Just speaking the truth, that's all."

"And so was I." Simone took some bills from her bag and pressed them into his hand. "If that's not enough, you be sure and tell me. Perhaps I could mention what a handsome man you are, Doctor, as well as being an excellent physician."

Jeremiah crossed his brawny arms. "If the two of you are going to carry on this way, maybe I ought to leave."

"Not at all," Kent said briskly as he turned away from Simone and reached for his hat and his bag. "As a matter of fact, I must be going myself. I've patients that I must look in on."

Before he could leave, Michael stopped him by saying from the door of the other room, "Before you go, Doctor, I have to ask you a question."

Kent turned back. "Of course, Michael," he said. "What is it?"

"Was this . . . appendicitis or whatever you called it . . . was it caused by living out here on the frontier?"

Kent stared at the young man in surprise. After a moment he said, "Really, Michael, you should know better. Appendicitis can strike anyone, anywhere. To blame your wife's illness on the Wyoming Territory is . . . well, ludicrous."

"Even I could have told you that, Michael," Simone put in, "and I'm not a doctor."

"I just wanted to know for sure," Michael said. "I never would have forgiven myself if Delia had to go through this because I came out here to take the job at the paper."

"Put your mind at ease, my boy," Kent told him. "This was sheer happenstance, nothing more. Just be glad your little girl came to tell you what happened and that I was summoned immediately."

Michael stepped across the room and put out his hand. "I am glad," he said. "Thank you, Doctor. There's just no words . . ."

"You've already said enough," Kent assured him as they shook hands. "Someone should stay here with Mrs. Hatfield until I get back, then I can watch her for the rest of the evening."

"I'll stay," Simone said immediately.

"No need." Michael looked over his shoulder at the still form of his wife. "I'll be here. I'll be here while she's sleeping, and I'll be here when she wakes up. . . ."

Night had fallen before Cole and Casebolt reached the Diamond S. Cole had approached the ranch in the darkness before and knew what to expect. So when he saw several small fires burning ahead of them, in addition to the normal lights from the ranch house and the bunkhouse, he felt a surge of relief.

"Cookfires for those troopers," he said to Casebolt, pointing at the flames glowing in the night. "I was worried that Burdette might be so anxious to kill some Indians that he'd pull out tonight."

"Not enough light from the moon and stars to do any trackin' tonight," Casebolt commented. "Looks like we're in time to put a stop to this, Marshal."

"We can hope so, anyway," Cole said. He wasn't convinced, though. Still, they had to make the effort to get Burdette to listen to reason.

A few minutes later, as they rode close enough to make out the ranch buildings looming in the darkness, as well as the tents pitched by the soldiers, a voice called sharply from the shadows, "Halt! Identify yourselves!"

Cole hoped the sentry didn't have an itchy trigger finger. He said, "Marshal Cole Tyler from Wind River, and this is my deputy, Billy Casebolt. We're here to see Major Burdette."

The guard moved out from a clump of cedar trees. "How do I know you're telling the truth?" he demanded. He sounded a little nervous now, and from his accent, Cole figured he was a newcomer out here on the frontier, too.

"Well, if I was up to any mischief, I could've shot you by now if I'd wanted to," Cole pointed out.

"Three or four times," Casebolt added. "More'n that, if the marshal here wanted to fan that Colt of his. 'Course, he ain't no show-off, and besides, fannin' usually don't hit half of what you aim at. Now if that ain't enough to convince you, soldier blue, you just go and fetch Kermit Sawyer out here. That ol' mossyhorn knows who me and the marshal are."

Another voice called out of the darkness, "Old mossyhorn, am I? That must be you, Casebolt. Ain't nobody else works their mouth as much and says as little as you do." Sawyer walked up beside the guard, an indistinct figure in his black clothes. "Let 'em through, sonny. They ain't much good, but they're who they say they are."

Cole bit back an angry comment and heeled Ulysses into motion. Casebolt followed on the chestnut mare he had borrowed from the livery stable in town.

Sawyer walked beside them, gesturing as he said, "Major Burdette's tent is over there. I was talkin' to him when we heard riders comin'. Told him I'd see who it was."

"We've got important news, Sawyer," Cole told the cattleman. "You were wrong about some things."

"We'll damn well see about that," Sawyer grunted. "Come on."

He led them to Burdette's tent, the largest of the canvas shelters. The entrance flap was open and a lamp had been lit on a folding table set up inside. Burdette stood up from a stool to greet them as they dismounted and came into the tent. He had taken off his hat and jacket but otherwise was in regulation uniform.

"Good evening, gentlemen," he said. "What brings you out here, Marshal?"

Cole jerked a thumb at Casebolt. "This is my deputy, the one I was telling you about earlier today."

Burdette glanced at Casebolt and gave that smug, irritating smile. "Yes, the fellow who is . . . friendly . . . with the redskins."

"Reckon I ought to be friendly with 'em," Casebolt said indignantly. "Two Ponies and his people saved my bacon not that long ago. Picked me up on the prairie when I'd been shot by a thievin' sidewinder and took care of me till I was damn near good as new."

"Well, that was kind of them, I'm sure," Burdette said. "It doesn't mean, however, that they haven't turned hostile since then."

Casebolt bristled. "The Shoshones ain't turned hostile, and I can prove it. I was with 'em last night, when Sawyer here says they

227

was killin' his hands and runnin' off his cows."

Burdette looked interested at last, and Sawyer's leathery features flushed. "Are you callin' me a liar, Deputy?" the rancher snapped.

"No, sir, I'm not," Casebolt replied. "But I sure figure you're honestly mistaken about them Shoshones. They're still peaceable, long as they're treated right."

"Then how do you explain the unshod hoofprints both here and at that homesteader's farm, as well as the moccasin tracks?" the major asked. "The signs certainly indicate that Indians were responsible for those atrocities."

Cole said, "Anybody can wear moccasins and ride an unshod horse, no matter what color his skin is."

"You're sayin' white men are to blame for this trouble?" Sawyer said angrily. "I never heard such a load of horse droppin's!"

"I'm not saying white men killed your hands or wiped out that settler and his family," Cole said. "But there weren't any arrows or lances found at either place."

"They were scalped, damn it, and so were those railroad men!"

Cole shrugged. "A white man can use a scalping knife, I reckon. For that matter, so can a Sioux. And they're damned good at it, too."

Burdette looked at Casebolt. "You realize, don't you, Deputy, that you're asking me to take the word of a savage?"

"No, sir, I'm askin' you to take my word. I know Two Ponies and his people, and they were all in their camp last night. I can swear to that on a stack of Bibles."

Cole asked Sawyer, "How old were the tracks you found around where your boys were killed?"

For a moment Sawyer didn't answer, then he said grudgingly, "Fresh enough we could tell it happened last night. The bodies told us the same thing."

Cole turned his gaze to the cavalry officer. "There you go, Major. You've got the proof you need to clear Two Ponies and his band of Shoshone. You go after them now and it'll be pretty clear you're nothing but a glory hunter."

Burdette stared angrily at him and said, "By God, you like to push your luck, don't you, Marshal?"

"Just telling the truth," Cole said flatly.

Sawyer said, "What if we follow those tracks and they lead right to that Shoshone village?"

"They won't," Cole said, and he hoped he

was right. It was always possible that who-ever was responsible for the series of depre-dations in the area might try even harder to lay the blame for the raids on the Shosho-nes. The stolen animals might have been driven into the vicinity of Two Ponies' camp for just that reason.

"I might could get Two Ponies to come in and talk with you, Major," Casebolt sug-gested. "Him and his people are pretty leery of towns, but I could give it a try."

Burdette shook his head. "That won't be necessary. I'm going to accept your word on this matter . . . for now."

"What?" Sawyer exclaimed. "Beggin' your pardon, Major, but if you don't go after those savages, me and my boys will!"

Burdette turned to the cattleman. "You'll do no such thing, Mr. Sawyer. Dealing with the Indians is the job of the army, and I fully intend to get to the bottom of this mat-ter. My men and I will follow those tracks and see where they lead. If the Shoshone are involved, I assure you we'll find out about it and deal with them severely."

"Yeah, well, that's fine," Sawyer said bit-terly. "In the meantime, what do I tell my men? Keep a gun close by and one hand on your hair?"

"Words to live by," Cole said, enjoying the

angry glare Sawyer threw at him. "Do I have your word, Major, that you won't attack the Shoshones without good reason?"

"I never intended to," Burdette replied stiffly. "But if they are responsible for those killings, then God help them."

"They ain't," Casebolt said. "You'll see, if you'll just be patient and do a little pokin' around."

"That's exactly what I intend to do. Now, if you gentlemen will excuse me, it *is* getting rather late, and my men and I rode a great distance today."

"Sure," Cole said. "Glad we got here in time to keep you from making a mistake."

"We shall see about that," Burdette said pointedly.

Cole and Casebolt turned and left the tent, striding over to their horses. Sawyer followed them, and he said quietly, "By God, if any more of my men are killed by those savages while the major and his soldier boys are piddlin' around on your say-so, Tyler, I'm goin' to hold you responsible."

Cole swung up onto Ulysses and returned Sawyer's cold stare. "Maybe you ought to start thinking about who really killed your hands, since the Shoshones aren't to blame for it," he suggested. He wheeled the sorrel around and heeled it into a trot. Casebolt followed. Both lawmen could feel Sawyer staring after them, hatred in his eyes.

When they were out of earshot, Casebolt sighed and said, "That major sounded like he was goin' to hold off on startin' a shootin' war with the Shoshones. I reckon that's another bullet we dodged, Marshal."

"Yeah," Cole grunted. "But around here, there's always at least one more cartridge in the cylinder."

14

To Cole's surprise, things were quiet in Wind River for the next couple of days. Many of the Union Pacific workers were still on strike, so many, in fact, that all construction on the railroad came to a temporary halt. Jack Casement and General Dodge wired their superiors back east, asking advice on how to proceed, but so far there had been no reply except to stand pat while the situation was assessed. In the meantime, the striking workers spent most of their time in the saloons, which meant a booming business for Hank Parker, Abner Langdon, and the other saloon owners. Fights were rare; the men were more interested now in drinking and trying to forget their troubles than they were in brawling. Nor had Major Burdette's troop of cavalry returned from its attempt to trail whoever had raided Sawyer's ranch.

Two nights after the visit by Cole and Billy

Casebolt to the Diamond S, the marshal was making his rounds in town when the sudden noise of a scuffle in the alley he was passing came to his ears. Cole swung around and called, "Who's there? What's going on back there?"

Somebody yelped, "Help! Oh please, God, somebody stop him —"

The cry was cut off by a strangled scream. Cole yanked his revolver from its holster and plunged into the shadows of the alley, not sure what he was getting himself into but knowing he couldn't ignore the cry for help. He ran down the alley, tripping over something and almost losing his balance as he stumbled forward.

An indistinct figure loomed in front of him. Something slashed through the air, and Cole felt a blade tear the sleeve of his buckskin shirt before drawing a fiery line across his forearm. The man grunted with the effort of the blow.

Another few inches, and that knife would have opened up his belly instead of just gashing his arm, Cole knew. He lashed out with the gun in his hand, aiming at the vaguely seen head of his assailant. The man twisted aside and took the blow on his left shoulder, at the same time cutting back the other way with the bloody knife clutched in his right hand.

Cole ducked back. Somewhere farther along the alley, someone was sobbing in pain. Without warning, there was a rush of footsteps from Cole's left, and he knew he had *two* enemies here, not just one. He tried to wheel around and meet the charge, but he was too late. A foot slammed into his side in a vicious kick that sent him sprawling into the wall of one of the buildings.

That was damned well enough of that, he thought. His side ached, and his left arm burned like blazes where that knife had cut him. Aiming high, he triggered a couple of shots. The Colt was deafeningly loud here in the close confines of the narrow alley. The muzzle flash half-blinded Cole, but through slitted eyelids he saw a couple of men in dark clothes darting away. Another man lay on the hard-packed dirt of the alley floor.

The attackers weren't willing to stand up to the threat of a gun, and they were fleeing for all they were worth. Cole thumbed off a couple of more shots after them, but neither set of running footsteps broke stride and he knew his bullets had missed. He moved forward along the alley and went to a knee beside the man he had glimpsed earlier.

"This is the marshal," he said, not holstering the Colt just yet. "Are you all right?"

A hand clawed at his arm. Cole shook it off as the man said desperately, "Oh, Lordy, Marshal, they hurt me! Two of 'em jumped me, and they did somethin' to my head —"

Cole moved his free hand toward the direction of the man's voice and touched something hot and wet and sticky. The man howled in fresh pain.

"Marshal Tyler!" Casebolt's voice shouted from the mouth of the alley. "You down there?"

"I'm all right, Billy," Cole called over his shoulder. "Bring a light, and you'd better send somebody for Dr. Kent!"

Cole heard the deputy issuing curt orders to some of the bystanders who had been drawn to the alley by the yelling and the gunshots, and a few moments later Casebolt came down the alley with a bull's-eye lantern held high in his left hand. His right gripped the old Gunnison and Griswold revolver he carried.

As the light washed over Cole and the man beside whom he knelt, the marshal saw about what he expected to see. The man lying in the alley was one of the striking railroad workers, and more than that, he was one of the men who had nearly gotten himself thrown in jail for rioting the night the Chinese family had arrived in Wind River. He was writhing in pain, one hand pressed to his head in a futile attempt to stop the blood welling from where his ear had been.

Cole knew firsthand how sharp the knife wielded by one of the shadowy attackers had been. It had ripped through the sleeve of his buckskin shirt, which was a lot tougher than the flesh of a man's ear. The railroad worker's ear had been sliced off cleanly, next to the head.

"Blast it," Cole grated. "I was hoping we'd seen the last of this sort of thing."

Casebolt let out a low whistle. " 'Nother'un, huh? What do you reckon's behind this, Marshal?"

"Don't know yet," Cole replied with a shake of his head. He leaned over the injured man and asked, "What happened? Did they rob you?"

The man was able to nod weakly. "I'd been drinkin' at Langdon's place, and I was cuttin' through here to get back to the railroad yard. Somebody . . . somebody jumped me, knocked me down, rifled my pockets. Then I felt one of 'em grab my ear and pull on it. . . . Oh, Lordy, it hurt then! It's gone, ain't it, Marshal?"

Cole didn't answer the question directly.

He said, "Shine that light around the alley, Billy."

Casebolt swung the lantern from side to side. "I don't see it nowheres," he announced. "Reckon them fellers must've got off with it, just like those other times."

"That's what I figure," Cole said. "Sorry, mister, but your ear's gone."

The mutilated railroad worker whimpered in his pain and distress. Cole stood up and moved back as several more men came down the alley, Dr. Judson Kent in the lead.

"I hear there's an injured man here," Kent said briskly.

"Another missing ear," Cole told the doctor. "Think you can tend to him?"

"Of course," Kent replied as he knelt beside the victim and set his medical bag on the ground. "I'll get a dressing on here to slow down the bleeding, then take him down to my office so that the wound can be cleaned and stitched. Deputy Casebolt, if you would, shine that light down here so that I can see what I'm doing. . . ."

Cole put a hand on Casebolt's shoulder as the deputy followed the physician's orders. "Stay hare and do what you can to help the doc," Cole said in a low voice. "I'm going to take a look around."

Casebolt glanced shrewdly at him. "You

got an idea who's been doin' this?"

"Just a hunch." Cole shrugged. "I'll see you later."

The crowd of curious bystanders parted to let him through, and he strode quickly along the alley back to the street.

Coincidences were piling up, and Cole didn't like them. This new attack confirmed there was a link between the victims — all of them had harassed Wang Po and his family when the Chinese cook arrived in Wind River. And Cole remembered how quickly the Chinese patriarch's sons had drawn knives when they were threatened. The robberies were secondary, Cole believed now; the real reason behind the attacks was vengeance.

Would anybody be that touchy, that protective of what they considered their honor? Cole knew little about the Chinese, their customs and culture, but given the circumstances, he had to think it was possible. When he reached Grenville Avenue, he turned toward the Territorial House.

It was time to get to the bottom of this, before anybody else got hurt.

Rose Foster had just drawn the door of her café closed and locked it behind her when the rider reined up in the street in front of the building. As she turned automatically toward the horsebacker he reached up and tugged off his hat, holding it in front of his chest. "Evenin', Miss Rose," a young man's voice said enthusiastically. "How are you tonight?"

"I'm . . . all right," she replied hesitantly. She recognized the rider's voice and knew him to be Lon Rogers, one of Kermit Sawyer's cowboys from the Diamond S. Lon had been in town quite a bit lately, Rose knew, and he usually managed to time his visits so that he could take a meal at the café. She had a pretty good idea why he had been doing that, so she added, "I'm rather tired, and I have to get home, Mr. Rogers. It's been a long day."

"Reckon most of them are for you, ma'am," Lon said, still holding his hat. He lifted his right leg, swung it over the horse's neck in front of him, and slid down from the saddle in one lithe motion. "I never saw anybody who puts in such long hours at their business, not even cowpokes."

Instinctively, Rose moved back a little as Lon stepped up onto the boardwalk. She murmured, "Thank you, but if you'll excuse me —"

"It'd be an honor if you'd allow me to walk you home, Miss Rose," Lon said, the words tumbling out of him in a rush. Rose wondered how long he'd had to work up his courage to say them.

"That's not necessary," she began. "It's only a short way —"

"Oh, that's all right," Lon broke in again. "It'd be my pleasure." He turned and whipped the reins of his mount around the hitch rail. "I'll just leave my horse here."

He was going to be stubborn about this, Rose thought with a sigh. She had seen the expression in his eyes when he came to the café, listened to the shy, stumbling compliments about the food and about how pretty she looked each time he came to town. There was no longer any doubt in her mind.

Lon Rogers was in love with her. Or, at the very least, he had an intense crush on her.

And Rose knew she could not allow anything to come of that. She had to keep her distance, not allow anyone to know the truth, not even some callow young cowboy who didn't really represent any obvious threat to her. . . .

Old habits were difficult to break, however. The long months of hiding and secrecy had trained Rose to be cautious. She didn't want anyone finding out who she really was, even by accident. Lon seemed to be trustworthy, but Rose knew better than to depend on that impression.

She had been wrong about men before — deadly wrong.

He was still watching her in the faint light that filtered onto the boardwalk from neighboring buildings. "I'm not going to take no for an answer," he said.

Rose allowed a tiny smile to creep onto her lips. "You Texas boys are stubborn, aren't you?"

"Yes, ma'am." Lon grinned at her. "Some folks've been known to say our heads are harder than a mule's."

"Well, I don't know that I'd go that far. . . ." Rose made up her mind. The quickest, easiest way to get rid of Lon would be to go along with what he wanted, and if that led to more trouble in the future, she would deal with it then.

She let him loop his left arm through her right, and they started down the street toward the Paines' boardinghouse, where she was renting a room. There was some sort of commotion down at the other end of town, past the hotel, and Rose had thought she heard some gunshots a few minutes before closing the café. The trouble was nothing to do with her, however, and she wanted to keep it that way. Here on this side of town, away from most of the saloons, Grenville Avenue was fairly quiet, all the businesses in this stretch already closed for the night. Rose had been the last one to shut her door. There were a few pedestrians on the opposite boardwalk, but she and Lon had this side to themselves at the moment.

"I'm surprised you've been able to get into town as much as you have lately, Mr. Rogers," Rose ventured. "I understand there's been a lot of trouble out at Mr. Sawyer's ranch."

"More'n our share," Lon admitted. "But the boss is pretty good about letting the boys have some time off if they get their work done. None of us would want to let Mr. Sawyer down."

"I've never really met him. He seems like an . . . an intimidating man."

Lon chuckled. "He rides tall in the saddle, all right, and when he clouds up and rains, you don't want to be caught in it. But he's taught me just about everything I know about ranch work, and I reckon I'd ride right off a cliff if he told me to. He was mighty good to my ma, down there in Texas. Gave her a job and all after my pa died."

Rose found herself interested in this young man's story despite herself. "What happened to your father?" she asked. "If talking about it doesn't bring up bad memories, that is."

"No, ma'am. I don't hardly remember him. He had a little spread, nothing like Mr. Sawyer's, mind you, but not a bad ranch. This was back in the late forties, when folks first started settling that country, and from what I've heard, it was pretty wild, let me tell you. The Comanches sure didn't like white settlers coming out there."

"Did the Comanches kill your father?"

"Oh, no. A bad horse he was trying to break threw him and stepped on him, busted him up so bad inside that there was no way he could recover. I heard stories about that horse later. It was pure wild, and nobody ever rode it. Don't know how come Pa even tried; he was no bronc buster. But the day my pa died, Ma went out to the corral with a rifle, and I figured she was going to shoot that horse. Maybe she meant to. Instead, she turned him loose, just pulled the gate open and let him run off into the hills. Took most of our mares with him, but Ma didn't care. She knew she couldn't keep the spread going without Pa. The next day Mr. and Mrs. Sawyer came over to our place with a wagon, loaded us up, and moved us to their spread. Ma went to work for them, and I grew up there." Lon hesitated, his voice far away when he resumed. "She's still there, I reckon. She said she was too old to make the trip all the way up here. But Mr. Sawyer, he couldn't stay in Texas after his wife died. I reckon he had to have some new challenge, otherwise he wouldn't have been able to get on with his life. He looks a lot better now. Wyoming Territory's been good for him."

"What about you?" Rose asked softly. She had never heard Lon talk this much, and she had been drawn into his story. "How do you feel about Wyoming?"

"Why, I love it. It's mighty big country. Not what you'd call pretty, really, but there's places that'll take your breath away, sure enough." He chuckled sheepishly. "Shoot, I've been going on and on about myself, and that ain't polite. Tell me about you, Miss Rose. How'd you come to settle here in Wind River?"

Rose stiffened before the words were finished coming out of his mouth, and he must have felt it because he went on hurriedly, "Not that it's any of my business, you understand. I shouldn't ought to pry into other folks' lives —"

"No, that's all right, Lon," she told him. "It's just that my story isn't very interesting. I always wanted to run a restaurant —

don't ask me why — and this was a chance to have a business of my own, instead of always working for somebody else. I've been happy here, too."

That much was true, at least, even if the rest of what she had told him was a lie. She liked it here in Wind River, liked the people and the town even though she was working harder than she had ever worked in her life. She went to bed tired at night, but she also went to bed satisfied that her past was far, far behind her. She hoped as well that it stayed that way, that it never caught up to her here in this isolated settlement.

"Well," she said, forcing an artificial brightness into her voice, "here we are. I hadn't really noticed, but that's the board-inghouse."

"Yes, ma'am, I reckon it is." Lon whipped off his hat again. "I'm mighty obliged to you. I enjoyed our walk."

"So did I. Good night, Lon."

"Good night, Miss Rose."

He didn't ask her to linger, didn't try to steal a kiss, and Rose was grateful for that. She just hoped he would be satisfied with the time they had spent together tonight and not press her for more in the future. Lon Rogers was a sweet boy, and she didn't want anything happening to him.

She didn't want him to die, too. . . .

Michael Hatfield hurried along the street, a pencil in one hand, a pad of paper in the other. He had heard the shots while he was at Dr. Kent's house, sitting with Delia in the bedroom where she had been moved to recover from the operation that had saved her life. She was sleeping fairly restfully, as she seemed to most of the time, and he was sitting in a rocking chair beside the bed, a book open in his lap. He had been unable to concentrate on the words, however, because his gaze kept straying to Delia's face in the dim light from the turned-down wick of the lamp on the bedside table. Michael knew he had come close, much too close, to losing her, and he was determined that nothing like that would ever happen again.

Then he had heard the distant double explosion of two shots, followed a moment later by two more that sounded like they came from the same gun. His head had jerked up from the book and his reporter's instincts tried to pull him out of the chair.

He stayed where he was. He wasn't going to leave Delia's side, not even if all hell was breaking loose outside. Not even if the biggest story since he had come to Wyoming

Territory was taking place right under his nose.

A few minutes after that, an urgent knock had sounded on the front door of the house. Someone was looking for Dr. Kent, and that meant somebody was hurt. Michael was sure there was a connection with those shots. He heard Kent bustle out of the house with whoever had come to fetch him.

Delia stirred a little, turning her head on the pillow and shifting her body just slightly under the covers. She didn't wake up, however. She seemed to settle back down into an even deeper slumber than before.

He could probably get up, go see what was happening outside, and be back here before she ever woke, he told himself. He could run down the street, jot a few notes, and hurry right back.

He was waging a losing argument with himself, and he knew it. Taking his pad and pencil from the night table, he stood up and slipped quietly from the room, heading for the front door of the house.

Now here he was, heading for the light and the cluster of people he saw gathered at the mouth of an alley on the east side of town. As Michael reached the alley the crowd parted, and Dr. Kent and Billy Case-bolt came through the opening, supporting another man between them. The man had a bloody bandage pressed to the side of his head, with several strips of cloth wrapped around his skull and tied to hold the dressing in place.

"What happened?" Michael asked Casebolt as he fell in alongside the deputy. The little group turned toward Kent's house, with the rest of the bystanders trailing along behind.

" 'Nother feller got hisself waylaid and robbed," Casebolt replied. "Hombres who did it sliced his ear off, slick as a whistle."

The injured man let out a groan, and Dr. Kent said, "Really, Deputy Casebolt, I think we can dispense with reminding this poor unfortunate of what happened to him."

"Uh, yeah, I reckon so. Sorry," Casebolt said.

Michael scribbled notes as he hurried along beside them, unsure whether he would be able to read them later. Most of the details would stay fresh in his mind, though. He asked, "Where's Marshal Tyler?"

"Gone to look for somebody or somethin'," Casebolt answered. "That was him firin' off his gun a while back, but he said he didn't hit either of the polecats. Seemed to think he had a pretty good idea where to find 'em."

He would have to go looking for Cole, Michael realized. The marshal held the key to this story. Maybe by the time Michael caught up with him, Cole would have found whoever had been cutting the ears off of robbery victims.

He was about to say something to that effect, feeling guilty about leaving Delia alone for an even longer time, when Casebolt abruptly stopped and exclaimed, "Tarnation! Would you look at that?"

Dr. Kent came to a halt, too, meaning that the injured man stopped as well. All of them, including Michael, gazed down at the western end of Grenville Avenue, where several dozen tired-looking men in blue plodded along on even tireder-looking horses.

The United States Cavalry had returned to Wind River.

15

Cole slapped open the front doors of the Territorial House and strode into the lobby. A few guests were sitting in the wing chairs scattered around the room, reading copies of the *Sentinel.* Most of them were drummers who had come to Wind River to hawk their wares. Cole paid no attention to them as he walked over to the registration desk.

The clerk behind the desk had slicked-down hair and a gaudy stick pin in his cravat. Despite his fancy appearance, there was a frontier twang to his voice as he said to the grim-faced Cole, "Howdy, Marshal. Somethin' we can do you for this evenin'?"

"Is Mrs. McKay here?" asked Cole.

"Naw, sir, she ain't. I 'spect she's gone home for the night. She was by here earlier, but she didn't stay long."

"What about Wang Po?"

The clerk frowned. "That Chinaman? Why, he's out back, I reckon. Kitchen's already closed for the night, you know."

"Out back?" Cole repeated.

"Sure. That's where Mrs. McKay moved the whole lot of 'em, into that shed next to the barn. Said they oughtn't to be stayin' under the same roof as white folks."

Again Cole was struck by how much that didn't sound like the Simone McKay he knew, but there wasn't time to worry about such things. He started toward the hallway that led to the rear door of the hotel, saying, "That shed's next to the barn, you said?"

"That's right, Marshal." The clerk leaned over the counter to call after him, "Hey, what do you want with them Chinamen, Marshal?"

Cole ignored the question. He strode rapidly down the corridor, opened the rear door, and stepped out into the small wagon yard behind the hotel. There was a barn back here where wagons and carriages could be parked and their teams stabled. Leaning against the barn was a shed that would probably look ramshackle eventually; it was still too new to have such an appearance now. There was no window in the shed, but Cole saw lines of light around the closed door that told him a lantern was burning inside.

He reached for the door's latch, intending to jerk it open, then stopped himself. He didn't have any proof Wang Po or any of the other Chinese were responsible for the attacks on the railroad workers. The badge pinned to his shirt meant he had to follow some rules at least part of the time, wearisome though it was.

Cole rapped sharply on the door. He heard a burst of words inside, hissed low so that he couldn't make them out. Of course, he likely couldn't have understood them anyway, since the shed's inhabitants were probably speaking their native tongue. Cole knocked again with his left hand and waited, his right hand resting on the butt of the revolver at his hip.

After a couple of moments he heard a sharp command inside the shed. Chinese, sure enough. Then the latch rattled, and the door swung open. Light slanted out and fell over Cole's tense form.

"Marshal Tyler!" Wang Po exclaimed, sounding surprised. "What brings you to our humble home?"

Cole wondered if the middle-aged Chinese was feigning the reaction. Under the circumstances, it seemed probable. He said, "Evening, Wang. I need to talk to you and your family."

Wang Po stepped back even more and opened the door wider. "Of course. Come in, Marshal, come in. You must excuse our humble accommodations."

Humble was right, Cole thought as he stepped into the shed and glanced around. Eight people were living in a space that could have more easily held half that number. The floor was packed dirt, and sleeping mats had been spread directly on the ground. The few belongings the family had brought with them to Wind River — a small wooden chest with some fancy engraving on the lid, a short-legged table, and several little wooden carvings — were scattered around the cramped room. There was a small stove tucked into one corner for cooking and heating the place.

"I'm told that Mrs. McKay had you moved out here," Cole said, not beginning the conversation the way he had intended. The words were out of his mouth before he could stop them, though.

Wang Po laced his hands together in front of him and bowed slightly. "Such is her right. The hotel is hers, and I and my family are but humble servants."

"Yeah," Cole snapped. "But still —"

"We bear no ill will toward Mrs. McKay, if this is what you have come to discuss with us," Wang Po said.

Cole shook his head. All eight members of the family were in the room, and the air was close. Lingering smells from the dinner they had had earlier, smells that Cole couldn't identify, made him edgy. Wang Po's wife was sitting in a corner, eyes downcast, practically invisible against the wall in her drab robe. Cole realized he didn't even know the woman's name. He hadn't heard it spoken in all the time the family had been in Wind River. Nor did he know the names of Wang Po's sons.

They were hard to overlook, though. They stood ranged along the far wall, arms crossed, regarding the visitor with glares of suspicion and dislike.

"I've come to ask if any of you happened to be in an alley up the street a little while ago," Cole said.

"We have been here all evening, since concluding our duties in the hotel kitchen," Wang Po replied smoothly.

Cole went on as if he hadn't heard the Chinese. "There was a fella jumped in that alley, knocked down and robbed. Whoever attacked him cut off his ear, too. Tonight's the third time it's happened in the past week or so."

Wang Po murmured, "Surely you do not

suspect I or my family had anything to do with such a crime. We are law-abiding people."

"Maybe so, but this time I got a look at the gents who lopped off the fella's ear. They were wearing dark clothes — a lot like the outfits your sons are wearing, in fact."

Wang Po's wife suddenly let out a wail. Her husband's eyes darted toward her and he spoke sharply in Chinese.

"Sounds like your wife's upset about something," Cole said as he moved closer to Wang Po. "What's wrong?"

Summoning up a smile, Wang Po said, "Nothing is wrong, Marshal. She is not completely accustomed to the ways of your country, even after all the years we have been here. She does not understand that the authorities here will not blame someone for a crime without proof. In our land, the word of the warlords is law, and they care nothing for evidence of wrongdoing. Their belief is all that matters."

Cole took a deep breath. "Well, I believe your boys have been responsible for those robberies, and for cutting off the ears of those railroaders. Every man who's been attacked so far was in the bunch that tried to cause trouble for you the night you got here."

Still smiling, Wang Po spread his hands. "But there is no proof of this, Marshal, despite your belief, and you cannot act on what you Americans call a hunch. You must uphold the law."

Cole felt frustration growing inside him. Wang Po was right; he had pinned on the badge, and that meant he had to do things right and proper — even though it was obvious his suspicions about the man's sons were correct.

"All right," Cole said abruptly as a thought occurred to him. "But I don't reckon you'll mind if I take a look around." His eyes darted around the cramped room and fastened on the most likely hiding place. "Say, in that little chest there." He took a step toward the wooden chest with its carved lid.

Wang Po moved to get in front of Cole, but the lawman was quicker. Not as quick, however, as the nearest of Wang Po's sons, who darted between Cole and the chest. A knife appeared in the young man's hand.

Cole's left hand shot out and grabbed the young man's wrist, twisting the knife to the side. At the same time, Cole palmed out his .45 and chopped a blow at the young man's head. Before it could land, another of Wang Po's sons let out a high-pitched cry and leaped high in the air, his foot lashing out toward Cole. The kick caught Cole on the shoulder and staggered him. He let go of the man with the knife.

"No!" Wang Po cried. "Do not do this!"

It was too late to put a stop to the fight. Cole stumbled back against the wall of the shed, pressing himself against it so that they couldn't come at him from all directions. He didn't want to shoot anybody, but the way knives were appearing in the hands of Wang Po's sons as if by magic, he knew he might not be able to avoid hurting them.

One of the blades flickered toward Cole. He ducked desperately. The knife thudded into the wall, its point sticking there, so that the hilt quivered from the impact. Cole thumbed back the hammer of his Colt and yelled, "Drop those knives, damn it!"

None of them did, so he triggered off a shot into the ground at their feet. Wang Po's wife let out a scream and tried to fling herself across the room, maybe intending to get between Cole and her sons, but Wang Po caught her and held her tightly.

The young men were still closing in around him, and Cole knew he had no choice. He fired again, the bullet catching one of the men in the shoulder and spinning him around. The rest of them stopped.

"I know at least some of you speak English," Cole rasped. "I'll kill the next one who makes a move toward me."

He should have brought Casebolt with him, he thought. He could have left the deputy outside to get the drop on the Chinese if they tried to make a fight of it — which was exactly what they had done. But it was too late to worry about that now; he was on his own.

With three bullets left in the cylinder of his gun, and five very angry young Chinese facing him, all of whom were still holding knives.

He had faced down worse odds before, Cole told himself. As long as they knew he was in command, there was a chance he would get out of this.

"Wang Po!" he said. "Bring me that box."

"My son is injured," Wang Po said stiffly.

"You can tend to him — after you bring me the box."

Wang Po's wife was sobbing and jabbering. He put his hands on her shoulders, moved her firmly to one side, then stalked over and picked up the carved chest. He carried it over to Cole.

"Open it," Cole grated.

His face as impassive as if it had been carved from stone, Wang Po lifted the lid and tilted the chest so that Cole could see inside it. Coins gleamed in the lantern light, and there were several wadded-up bills in the chest as well. There were also two ugly, dried-up things that had once been human ears, along with another ear that still had drying blood on it. It had been cut off, Cole knew, less than an hour earlier.

"Why, Wang Po?" He couldn't stop the question, even under the circumstances.

"Do you know what it is like to be spat upon everywhere you go?" Wang Po asked, his voice bitter. "Do you understand, Marshal, what it is like to be less than human in the eyes of everyone around you? The guests in the hotel, they eat my food, they praise my skill, but still my family and I are forced to dwell in this miserable shed. And why is this? Because we are not fit to live with white people! No," Wang Po concluded, answering his own question, "I do not think you know what this is like."

"That's still no reason to go around cutting off people's ears," Cole argued. "Not to mention robbing them."

"The money is a token, nothing more. The loss of an ear . . . that is a reminder which will stay with those men forever. A reminder of how they mistreated a humble man and his family for no reason."

One of Wang Po's sons spoke up. "Our father knew nothing of this, Marshal. It was all the idea of my brothers and myself."

"I don't reckon that's true," Cole said. "He knew what was in that chest, right enough."

"Of course I knew," Wang Po declared. "What my son says has a kernel of truth in it. I did not know what they intended to do until the deed was already done the first time. But after that there was no way they could conceal the truth from my wife and me. I wished my sons would not do this thing, but I understand the rage that burns within them. I could not tell them they were wrong to seek revenge on those men."

"Well, they're going to have to pay for what they did."

One of the young men said, "We will not go to your jail, Marshal. We will kill you first."

"That just means you'd get strung up from a gallows," Cole warned them. "Your ma and pa would probably be hanged along with you. That's not what you want, is it?"

For a long, tense moment Cole stood there, his eyes locked with those of the young men watching him. Then, one by one, Wang Po's sons began dropping their knives. Wang Po and his wife knelt beside the youngster Cole had winged. The impending violence that had filled the air only seconds earlier seeped out of the room.

"Marshal!" Billy Casebolt called anxiously from outside. "You in there?"

"Yeah, Billy," Cole replied, lifting his voice. He angled his head toward the open door. "Take your family on out, Wang Po. We need to get your son down to the doc's so that bullet hole can be patched up."

Glumly, Wang Po shepherded his wife and sons out of the shed, the wounded son being supported by two of his brothers. Cole followed them out and found Casebolt standing there, a shotgun in his hands and a confused expression on his grizzled face.

"There won't be any more ears cut off around here," Cole told his deputy. "We've got an injured man. See that Dr. Kent takes a look at him."

"Sure," Casebolt replied. "What about these other folks?"

"We're going inside the hotel," Cole said. "Once that wound is taken care of, bring the fella back here. The rest of the family will be in one of the rooms; you can find out which one from the clerk."

Wang Po shot a surprised glance at Cole. "What do you intend to do with us, Marshal? I thought we were going to jail."

"Wind River doesn't have a jail," Cole told him. "Besides, I've got some other ideas."

Casebolt spoke up, saying, "Reckon you've got a full plate already, Marshal, but I figured you'd want to know — that cavalry troop's back. Major Burdette wants to talk to you, and he's waitin' in the office."

Cole stiffened. "Did they find out anything about those raids?"

"Don't rightly know," Casebolt said with a shake of his head. "They rode in whilst Doc Kent and me was takin' that feller down to the doc's place. Burdette asked me where you were, and I told him I didn't know, but that I figured I could find you. That's when he said he'd wait for you at the office. Then, a few minutes after that, I heard a shot come from down here some-wheres, so I came a-lookin'."

"All right, thanks. I'll go talk to the major in a few minutes. I've got this chore to fin-ish first."

Cole herded Wang Po, his wife, and four of their sons into the hotel. The other uninjured son went with his wounded brother and Casebolt down to Dr. Kent's. Cole warned Casebolt to keep a close eye on them, explaining that they were behind the robberies and mutilations of the railroad workers.

The clerk gaped at Cole and his prisoners as they entered the lobby. Cole said, "Give me the key to a vacant room."

"What's goin' on, Marshal? I thought I heard a shot —"

"You did. I'll take that key now."

The clerk fumbled a key off the board and handed it across the desk. "Room Eighteen," he said. "That be all right?"

"As long as it's got a lock on the door."

All the fight seemed to have gone out of the Chinese. Their shoulders slumped in despair as Cole took them upstairs at gunpoint and locked them into Room 18. The room had a single window, and Cole wished he had someone to watch that window from outside. It didn't open onto a balcony or a set of fire stairs, though, and Cole thought it unlikely either Wang Po or his wife would be up to making such a drop to the ground. He didn't expect the young men to desert their parents, either.

When he returned downstairs, the clerk came out from behind the counter and asked, "What'd them Chinamen do, Marshal?"

"I'll talk that over with Mrs. McKay." Cole gave the key back to the man. "Deputy Casebolt will be bringing the rest of the bunch back here in a little while. They go in

264

Room Eighteen with the others."

The clerk bobbed his head up and down. "You bet. I can handle that."

Cole stalked out of the hotel, weariness gripping him. He had figured out who was behind the attacks and had captured the thieves without too much bloodshed, but damned if he knew for sure what to do next. He had an idea, but he didn't know if anybody involved would like it. . . .

That would have to wait for a while, however. Cole headed for his office, figuring that Major Burdette would be getting a mite impatient by now.

That was definitely the case, Cole saw as he stepped into the marshal's office a few minutes later. Burdette was pacing back and forth in the small room. He swung around to face Cole, an angry frown on his face. Trail dust clung heavily to his uniform.

"Hello, Major," Cole greeted the officer. "Find out where those tracks went?"

"I think you probably know the answer to that," Burdette snapped.

Cole shrugged as he moved behind his desk. "I can guess. Billy didn't say anything about you having any prisoners, nor about any of your men being shot up, so I'd say you lost the trail somewhere after following it for a good ways."

"We rode across miles and miles of some of the most godforsaken wilderness I've ever seen!" Burdette said bitterly. "The trail led to the southwest from Sawyer's ranch. I thought several times we had lost it, only to find it again later. But then we reached a stretch where the ground was solid rock, and that was the end of it. There were no more tracks to follow."

Cole was a little disappointed. He had been hoping that Burdette would catch up to whoever had killed Sawyer's men and stolen the Texan's stock, because Cole was convinced Two Ponies and the other Shoshones hadn't had anything to do with it.

"So you haven't eliminated the Shoshones as suspects," he said.

"Of course not. We have no more answers than we did before. I decided to return to Wind River to see if there had been any further developments while we were in the field."

"Any more raids, you mean?" Cole shook his head. "None that I've heard of. We've had some trouble here in town, but I rounded up the ones responsible for that. They don't have anything to do with your problem." Cole sat down. "Did Sawyer ride with you?"

"No, but he sent his foreman and a couple

of his men. They've already ridden back to the ranch with the news. There was no point in them coming all the way into town with the troop."

"Sawyer's liable to mount an expedition of his own against the Shoshones," Cole cautioned.

"Not if he knows what's good for him. He'll just have to be patient until we can prove what the savages are up to."

Cole chuckled humorlessly. "Patient and Kermit Sawyer don't go together very well, Major. What do you intend to do now?"

"We're going to patrol the area regularly, and I may try to talk to this Two Ponies your deputy mentioned."

Cole nodded, a little surprised Burdette was being so reasonable. The major had seemed the type to jump the gun, right from the first.

"At any rate, I wanted to let you know about our lack of success so far," Burdette went on. "But rest assured, Marshal, we *will* get to the bottom of this matter."

"I'm sure you will, Major." Cole stood up again. "Now, if you'll excuse me, I've got an errand to run and some local law business to take care of."

"Of course. Anything I can give you a hand with?"

"Nope." Cole thought about Simone McKay. "This is something I'm going to have to handle myself."

16

Cole hesitated at the front door of Simone McKay's house on Sweetwater Street. He had worked out what he wanted to say to her on the way over here, but he had no way of knowing how she was going to react. He was beginning to believe that he didn't know Simone as well as he had thought he did.

The housekeeper answered the door, as usual, but tonight Simone had not yet retired for the evening, so Cole was ushered straight into the parlor. Simone looked up from the divan where she was working on some embroidery and greeted him with a smile. "Good evening, Marshal," she said. "Please, have a seat. What brings you here tonight? Not more trouble, I hope."

"I'm afraid so," Cole replied as he lowered himself carefully into a fancy, fragile-looking wing chair. "I've just been down at the hotel."

Simone laid aside her needlework and peered at him intently. "What's wrong?"

"Another railroad worker was attacked and robbed tonight. Reckon you've probably heard about what's been going on. The fella had an ear cut off, just like what happened to two other men in the past week or so."

"That's dreadful! And you say this incident tonight happened at the hotel?"

Cole shook his head hurriedly. "Reckon I'm getting ahead of myself. The holdup was in an alley on the other side of town. But this time I was able to find out who did it, along with proof that they were responsible for the other attacks, too."

"And *that* was someone at the hotel?" Simone demanded, making the logical connections from what Cole had told her so far.

"I'm afraid so." He nodded. "Wang Po's sons are the ones who have been jumping those railroaders."

Simone stared at him in surprise and disbelief. "But that's not possible!" she exclaimed after a couple of seconds. "They're such polite young men."

"Maybe so, but they're mighty proud, and they've got a code of honor as strict as any Indian's. All three of the men who were attacked were in that bunch that tried to run Wang Po and his family out of town the first night they got here. The robberies and the business with the ears were those boys' way of paying 'em back."

"And you say you have proof of this?"

Cole nodded. "I found some of the money they'd stolen, along with . . . well, along with the ears they'd cut off, stashed in a box in that shed where they're living now." He hesitated, then added, "I hear that was your idea."

"I'd had some complaints from the guests," Simone responded absently.

"I heard you said they shouldn't be living under the same roof with white folks."

Simone made a face and said crisply, "I'm a businesswoman now, Marshal. I sometimes have to say things I don't necessarily agree with in order to keep other people happy. You should understand what a delicate matter it is to deal with the public."

"I'm starting to," Cole said grimly. And he didn't much like it, either, he added to himself. He was used to dealing straight with people, but the more folks came out here to the frontier, the more difficult that was getting to be.

"What are you going to do about this?" Simone asked. "Have you arrested Wang

Po's sons?"

"I've got the whole bunch of them locked up in a room at the hotel," Cole said. "Except for the one I had to shoot —"

"You killed one of them?" Simone was aghast.

Cole shook his head. "Just nicked him in the shoulder. Billy took him and one of the other boys down to Dr. Kent's to get the wounded one patched up. He's probably got them back at the hotel with the others by now. As for what I'm going to do with them . . ." Cole stood up, unable to perch in the chair any longer. He strode back and forth across the thick rug on the parlor floor as he continued, "I want this kept quiet. If those railroad workers get wind of it, they're liable to form a lynch mob. As long as they're on strike, they're going to be bored and drunk, and that's a bad combination. So I want to get Wang Po and his family out of town without anybody knowing why."

"You're not going to press charges against them?"

"Not if they'll agree to leave and go back to California."

Simone frowned. "I went to considerable expense to bring Wang Po here so he could work for me, Marshal."

"Yes, ma'am, I thought about that. But

he's not going to be able to cook for you if he's strung up from the branch of a tree with his boys."

"You're the marshal. It's your job to prevent such things from happening."

"That's what I'm trying to do," Cole said, hanging on to his temper. He didn't want to argue with Simone. He had hoped she would be reasonable about this.

She looked down at the floor for a long moment, then lifted her head and nodded. "You're right, of course. The best solution is for Wang Po and the others to simply leave Wind River. Someone may figure it out eventually, but by that time they'll be far away."

"That's what I thought," Cole said, grateful that she had come around to his way of thinking.

"All right," Simone said. "I'll give them enough money to get them back to San Francisco. They still have their wagon and their mules, so they can load up their few belongings and leave first thing in the morning."

"At first light," Cole agreed. "And the less said about this, the better."

"Yes, you're right. What about the money they stole?"

"I'll see that it gets back to the right folks

— sooner or later."

Simone stood up. "Thank you for coming to see me about this, Cole. I understand that you're trying to do a difficult job here in Wind River."

He had to grin as he replied, "It's sure a lot more complicated than shooting buffalo for the Union Pacific. But I'm sort of getting to like it here."

There was genuine warmth in the smile she gave him in return. "I'm glad to hear that."

Cole paused in the arched entrance to the parlor and looked back at her. "By the way, Major Burdette and his men are back in town. They lost the trail of whoever killed Sawyer's men and stole his cows."

"You still don't believe the Shoshone are responsible?"

"No, I don't. But the major intends to stay around here until he finds out. Thought you might like to know."

"Is there any particular reason you thought that, Marshal?"

Cole wished now he had kept his mouth shut about this. He had gotten in deeper than he'd intended. "Well, you and the major seemed like you hit it off pretty well. . . ."

"Major Burdette is a very handsome

274

man," Simone pointed out.

"I reckon," Cole muttered. "I got to be going —"

"But I'm still in mourning for my late husband, Marshal," Simone went on, "and even if I wasn't . . . Well, I don't think there would be anything romantic between myself and Major Burdette. He's much too interested in his career. But I appreciate you letting me know."

Cole just nodded and headed for the front door, well aware that anything else he might say would likely just get him more flustered. He was glad to know, though, that Simone wasn't smitten with Major Burdette.

For some reason, he thought as he headed back to the Territorial House, that knowledge made him feel better than it should have. . . .

Wang Po and his family left Wind River *before* first light the next morning. Judson Kent had assured Cole that the wounded young man was not badly hurt and would be able to recuperate during the family's journey back to San Francisco. Except for the saloons, the town was still asleep as the wagon carrying the eight Chinese rolled down Grenville Avenue and out of town. Cole and Billy Casebolt stood on the boardwalk and watched them depart, and Cole was glad to see them go. Their arrival had signaled the beginning of a turbulent period for Wind River, and maybe with them gone, things would settle down a little.

Cole wasn't going to hold his breath waiting for that, however. Not with Major Burdette still in town and the threat of an Indian war looming on the horizon.

The morning passed quietly. Burdette came by the marshal's office to tell Cole that his troop would not be leaving on patrol until the next day; after the long ride earlier in the week, their horses needed some rest and the soldiers likely did, too.

As Burdette was about to leave he asked casually, "Have you spoken to Mrs. McKay recently, Marshal?"

"Talked to her just last night." Cole nodded, without explaining what the conversation had been about. He certainly didn't intend to mention that Burdette's name had come up.

"I see," the major said. "Since she's the most influential citizen in Wind River, I wonder if I ought to pay a call on her — strictly as a courtesy, you understand — so that I can let her know what my plans are regarding the Indian trouble around here."

Cole said coolly, "Do what you want to

do, Major. But I thought we'd cleared up this business about Indians being behind all the trouble. We don't know that."

"We don't know that they're innocent of wrongdoing, either," Burdette snapped.

Cole shrugged disdainfully, and Burdette turned on his heel and stalked out of the office before the discussion could deteriorate into a genuine argument. Cole leaned back in his chair and thought that he was going to be damned glad when Burdette moved on to another assignment. The glory hunter wanted to fight the Sioux, and it would be just fine with Cole if that was what Burdette wound up doing.

Casebolt ambled into the office a half hour later and said, "That major wants me to see about gettin' Two Ponies to come in for a parley. You reckon I ought to do it, Marshal?"

"I'm not sure it would do any good," Cole said bluntly. "Burdette has your testimony that the Shoshones weren't involved in any of those raids, and I don't know that he'd be more inclined to accept Two Ponies' word for it. I don't much think I trust him, either."

"You reckon once he got Two Ponies here, he'd have them soldiers blue arrest him?" Casebolt speculated shrewdly.

Cole nodded. "It could happen that way. Then all hell would break loose for sure." He thought for a moment, then went on, "Stall Burdette for now. If he gives you trouble, tell him I've got chores for you and won't let you go. I can handle Burdette if I have to."

Cole hoped that was true. So far they had been lucky that Burdette hadn't caused any real trouble.

While Casebolt held down the fort at the office Cole walked over to the boarding-house and had some of Abigail Paine's excellent chicken and dumplings for lunch. Gretchen Hatfield was staying at the board-inghouse these days, and the sight of her skylarking with the Paine children reminded Cole of the close call that Delia had suf-fered. He had heard about the sudden ill-ness and the emergency operation Dr. Kent had performed to save her life, but he hadn't talked to Michael in several days to find out how the young woman was doing.

"What do you hear about Delia Hatfield?" he asked Abigail as he spooned some greens onto his plate.

"She's doing quite well," Abigail replied. "Michael came by earlier today and took Gretchen to see her. He said that Delia should be able to come home in another few days. I'm going to continue taking care of Gretchen for a while, though. With the condition that Delia was in to start with, plus having to recover from that operation, she doesn't need a child underfoot right now."

Cole nodded, glad to hear the good news. "If you see Michael again, tell him I was asking about them. If there's anything I can do to help . . ."

"I'm sure Michael knows that." Abigail smiled.

After the meal, Cole headed back toward the office. He hadn't gotten there, though, when gunfire suddenly erupted behind him. He heard the rapid hoofbeats of a galloping horse, and men began to shout. Cole wheeled around, his hand going to the butt of his gun as more shots rang out.

The man doing the shooting wasn't aiming at anybody, though. He was emptying his six-gun into the air as he raced down Grenville Avenue. "Gold!" he shouted. "Gold in the Wind River range!"

Cole stiffened as more and more pedestrians took up the frantic cry. Men leaped into the street, tugging off their hats to either fling them into the air or use them to wave the rider on. People began running along the boardwalks, and kids and dogs scampered along in the wake of the shouting rider. The news brought to town by the man went through the settlement like a flash flood. The uproar grew and grew steadily, swelling until it had swept over everything in its path. The striking railroad workers came tumbling eagerly out of the saloons where they spent their days and took up the cry louder than anyone else.

Gold! The word had a magic sound to it, especially here on the frontier. Twenty years earlier, the news had come out of California, launching a rush to the West that still hadn't completely stopped. Ever since the gold fields in California had practically played out after a wild, tempestuous few years, people had been waiting for the next big strike, confident that it would come sooner or later. Now, evidently, it had, and within a few days' ride of Wind River to boot, in the mountains to the north that had given the settlement its name.

Cole stood there, watching the chaos building around him, knowing there wasn't much he could do to stop it. Not that he had any authority to. If people wanted to go looking for gold, they had every right to do so.

But they weren't going to find any in the Wind River range, he thought. He had been all over that country, just like his father before him. There had been a time when the mountains were rich with beaver, but even that day was over now. Cole was confident that if there had been any significant gold deposits up there, some of the hordes of fur trappers would have found them before now.

Nobody was going to listen to him. They were too busy rushing to the general store to lay in some supplies before they headed north. Casebolt emerged from the marshal's office, spotted Cole down the street, and made his way through the crowd to join him. "You ever see anything like this in all your borned days?" the deputy asked in amazement.

"Nope. I wasn't at Sutter's Mill in forty-eight, though," Cole replied. "Reckon we're seeing the same thing here, only on a smaller scale."

"Who started this fandango?"

Cole thought back to the man who had galloped down the street past him. He shook his head. "Never saw him before. Looked like a drifter, maybe a cowboy." He looked up and down the street and didn't see the man in the growing mob. "I don't know where he went. Maybe he headed back to the mountains to get the jump on everybody else?"

"You believe it?" Casebolt asked over the din. "You figure there's really gold in that range?"

Cole shook his head again. "I'm not saying there's no dust in the streams, or no nuggets scattered here and there. But there's not enough to justify . . . *this*."

Casebolt said dryly, "I ain't sure folks'd like to hear you say that, Marshal."

"They wouldn't pay any attention to me if I tried."

Cole heard his name being called and looked down the street to see Major Burdette striding rapidly along the boardwalk toward them. The officer had a concerned frown on his face. As he came up to Cole and Casebolt he demanded, "What in blazes is all this?"

"It's a gold rush, Major," Cole drawled, "in case you hadn't noticed. Somebody rode into town a little while ago yelling his head off about a gold strike up in the Wind River range, and you can see for yourself what happened."

"Aren't you going to do anything about it?" Burdette snapped.

"What do you suggest? You want me to arrest damn near everybody in town? What's the charge, Major? Making damn-blasted fools out of themselves?"

Burdette frowned darkly. "You're being uncooperative, Marshal."

"No, sir," Cole said flatly. "Just realistic. It only takes a few minutes to start something like this, but it takes a hell of a lot longer to end it. People are going to have to go up there and see for themselves there's no gold to be found. Then they'll come back, dragging their tails between their legs."

"But it's not safe for a lot of civilians to be wandering around the countryside!" Burdette protested. "This is just going to cause more trouble with the Indians."

Cole nodded. "You could be right."

Casebolt added, "I don't reckon Two Ponies and his people'll want anything to do with this, Major. They'll just figure all the white folks've gone crazy, which the Shoshones consider most of 'em to start with. You'll see; this'll blow over in a few weeks."

"I hope so. I don't have enough men to protect a horde of gold seekers, and besides, I've no orders to do so." Burdette nodded grimly at the evidence of the madness, the gold fever, gripping the town. "These people will just have to fend for themselves."

Cole didn't much like that, but he knew Burdette was right. One troop of cavalry wasn't enough to police an entire gold rush.

There was another angle to be considered, too. With Wang Po and his family gone, Cole had hoped the striking railroaders would see that their jobs weren't in jeopardy from any source except their own contrariness. He had thought there was at least a chance that the dispute could be settled quickly and the Irishmen would be back at work on the Union Pacific.

Now, with this gold rush, the track layers, the gandy dancers, the spike pounders would all head for the mountains in search of a fortune that would doubtless prove elusive. They would come back eventually, but for the time being, the railroad was still being held up, and every day of delay meant less money for the Union Pacific once the transcontinental link was finally made. Cole didn't give a damn who wound up making the biggest profit, the Union Pacific or the Central Pacific, but he did care about restoring law and order here in Wind River. He figured things wouldn't really settle down until the railroad construction was back in full swing.

Major Burdette broke into Cole's reverie by saying, "Gold rush or no gold rush, my men and I are riding out on patrol again tomorrow, and we're heading west. I still want to try to pick up the tracks of those stolen animals again."

"Well, good luck, Major," Cole said. "Reckon you'll need it."

He looked at the insanity surrounding them, sighed, and added to himself, Likely we all will.

17

By the next morning, Wind River wasn't a ghost town — but it was considerably less populated than it had been the day before. As Cole walked down to the Wind River Café for breakfast, he thought there were fewer people on the streets than he had ever seen at this time of day. Some of the businesses were closed, their boarded-up doors and windows mute testimony that their owners had been gripped by the same gold fever infecting the rest of the town.

The general store and the hotel were still open, of course, and as Cole passed on the opposite side of the street from the newspaper office, he saw Michael Hatfield through the window. The young editor was working on something, probably getting ready to print the next edition of the paper. Wouldn't be near as many people in town to read it, though, Cole thought.

The café was open, too, and he was glad

to see that. As he went inside he saw that only one table and a couple of stools at the counter were occupied. Rose Foster was standing at the end of the counter, obviously not busy. She smiled when she saw Cole.

"Good morning, Marshal," she said. "You didn't take off your badge and go gold hunting like the rest of the town?"

"I've got more sense than that," Cole replied as he sat down on the stool nearest Rose. "There's not enough gold in those mountains to make it worth anybody's while to look for it. I'd rather have some breakfast instead."

Rose's smile widened. "We've got plenty. Monty cooked like he normally does, and I'm afraid a lot of it is going to go to waste. So eat hearty, Marshal; everything is half price this morning."

"Can't beat that deal." Cole grinned at her. "Start me off with some flapjacks, ham steaks, and a big pile of fried eggs. Plenty of coffee."

"Sure thing." Rose ducked back to the kitchen to tell the cook, Monty Riordan, what Cole wanted to eat, then returned to pour his coffee.

Cole took an appreciative sip of the strong black brew, then asked, "Have you heard whether or not Sawyer's ranch hands are going off to look for gold, too?"

Rose flushed slightly. "Why would I know anything about Mr. Sawyer's hands?"

"I just figured, what with young Lon Rogers sweet on you, he might've come by here and said so long before he took off for the mountains."

The pretty glow on Rose's face deepened, and she asked quietly, "Does everybody in town know about Lon?"

"About him courting you? I imagine most folks do. This is a good-sized settlement, but not so big that people can't keep up with other people's business."

"Well, for your information, Marshal, I haven't seen Lon Rogers for a couple of days, and he's *not* courting me."

Cole grinned again and drank some more coffee. "Does he know that?"

"You can be an annoying man, Cole Tyler," Rose snapped. "I'll see if your food is ready."

She disappeared through the swinging door to the kitchen, then came back a minute later with a big plate that was heavily laden with food. She set it down in front of Cole with a clatter and added insincerely, "Enjoy your breakfast." Then she went to check on her other customers.

Cole smiled to himself as he started eating. He liked Rose, but he could see the humor in the way the young cowboy had started following her around like a lovesick calf. It was one of the few things lately that had given him any cause to smile.

He was halfway through breakfast when the door of the café opened and someone with a heavy step came inside. A voice he recognized said harshly, "I been looking for you, Marshal."

Cole looked over his shoulder and saw Hank Parker striding toward him. The burly, one-armed saloonkeeper was up either late or mighty early for somebody in his profession. Parker didn't look happy, either, but that was nothing new. He'd been on the prod for one reason or another ever since arriving in Wind River.

"What's wrong now, Parker?" Cole asked wearily. "Another fight in your saloon?"

Parker gave an explosive snort. "Hell, there's not enough people in there drinking to start a good fight! No, I just came to tell you that you've got to do something about Langdon."

"Abner Langdon?" Cole asked with a frown.

"Who the hell do you think I mean? Yeah, Abner Langdon and that enforcer of his,

Bert Sweeney. They're nothing but a couple of thieves."

Cole tried not to sigh. Parker was the belligerent type who had trouble getting along with anybody. Cole had listened to his complaints about Langdon — and other saloon owners, for that matter — stealing his business in the past. Protecting somebody from competition wasn't part of a marshal's duties, however, and for the most part he had ignored Parker's bitching.

"What've they done now?" he asked, not really wanting to know the answer but all too aware that Parker wouldn't be satisfied and leave him to finish his breakfast without at least a show of interest.

"Bribed one of the freight clerks at the depot to let them have some cases of whiskey that *I* had shipped in."

That statement brought a glance of surprise from Cole. He said, "You mean you actually bring in that who-hit-John from somewhere else? I figured you got a little gunpowder and arsenic and rattlesnake venom and mixed it up yourself."

"I don't sell anything but the finest stock, Marshal," Parker said stiffly. "You ought to know that. And now Langdon's stolen it from me, and I'm not going to let him get away with it! I want him arrested!"

With everything else that had been going on, Cole didn't want to get mixed up in a petty dispute between Parker and Langdon any more than he had to, but Parker was making an official complaint. Cole knew he was duty-bound to investigate it. He nodded reluctantly and said, "I'll go talk to Langdon in a little while, see what he has to say about it. I'm not going to promise to arrest anybody until I'm sure what happened, though."

"I told you what happened," Parker said. "Langdon and Sweeney are no-good, thieving bastards. Either you run 'em out of business, Marshal, or the rest of us honest saloon owners will."

Curtly, Cole told him, "Don't go making threats, Parker. It's my job to look into things like this, and you're not going to take the law into your own hands."

"Somebody ought to," Parker said. "It's not bad enough that Langdon undercuts the rest of us on the price of his drinks so that he can lure all those railroad workers into his place, but then he gets 'em all worked up by feeding 'em a pack of lies along with his whiskey — *my* whiskey, now."

One of Parker's angry comments had caught Cole's attention. He asked, "What do you mean, feeding them lies?"

"Well, that business about the Chinamen coming in and taking over all the jobs on the UP, for one thing. Langdon and Sweeney started that rumor. Reckon I can see why. The unhappier those apes are, the more booze they put away — and Langdon sells it cheaper than anybody else."

Cole frowned in thought. "Are you sure Langdon and Sweeney were responsible for those rumors?" he asked.

"Damn right. More than one of the railroaders told me how they first heard the stories about Chinamen in Langdon's place."

"You wouldn't be making this up because of hard feelings between you and Langdon, would you, Parker?" Cole asked sharply.

The saloonkeeper shook his bald head. "I don't care whether you believe me or not, Tyler, but I know what I've seen and heard. Langdon got 'em stirred up to start with, and he kept 'em stirred up." Parker shrugged his broad shoulders. "It worked, I reckon. His place has been packed nearly twenty-four hours a day ever since all this trouble started."

That was true, Cole reflected. He disliked Hank Parker, but the man might be onto something. "I'll go down and talk to Langdon as soon as I finish my breakfast," he promised.

"You do that," Parker said with ill grace. "Make him tell you the truth. Ask him about that Indian business, too."

Cole stiffened. "What Indian business?"

"It wasn't just the Chinamen him and Sweeney and the bartenders down there kept talking about. To hear them tell it, the whole country's about to break out in an Indian war. If all this yelling about gold hadn't come along, those railroaders would have been ready pretty soon to go out and start taking potshots at any Indians they could find."

Cole didn't like the sound of that at all. He was curious enough to ask, "How come you didn't go look for gold with everybody else?"

Parker snorted in derision. "I ain't interested in digging my fortune out of the ground, Marshal. I'd rather collect it from the poor sons of bitches who dig it out of the ground when they buy my whiskey — if you can get back what Langdon stole from me, that is!"

Cole glanced at his food. He knew it had already gone cold while he and Parker were talking, and he sighed in regret. "I'll go have a talk with Langdon and Sweeney right now. No point in putting it off."

"Good," Parker grunted. "Be careful, Tyler. You can't trust those bastards."

Cole didn't trust Parker any more than he trusted Langdon and Sweeney, but he didn't point that out as he put some coins on the counter to pay for his unfinished meal, drank the last of his coffee, and then got up to leave the café. He waved to Rose on his way out, but she didn't return the gesture. Nose was still out of joint about his joshing over Lon Rogers, Cole supposed.

Parker followed him out of the café, but Cole told him, "You go on back to your saloon. I don't want you with me while I'm talking to Langdon and Sweeney."

"I got a right —"

"No, you don't. I've heard your story, now I want to hear theirs. Besides, you're so hotheaded you're liable to take a swing at one of them, and then I'll have another brawl on my hands."

Pointing a blunt finger at Cole, Parker said, "Don't you let 'em fool you, Tyler. They're mighty slick operators, the both of 'em."

"I'll get the truth out of them," Cole promised.

Reluctantly, Parker headed back toward his tent saloon. Cole let him go, then started in the same general direction himself, since

Langdon's place, like Parker's, was on the east side of town.

The difference this morning was even more noticeable over here, Cole thought. This section of town had always been the busiest of all, but while there were still men moving around the saloons and taverns, the area was less crowded than Cole had ever seen it. He didn't think he would have to worry too much about brawls around here until the disgruntled railroad workers began drifting back into town. And that wouldn't happen until they had discovered for themselves that their dreams of finding a fortune in gold were just that — dreams.

The entrance flap of Langdon's tent was closed but not tied, and when Cole pushed through it, he saw that the place was still doing a little business. About a dozen drinkers were lined up at the crude bar. A skinny bartender with a prominent Adam's apple was serving them. Cole glanced around but didn't see Abner Langdon or Bert Sweeney.

He walked over to the bar and waited until the bartender noticed him. The man came over and asked in a surly tone, "What'll it be?"

"Langdon or Sweeney, or both of 'em. Where are they?"

"Not here," the bartender replied curtly.

"I can see that," Cole said, making an effort to hold on to his temper. "I'll ask you again. Where are they?"

The bartender's eyes flicked toward the rear of the tent, but he shook his head stubbornly. "Ain't seen 'em this mornin'. Come back later, Marshal. It's mighty early."

Cole wasn't sure what was in back of this tent, but he was certain he hadn't imagined the look that the bartender had cast in that direction. Assuming that the man wasn't trying to trick him somehow — and judging from the lack of intelligence in the dull eyes, that was a safe assumption — Cole decided it was time to take a look around back there.

"Thanks anyway," he said to the bartender, then turned to leave. He went toward the back of the tent, however, rather than the front.

"Hey!" the bartender called after him. "That ain't the way out."

Cole had already spotted a smaller flap in the rear wall of the big tent. "It'll do," he said lightly as he strode toward the flap.

No one tried to stop him, although a glance over his shoulder told him that the bartender had started to fidget around nervously. More convinced than ever that he was onto something, Cole pushed open the rear flap and ducked through it, having to stoop a little to do so.

He straightened as he let the flap fall shut behind him. There was a shack back here, facing the rear of the tent. If there was a window in the building, it had to be where he couldn't see it. The shack wasn't much bigger than an outhouse, but it had a chimney on its roof, and smoke was curling from it into the morning sky. Cole caught a faint whiff of coffee and grinned.

Langdon probably used the shack as a combination home and office. There wasn't a good place inside the saloon itself for a man to sleep or go over his books. Cole strode toward the door, intending to knock on it.

Instead he paused abruptly as he reached the shack. There was a gap around the door where it hadn't been hung properly, and conversation filtered through the opening. Cole heard a voice he recognized as Langdon's saying, ". . . good job you did, Parton. Those apes won't be back anytime soon, and by the time they are, the Union Pacific will have a lot more trouble on its hands than just some strike."

"Thanks, boss. It was easy, like you said. All I had to do was yell 'Gold!' a few times and shoot off my gun. Those dumb Irishmen did all the rest."

Cole didn't recognize the second voice, but he could figure out from what it was saying who it belonged to. The man who had started the gold rush was inside that shack with Langdon and had called him boss.

The implications of that sent waves of anger and shock through Cole. He stiffened as he thought about what he had learned this morning, both from Hank Parker and from these few moments of eavesdropping. Cole had believed it was a coincidence that trouble seemed to be breaking out on so many fronts all at once. Now it appeared that almost everything that had happened over the past week or so had been a carefully thought-out plan with a single plotter behind it.

And that plotter was Abner Langdon.

Cole didn't know what was behind it, but that could wait. For now, he wanted to get the drop on Langdon and his accomplice; then all the questions could be answered. He put his right hand on the butt of his gun and reached for the door latch with his left.

He paused before grasping it, because the men inside the shack were saying something else he wanted to hear. He leaned closer so there would be no mistake.

Langdon chuckled and said, "Once Bert

gets through today we won't have to worry about the UP getting any work done for a long time. They'll all be too busy dodging arrows to lay any track." Langdon paused, then asked, "You're sure about which way those soldier boys were heading?"

"I followed 'em for several miles before I turned back," replied the man called Parton. "They were riding west, just like I told you."

"And the Shoshone camp is southwest?"

"Yep. Scouted it out yesterday after doin' my part to start the gold rush."

Langdon laughed harshly. "A gold strike to the north and an Indian war to the west. Yes, this'll cripple the Union Pacific, all right. I'd say we've all earned our money, Parton." Cole heard a chair scrape back, then footsteps began to pace back and forth across the puncheon floor of the shack. Langdon went on, "Bert and the rest of the boys ought to be ready to hit those troopers when they stop at noontime. Then it's just a matter of leading that dumb major back to the Shoshone camp. Hell, if Burdette hadn't lost the tracks of those cows we stole from Sawyer's place, the war would've already broken out."

Cold sweat broke out on the marshal's forehead as he listened outside the shack.

Langdon's boasting had unwittingly laid out the entire plan for him. Cole still didn't know exactly what was behind it, but it was clear now that Langdon and Sweeney and some hard cases they had working for them had been responsible for the raid on the Jessup farm, the butchering of the Union Pacific workers, and the murder of Kermit Sawyer's cowboys, along with stealing some of the rancher's stock. In addition, they had spread rumors about Chinese coolies and taken advantage of Wang Po's coincidental arrival in town to make that situation even worse. Or maybe it hadn't been coincidence; maybe Langdon had found out someway that Simone McKay had hired a Chinese family, and that had given him the idea for the rumors. Then there was the phony gold strike. . . . About the only thing he couldn't lay the blame for at Langdon's feet, Cole realized, was the gruesome revenge Wang Po's sons had taken on the men who offended their family honor. Everything else had been designed to spread tension, cause trouble, and generally wreak havoc on the pattern of life in Wind River and the vicinity. Why? Cole asked himself.

Only one reason he could see, and Langdon had said as much. All of it had been aimed at disrupting, delaying, and even stopping the construction of the Union Pacific Railroad.

And if a lot of innocent people got killed in the process, that was just too damned bad. . . .

Cole had heard enough. With his lips pulled back in a grimace of anger, he palmed out his Colt, jerked the door open, and stepped into the shack. He leveled the gun at the two startled men inside and barked, "Don't move, damn it! I'd be glad to shoot either one of you if you want to try anything."

Langdon was staring at him in shock. The other man, whom Cole recognized as the rough-looking hard case who had galloped down the street yelling about gold, seemed to be just as surprised. After a moment Langdon tried to summon up some offended dignity and demanded, "What's the meaning of this, Marshal? You can't just come busting in here —"

"Shut up, Langdon," Cole snapped. "I know what you've been up to. You sure had everybody fooled, but it's over now. I'm going to lock up the two of you, then get a posse and go after Sweeney to keep him from ambushing that cavalry patrol."

Those words dispelled any hopes of Langdon's that Cole didn't know what was actually going on. It was obvious the marshal had overheard enough to figure out the entire scheme. Cole saw that angry, disgusted realization in Langdon's eyes.

Still, the saloonkeeper wasn't going to admit defeat that readily. He said, "I don't know what you're talking about, Marshal, but I can assure you I'm going to complain to Mrs. McKay and the other civic leaders about your behavior. You can't get away with harassing an honest merchant —"

Cole laughed humorlessly. "You're about as crooked as a Texas sidewinder, Langdon." His eyes flicked back and forth between Langdon and the man called Parton, who were standing about six feet apart. He could cover both of them at the same time as long as they were that close together. "I reckon you're both packing iron. Shuck it." The coldness of his tone left no room for argument.

Parton had a holstered revolver strapped around his waist. Slowly and carefully, he unbuckled the belt and lowered the rig to the floor. He bent and added a knife that he pulled from the top of a boot.

"You, too, Langdon," Cole snapped.

"I'm not armed —"

"I know better than that. Shed that belly gun, and the one under your arm, too."

Both of those were guesses on Cole's part, but accurate ones, as it turned out. Grudgingly, Langdon opened his frock coat and took a small pistol from a holster clipped to his belt for a cross draw, then reached under his arm and removed an even smaller revolver from a shoulder rig. He placed both weapons on a roughhewn table that he had evidently been using for a desk. There were a few papers scattered on top of the table as well.

Langdon wasn't bothering to deny anything anymore. He said, "You're too late, Marshal. Everything is already in motion. Things won't get back to normal around here for a long time, if ever. Wind River's heyday is over almost before it got started good."

"I wouldn't be bragging too soon. All that money the Central Pacific was going to pay you won't do you a hell of a lot of good when you're either in jail or hanging from a gallows. It'll be up to a judge which one."

The thrust about the Central Pacific was a guess, too, but from the look in Langdon's eyes, Cole knew it was a good one. The Big Four, the ruthless financiers behind the Central Pacific, stood to benefit if the Union Pacific was badly delayed in its construction. Each mile of track meant more money from the government for the railroad that laid it, and the UP already had a big lead on the Central. It stood to reason that Langdon, Sweeney, and Parton were acting as agents for the Central Pacific, even though their bosses in San Francisco might not be aware of just how ruthless their delaying tactics had become.

Suddenly Langdon smiled, and his voice was mocking as he said, "I'm not the one who's bragging too soon, Marshal. You should have brought someone to help you." He nodded serenely toward something behind Cole.

Cole started to shake his head, surprised that Langdon would try such an old trick, but then the scrape of shoe leather on the ground made him whirl desperately. He caught a glimpse of the bartender with the big Adam's apple. The man was swinging a bungstarter toward his head. Cole threw up his left arm in an attempt to block the blow, but he was too late. The bungstarter crashed into the side of his head.

At the same time, Parton jumped him, grabbing the wrist of Cole's gun hand and forcing it down. He looped an arm around Cole's throat and jerked it tight to cut off any yells for help. Cole felt himself going down.

"Hit him again, blast it!" he heard Langdon hiss viciously. Cole tried to throw himself to the side, but with Parton hanging on to him, he couldn't get out of the way. This time the brutal blow from the bung-starter caught him on the back of the head.

Cole didn't feel the impact when he hit the floor. He was out cold.

18

Michael Hatfield felt better than he had at any time in days. Delia would be home soon, and their lives could return to normal. In another few weeks, Dr. Kent had told them, they could expect the new baby to be born, and the doctor was not anticipating any problems with the birth.

Under the circumstances, Delia had urged Michael to stop neglecting his work and get ready to print the next edition of the *Wind River Sentinel,* which was due to be published in a couple of days. He was hard at work doing that very thing right now, setting the type for some hastily composed stories about the disturbing events of the past week. While Michael's personal life might be improving, he knew all too well how unsettled things were in the area, what with rumors of gold strikes and Indian uprisings. Major Burdette's cavalry troop had left early that morning, breaking their camp just outside of town and heading west in another attempt to pick up the trail of whoever had murdered a couple of Kermit Sawyer's ranch hands and stolen quite a few cattle and horses.

Michael was alone in the office when the door opened and Judson Kent came in. The doctor's face was haggard and gray, and Michael knew immediately that something was wrong. Fear shot through him. Something might be wrong with Delia!

"What is it, Doctor?" he exclaimed as he shot to his feet, jostling the tray of type and knocking some of the little bits of metal out of place. He didn't care about that, not now. "Is it Delia?"

Kent looked up in surprise. "What? Oh, I'd forgotten how observant you are, lad. There's a problem, all right, but not with your lovely wife."

Michael's concern eased a little. He asked, "It's not the baby, is it?"

"Not yours," Kent answered. He ran a hand over his face, trying to scrub away some of the weariness that obviously gripped him. "No, I've been over at Harvey Raymond's house since two o'clock this morning."

Michael knew that Kent had been off seeing a patient; Delia had told him as much when he stopped by the doctor's house to see her earlier this morning. But neither Delia nor Michael had known that patient was Estelle Raymond, nor that Kent had been summoned there in the middle of the night. Estelle Raymond was pregnant, too, and due to deliver sooner than Delia. . . .

"Something's wrong with Mrs. Raymond's baby, isn't there?" Michael asked, a cold certainty suddenly gripping him.

"I'm afraid so," Kent replied dully. "I was worried that she would have a difficult time of it, but I didn't expect . . ." The doctor sighed. "The child was positioned incorrectly. Not only that, but Estelle Raymond was a rather small woman, and this was her first child. I didn't really know what to expect."

"Was?" repeated Michael.

Kent nodded, his face a bleak mask. "I wasn't able to save either one of them. This is a tragedy, a terrible tragedy. . . ."

Michael felt sorrow wash over him, sorrow for Harvey Raymond and the man's devastating double loss, but mixed with that emotion were a couple of others. Fear and anger both made Michael's heart slug wildly in his chest.

"Why did you come here to tell me this?" he asked tightly.

Kent looked up at him. "I wanted you to hear about it from me, rather than someone else. I know how concerned you've been about Mrs. Hatfield and her condition, and I wanted you to understand that her situation is nothing like that of Estelle Raymond's. Delia is in no great danger —"

"You just admitted you couldn't save either the Raymond woman or her baby," Michael broke in, his voice rising and cracking. "What kind of doctor *are* you, anyway?"

Resentment flashed in Judson Kent's eyes. "I'm a damned good doctor, and you know it, lad. But I'm not a miracle worker. You've nothing to worry about where your wife is concerned —"

"Just that she's being taken care of by some sort of . . . some sort of quack!"

Kent stiffened and stood up straighten. "I'm going to forget I heard you say that, Michael. But I'd remind you that it's only been a few days since I saved your wife's life by removing her appendix."

"Yeah — if that was really what was wrong with her!"

A small part of Michael's brain knew he was being unreasonable. He had seen countless examples of Judson Kent's medical skills and knew the Englishman to be a caring, highly competent physician. But at the moment Michael's anger and fear — mostly fear — easily overwhelmed that knowledge.

He came out from behind his desk, moving like a panther, and gripped Kent's arm. Through clenched teeth, he told the startled doctor, "If anything happens to Delia —"

A voice from the door said, "Here now! What's goin' on?"

The surprised but steady tone cut through the fog of emotion clouding Michael's brain. He glanced at the door and saw Billy Casebolt standing there, a worried frown on his leathery, beard-stubbled face. Michael looked back at Kent and found the doctor regarding him with a mixture of resentment and pity.

"I'll thank you to let go of my arm," Kent said stiffly, and Michael did so, stepping back and lifting a hand to rub the back of it across his eyes.

"Sony, Doctor," he muttered, utterly ashamed of himself. "You know I didn't mean —"

"I know we sometimes say things when we're worried about a loved one that we might not say otherwise," Kent told him. "You can put this little incident behind you, Michael . . . but I would appreciate it if you'd not be impugning my skills again without good reason."

"I won't," Michael promised.

Casebolt walked into the office and said, "Don't know what this ruckus was about, but I'm glad to see you two got it worked out all right. Now I can ask you what I come over here to ask you, Michael, and you, too, Doc, since you're here."

"What's that?" Michael said.

"Either one of you seen Marshal Tyler this mornin'?"

Kent shook his head. "I've been quite busy with a patient, I'm afraid."

"I haven't seen him either," Michael began, then shook his head. "No, wait a minute. I think I did see him go past on the opposite boardwalk a little while ago, but I don't have any idea where he was going."

"Which way was he headed?" Casebolt asked.

Michael thought again, then said, "East, I believe. Is something wrong, Deputy?"

Casebolt scraped a thumbnail over his lean jawline and shook his head. "I ain't sure. Nothin' that I know of, but I got a feelin'. . . . Anyway, I ain't seen Cole this mornin', and he's usually down at the office 'fore now. I wondered if he'd stumbled onto some trouble. Ain't heard no shootin', though."

"Neither have I," Michael said. "The town

311

seems exceptionally quiet this morning, what with so many of those railroad men gone north to look for gold." There was going to be a story about that in the paper, too, if he ever got around to writing it and setting the type.

"Well, I'll mosey on down to that end of town and poke around in some o' them saloons." Casebolt looked intently at both Michael and Dr. Kent. "You two ain't goin' to go to argufyin' again, are you?"

Michael shook his head and smiled sheepishly at the doctor. "No, I can promise you that won't happen, Deputy."

"Good," Casebolt said emphatically. He nodded to both of them, turned, and left the office in his disjointed stride.

"I owe you an apology as well, Michael," Kent said. "I should have been more sensitive and realized you'd be upset when you heard about Mrs. Raymond."

"Well, I reckon we ought to pray for Harvey, and for poor Estelle and the baby, too. I'm sure Jeremiah will hold a service for them."

"I'm on my way to see Mr. Newton right now," Kent said.

"Sorry again," Michael called after the doctor as Kent left the office and started toward the blacksmith shop. Kent just smiled tiredly and waved. Michael leaned against the doorjamb and looked up and down Grenville Avenue. Wind River did seem to be mighty peaceful and quiet this morning, but Michael knew all too well that appearances could be deceiving. Death could lurk anywhere, no matter how placid the surface might seem.

With that troubling thought in his head, he turned, reentered the office, and got back to work.

Cole figured he had been unconscious for only a few minutes when reason seeped back into his head, along with a throbbing pain. He tried to ignore the pain and concentrate instead on his current situation. He remembered confronting Langdon and Parton in the shack behind Langdon's saloon. From the feel of the rough wooden floor pressed against his face, he might still be there.

The first thing he did was check to see if his arms and legs would move. None of his limbs would budge, he discovered. He was tied hand and foot, trussed up like a turkey.

Somebody moved around in the room, and Cole was glad he had been careful about revealing that he was conscious again. If his captors knew that, they would probably just hit him in the head again and knock him out. The next blow might well be fatal. He kept his eyes pressed shut and listened intently, hoping for some clue that would tell him what was going on.

Whoever was in the shack with him lit a cigar. The pungent smell of the tobacco assailed Cole's nostrils. That meant his guard was probably Abner Langdon; Cole had seen Langdon smoking cigars on plenty of occasions.

A few minutes later that guess was confirmed. The door of the shack opened, and Parton's voice said, "I got that robe, boss, just like you said. Is it going to be big enough?"

"It should do just fine," Langdon replied. "Spread it out on the floor."

Cole heard both men moving around, then hands grasped him and rolled him to the side. He let his head loll loosely, mimicking the look of a man who was still out cold. He felt coarse hair underneath him when they stopped rolling him, and another familiar smell surrounded him. They had rolled him onto a thick buffalo robe, the kind that many people used for rugs.

"All right, roll him up in it," Langdon commanded, and part of the smelly robe was thrown over Cole's face. He forced himself to stay still as he was rolled into the buffalo hide. Langdon asked, "Did you bring the wagon around?"

"Sure," Parton replied. "I did that before I got the robe."

"Let's carry him out, then."

Cole heard a pair of grunts as he felt himself being lifted inside the robe. They carried him out of the shack, and as they did Langdon said quietly, "Take him a long way out of town, make sure he's dead, and dump him in a gully somewhere. You can cave in the side to cover him up."

"Sure," Parton agreed. "Don't worry, boss. Nobody'll ever find him."

"Make sure they don't," Langdon said coldly.

An instant later the buffalo-wrapped bundle thudded down in the bed of a wagon. Cole didn't know if the bed was covered or not, but he would have bet that it was. With so many immigrants moving into the area, the sight of a prairie schooner with an arched canvas cover over its bed was a common one. Most folks wouldn't look twice at one like it.

The wagon shifted a little and its springs creaked as Parton climbed to the driver's box and settled himself on the seat. Cole didn't know if the vehicle was being pulled by horses, mules, or oxen, but whatever the draft animals were, they leaned against their harness as Parton snapped a whip and called out to them. The wagon began to roll forward.

Cole knew he couldn't wait much longer to make a move. But hog-tied and wrapped in a buffalo robe as he was, his options were limited. Langdon and Parton had neglected to gag him, so he could call out for help, but if no one heard his shouts immediately, Parton could lean back and pistol-whip him through the robe, shutting him up quickly.

The first chance he got, Cole realized, would likely be his only one. . . .

Billy Casebolt had visited three of the saloons in the east end of town without finding anyone who would admit to seeing Cole Tyler that morning. His next stop was Hank Parker's big tent, next to the permanent building that was being erected to house Parker's establishment. As he stepped inside he spotted the big, bald-headed proprietor standing behind the bar.

"Howdy, Parker," Casebolt said as he strode up to the bar. "You seen the marshal this mornin'?"

"Matter of fact, I have," Parker replied, "He was going over to Langdon's place to have a talk with that thief." Parker snorted contemptuously. "That's like having a talk with a rabid dog. It's not going to do a damned bit of good. Langdon and Sweeney ought to be in jail."

"We got to get around to buildin' us one of those," Casebolt said. "How come you're so het up about Langdon and Sweeney?"

"They stole some of my whiskey. I went to the marshal to complain."

Casebolt nodded. "I reckon Cole'd look into somethin' like that, all right. I'll just go over there and make sure he don't need a hand."

With a wave that drew a surly nod of farewell from Parker, Casebolt left the tent and walked toward another down the street. He would have gotten around to checking at Langdon's place sooner or later, but with Parker's help he had been able to save some time. Of course, Cole might not be there now, Casebolt realized. The marshal could have concluded his business with Abner Langdon and moved on somewhere else.

This was a good starting place, though.

Casebolt hadn't quite reached the entrance to Langdon's tent when a wagon came around the corner of the big canvas structure. Barely glancing at the vehicle, the deputy turned his attention back to the entrance flap of Langdon's saloon. He was about to push it open when he frowned suddenly and straightened, then looked at the wagon again. It was rolling west down Grenville Avenue at a sedate pace, pulled by six mules. Casebolt trotted after it and caught up within fifty yards.

"Hey, hold on there, mister!" he called to the driver. The man cast a glance at him but didn't seem to want to stop. He kept the mules moving until Casebolt drew alongside the box and reached up to grasp the man's arm. The deputy ordered sternly, "Stop that wagon!"

The driver hauled back on the lines and brought the mules to a halt. He licked his lips and asked, "What is it, Deputy? I'm sort of in a hurry."

"You ain't goin' nowhere," Casebolt said. "Didn't you look over this wagon 'fore you started out?" He pointed at the left rear wheel. "You got a cracked hub back there. That wheel'll work loose and fall off 'fore you go five miles. Best take it over to the wagon yard and get it worked on. Won't take too long to replace that hub, and it'll save you a hell of a lot of trouble later."

The driver leaned over, studied the wheel, and nodded. "Yeah, I reckon you're right, Deputy. I'll do that."

"Good thing I noticed," Casebolt said, stepping back from the wagon. He lifted a finger to the brim of his hat in a gesture of farewell.

That was when the muffled shout came from the back of the wagon. "Billy! Back here, Billy!"

Casebolt recognized Cole's voice immediately. That was enough right there to tell him something was wrong, but then the driver cursed bitterly, his face contorting in anger, and reached for the gun on his hip.

He was faster than Casebolt and had his revolver out first. His shot was hurried too much, though, and the bullet went wide of Casebolt to thud into the hard-packed dirt of the street. In the next instant, Casebolt's gun boomed heavily, sending a .36-caliber slug tearing into the driver's chest. The impact of the bullet drove the man backward and sent him slumping over the seat into the bed of the wagon.

Casebolt leaped up to the box with a spryness that belied his years. The driver had dropped his gun when he was hit, but Casebolt kept the Griswold and Gunnison trained on him anyway, just in case he was up to any more mischief. The man was dead, though, his eyes staring sightlessly up at the canvas cover over the back of the wagon. He was lying next to something wrapped in a buffalo robe.

That something was yelling, "Billy! Damn it, what's going on out there?"

Cords had been tied around both ends and the middle of the rolled-up robe. Casebolt holstered his gun and pulled a barlow knife from his pocket. He opened the blade and used it to cut the cords. The bundle fell apart, and Marshal Cole Tyler thrashed his way up out of the folds of the buffalo robe.

"What in blazes was you doin' in there, Marshal?" Casebolt demanded incredulously as he cut the ropes binding Cole's wrists and ankles.

Cole ignored the question and asked one of his own. "Is he dead?"

"Sure enough. I didn't much want to shoot him, but since he was throwin' lead at me —"

"You didn't have any choice," Cole assured him. "Anyway, you saved my life, Billy. Thanks." He quickly rubbed feeling back into his arms and legs, which were obviously cramped from being tied up for a while. "We've got to get back down to Langdon's place."

"Langdon?" Casebolt repeated. "What's he got to do with this?"

Cole jerked a thumb at the dead man.

"That fella worked for him and Sweeney. They've been behind just about all the trouble around here lately. They've been trying to disrupt construction on the UP, and they've damned near succeeded."

Casebolt shook his head as he hopped down from the wagon behind Cole. "Sounds like the whole thing's pure-dee complicated, but if you say Langdon's to blame for it, that's good enough for me. Let's go get him."

Several people had run up to the wagon, drawn by the shots, among them Jeremiah Newton. The blacksmith was holding one of the big hammers he used in his forge. "Are you all right, Brother Tyler?" he asked.

"I will be," Cole replied grimly as he picked up the revolver the dead man had dropped. "You want to come along with Billy and me while we make an arrest, Jeremiah?"

"Some sinner has transgressed and broken the laws of God?"

"And the laws of man, too," Cole said. "Come on."

The three of them went quickly down the street toward Langdon's saloon, trailed by several curious bystanders. When they reached the tent, Cole told the townspeople curtly, "Better stay back. There could be more trouble."

Instead of going through the tent, Cole skirted the big canvas structure. He hoped Langdon was still in the shack out back so that they could confront him where there wouldn't be as many innocent folks around to get in the way of any flying lead.

Cole didn't hesitate when he reached the door of the shack. With Parton's gun clutched in his fist, he lifted his right foot and drove the heel of his high-topped boot against the door. It slammed open, and Cole was inside before the door could strike the wall of the shack. He leveled the gun and let his gaze dart around the room, then uttered a heartfelt "Damn!"

Langdon wasn't there.

Cole wheeled around and snapped, "Into the saloon!" He and Casebolt and Jeremiah headed for the rear entrance.

When Cole jerked the canvas flap aside and stooped to step quickly into the tent, the first thing he saw was Abner Langdon hurrying toward the front opening. Langdon threw a frightened glance over his shoulder, and as he spotted Cole his hand darted under his coat and came out with one of the pistols the marshal had forced him to drop earlier. The little gun cracked wickedly and the bullet hummed past Cole's head to tear a hole in the canvas of the rear wall.

"Everybody down!" Cole shouted, but Langdon's customers hadn't waited for the order. As soon as the shooting broke out, they went diving for cover, upending tables and rolling behind the whiskey barrels that supported the planks of the bar.

Langdon must have found out somehow — probably from someone who had come into the saloon from outside — that the marshal was looking for him. He reached the front entrance and dove through it. Cole had the man in his sights for an instant but held off on the trigger. If he missed, the bullet could hit somebody passing by on the street outside.

Langdon wasn't being as cautious. He triggered another shot as he vanished through the flap. The bullet missed Cole and thudded into one of the overturned tables.

"Circle around!" Cole rapped over his shoulder to Casebolt and Jeremiah. Then he ran straight through the saloon, vaulting over a chair that had gotten upended in the rush to escape the shooting. As he emerged from the front entrance a pistol spat from his right, the bullet again plucking at the canvas as it missed the marshal.

Cole whirled in that direction and saw Langdon stumbling along, running blindly and half turning to fire again. Cole went to one knee as the bullet passed over his head. He steadied the gun he had taken from the wagon, eared back the hammer, and squeezed the trigger. Langdon screamed as the slug bit a hunk of flesh from his right thigh. Cole fired again, and this time the bullet shattered the saloon owner's left knee. Langdon pitched to the ground with a shriek of agony.

Cole came to his feet and ran up to the fallen man. His boot lashed out and caught Langdon's wrist, sending the little pistol spinning away harmlessly. Cole brought his foot down on Langdon's shoulder, pinning him to the ground. He lined up the barrel of the gun with Langdon's twisted face, and for a couple of seconds, as the blood hammered in Cole's head, every nerve in his body cried out for him to put a bullet through the devious son of a bitch's brain.

Then Cole drew a deep, ragged breath and stepped back, although he kept the gun trained on Langdon. Casebolt and Jeremiah pounded up behind him, and the deputy said, "You got him, huh?"

"Damn right," Cole said. "And now he's going to tell us — he's going to tell the whole town — what he's been up to here in Wind River." He shook his head and grinned humorlessly. "You never should have gotten so greedy, Langdon. If you hadn't cheated Hank Parker out of a shipment of whiskey, I might not have ever tumbled to your real operation."

Langdon just groaned in pain from his wounds. Somehow, Cole couldn't bring himself to feel too sorry for the man.

Not when there was a whole troop of cavalry out there somewhere riding into an ambush. . . .

19

Major Thomas Burdette reined in with his left hand and raised his right in the signal to halt. His sergeant bellowed out the order, and the troop of cavalry came to a crisp stop. Burdette saw that as he glanced over his shoulder and felt pride swell his chest. Even out here in the middle of all this desolation, his men were disciplined and well trained. They were living examples of his skills as an officer and a leader of men.

Those skills would be appreciated even more by his superiors, Burdette thought, if someone would have the good sense to assign him to a more suitable task — such as tracking down and routing the Sioux who were making life miserable for both settlers and the railroad back in the eastern half of Wyoming Territory.

But that was a task for another day, Burdette told himself. For now, his duty was to find out who was responsible for the attacks in this part of the territory, and he intended to fulfill his mission. Of course, when he did run the culprits to ground, they would probably turn out to be only a ragtag band of Shoshone.

Any engagement, however, no matter how one-sided, would help advance his career. Thomas Burdette knew how to take his victories where he found them, he thought smugly.

"We'll stop here to rest the men and the horses, Sergeant," he told the noncom. "Thirty minutes, no more."

"Yes, sir!"

The sergeant called the order to dismount and fall out, and the troopers began complying gratefully. Burdette swung down from his own saddle and looked around.

The troop had stopped for nooning in a grassy swale between two small hills. A tiny stream, barely three inches wide, trickled through the middle of the depression. Following the sergeant's orders, the troopers held their horses back to keep the animals from trampling the creek and ruining it. The men took turns filling their hats from the stream and letting their mounts drink from the headgear. Canteens were also refilled. The men broke out their rations — hardtack, jerky, and dried beans — and began eating their meager meal.

Burdette took off his hat and used his yellow bandanna to mop sweat and dust from his face. Although he was still optimistic, he was also becoming more and more frustrated. The troop was quartering through the same general area where the tracks of Sawyer's stolen stock had been lost a couple of days earlier, and Burdette had hoped they would pick up the trail again before now. Obviously, he was just going to have to be patient.

Either that, or proceed directly to the Shoshone camp and wipe out the vermin who were no doubt responsible for the continuing atrocities in the area around Wind River. Perhaps there was no real proof of their guilt, but Burdette knew Sawyer would thank him, the Union Pacific would thank him, and his superiors would have no choice but to admire his initiative. He was convinced that the redskins were to blame for the trouble.

And besides, they were only Indians. It wasn't like they had any rights to be considered, Burdette mused. . . .

He was still trying to talk himself into the idea a moment later when a bullet ripped through his hat and jerked it off his head.

Burdette heard the crack of the rifle at the

same instant as his bullet-torn hat went sailing through the air. With an incoherent cry, he flung himself forward instinctively, landing so hard on the ground that the breath was knocked out of his lungs. As he lay there on the grass gasping for air, more shots blasted the still Wyoming air. Men screamed in pain as bullets ripped through muscle and bone.

"Up there!" the sergeant shouted. His sidearm was out and began cracking as he returned the fire.

Burdette twisted his head and looked in the direction the noncom was shooting. Puffs of smoke drifted up from the hill to the south. Ambushers must have crept up on the far side of the slope, Burdette reasoned, then opened fire on his unsuspecting men. A cowardly tactic, but an effective one. Thinking about strategy helped Burdette force into the back of his mind the panic he felt welling up inside him.

More of his men were fighting back now, going down on one knee and forming a rough skirmish line. The Springfields they carried began to crash as they returned the fire. Burdette saw four men lying on the ground, three of them still moving, the other motionless in the limp sprawl of death. Sickness clogged the major's throat as he saw the bloody mess where half of the dead trooper's face had been shot away.

This was not the first time Burdette had been under fire. He had seen some limited action four years earlier, during the waning days of the Civil War. That had been entirely different from this, however. Then everything had been out in the open, two opposing forces moving straight toward each other across a field. For some reason, this ambush was even more frightening. Burdette supposed that was because he couldn't see the enemy this time; the only evidence of the men trying to kill him was the haze of powder smoke hanging over the ridge to the south.

Burdette twisted around on the ground, staying low, and reached for the flap of his holster. He fumbled it open and grasped the butt of his revolver. As he drew out the weapon he realized that none of the shots from the ambushers had come close to him since that first one, the one that had knocked his hat off. Maybe they thought that shot had killed him. Maybe if he joined the fight, they would realize their mistake and concentrate their fire on him until he was nothing but a pile of bloody ribbons. It might be better if he simply lay there and was as still as possible.

He couldn't do that, and he knew it. His hand trembling only a little, he lifted the pistol, pulled back the hammer, and fired toward the top of the hill. It was impossible to tell if he had hit anything or not, but he didn't let that deter him. He cocked the gun and squeezed off another shot, then another. The blood was surging through his veins now as he found himself caught up in the battle.

"Hold your fire!" the sergeant shouted a moment later. Burdette growled a curse as the gunshots died away. He would have to have a talk with the noncom. *He* was the one who should have issued the order to cease firing. After all, he was in command of this troop.

Then he realized what had prompted the sergeant's order. When the soldiers stopped shooting, silence fell over the valley. The ambushers had given up the attack. Either that, or they were trying to lure the troopers into doing something foolhardy.

A moment later Burdette heard hoofbeats, a lot of hoofbeats. Quite a few men, a dozen or more, were riding away in a hurry. Galloping, in fact, like they were being pursued by demons out of hell. "They've fallen back!" he called excitedly. "We've got them on the run!"

Burdette sprang to his feet, too late remembering that this could be a trap. Nothing happened, though, as he turned to his men and shouted, "Mount up! We're going after them!"

No one argued with the order. Members of the troop had been wounded, and at least one had been killed. There had to be retribution. The soldiers leaped to their mounts and pulled themselves up into the saddles. Burdette left his hat where it had fallen and raced to his own horse. This was why he had joined the cavalry, he realized as he practically leaped onto the back of the animal. He was about to lead a charge that would utterly destroy the enemy, and he had forgotten all about the fear that had plagued him only moments earlier.

This was war, even though on a small scale, and Burdette gloried in it.

He led his men out of the swale and around the hill to the south. They were howling for blood as they rode, and Burdette had never been more proud of them. Those damned Shoshone would rue the day they had attacked the United States Cavalry, he vowed.

There was the dust cloud of the fleeing attackers up ahead. Through the haze, Burdette could see only that they were dressed in buckskins and brandishing rifles. He was confident, though, that the ambushers had been Shoshone.

And he intended to catch them if he had to chase them to the ends of the earth.

Cole leaned forward over the neck of the golden sorrel Ulysses. The horse was stretching its legs in a ground-eating gallop, trailed by Billy Casebolt's pinto. Both lawmen were urging all the speed possible out of their mounts as they rode straight toward the location of the Shoshone village. Cole hoped Two Ponies and his people hadn't moved their camp since Casebolt's visit there a few days earlier.

They had left Abner Langdon back in Wind River, being tended to by Dr. Kent while Jeremiah stood guard. The crooked saloon owner had spilled the whole story, unable in his pain even to think about lying. Cole's guess about the Central Pacific being behind all the trouble Langdon and Sweeney had caused was correct, although Langdon insisted that the Big Four knew nothing of the lengths to which he and his cohort had gone to delay construction of the Union Pacific. Cole wasn't convinced that the financiers wouldn't have condoned murder if they had known about it, but that didn't really matter either way.

What was important was reaching the Shoshone camp in time to prevent the final step in the plan from being realized.

By the end of this day an Indian war would have been averted — or it would be in full, bloody sway, sweeping over the Territory.

Cole's hat hung by its chin strap, bouncing against his back as he rode. The wind of his passage caught his thick brown hair and blew it out behind him. His own gun was back in its holster on his hip, having been retrieved from Langdon's shack. The sun was high overhead, and he glanced at it now.

A little after noon. Probably too late to stop the ambush on Major Burdette's patrol. But the plan called for the bushwhackers to withdraw after inflicting a little damage and then lead the cavalry back to the Shoshone camp before slipping away. Caught up in the heat of pursuit, Burdette and his men would sweep down on the peaceful village and massacre its inhabitants. But word of the atrocity would spread, and all the other tribes in the territory would rise in anger to avenge their fallen brothers. If, by some chance, the Shoshones were able to fight off the attack, and destroyed the cavalry troop instead, the army would immediately move to send more soldiers and would launch a massive campaign of reprisal. Either way, work on the Union Pacific would be effectively delayed for months.

It was a cunning scheme. Cole just prayed there was still time to put a stop to it.

His eyes scanned the horizon as he rode, and after a while he spotted some dust rising to the northwest. Reining in, he pulled Ulysses to a stop and lifted an arm to point toward the dust as Casebolt rode up alongside him.

"What do you think?" Cole asked.

The deputy squinted into the distance, adding even more wrinkles to his leathery face. "Could be them, I reckon," he said after a moment. "Looks like there's two bunches."

"That's what I thought," Cole agreed. "Sweeney and the rest of those hard cases pretending to be Shoshones are in front, and Burdette and his men are chasing 'em."

"We're still about three miles from Two Ponies' camp," Casebolt said worriedly. "Goin' to be close, Marshal."

"Then we'd better not waste any more time." Cole heeled the sorrel into a run again.

Even that brief respite had allowed the horses some rest, and they seemed stronger as they launched into a gallop once more. Still, the distance dragged by with agonizing slowness. Finally, several minutes later, Cole and Casebolt rounded a rugged-looking shoulder of rock and saw the Shoshone tepees along the cottonwood-lined banks of a small creek. Everything appeared to be peaceful.

But those columns of dust were closer now, and as Cole reined in again he could faintly hear the popping of gunfire in the distance.

"That's them," he snapped. "No doubt about it now."

"What are we goin' to do?" Casebolt asked.

Cole's lips pulled back in a savage expression that was half grin, half grimace. "Give Sweeney one hell of a surprise," he said. With that, he rode down toward the Shoshone village, Casebolt following closely behind him.

The Indians heard them coming, and so did the dogs. Several curs came bounding out from the scattering of tepees, snarling and barking. Men emerged from the conical shelters, all of them armed with rifles, lances, or bows and arrows. They shooed the women and children inside the tepees in case an enemy was attacking.

336

It quickly became obvious that the two white men riding hurriedly into the camp were friends, though. Cole had a palm lifted in the universal gesture of peace, and Casebolt was well known to these people. A tall, well-built warrior with graying dark hair stepped forward and greeted the two lawmen as they drew their winded horses to a halt. "Billy Casebolt!" said Two Ponies. "We did not expect to see you again so soon, but you and your friend are welcome."

Without dismounting, Casebolt said, "We may not be once you hear what me and Cole got to tell you, Two Ponies. By the way, this here's my boss, Marshal Tyler from Wind River."

"Howdy, Two Ponies," Cole said. "I'm afraid there's trouble on the way." He knew he was dispensing with the formality that the Indians loved so well, but there was just no time for it today.

Two Ponies must have sensed the seriousness of the situation, because he frowned and asked, "What is this trouble?"

Cole hipped around in the saddle and pointed. "See that dust? A bunch of white renegades attacked a cavalry patrol a little while ago, and now they're leading those soldiers right toward your village here. They'll duck off out of sight at the last

337

minute so that the soldiers will think your people are to blame for the ambush."

Two Ponies stiffened. "There will be much fighting," he declared. "Many of my people and many of the white soldiers will die."

"That's just what those skunks want," Cole said. "We've got to stop 'em."

"The Shoshone will do anything they can to help prevent this."

Casebolt added, "You got any ideas, Marshal?"

"Maybe one," Cole said slowly. "There's only one way to convince Burdette that the Shoshones are innocent, and that's to show him who the real killers are. He'll have to see it all at once to believe it." He looked intently at Two Ponies. "Have your men get their horses ready. We have to meet that charge before it ever gets here."

Two Ponies nodded curtly, understanding what Cole had in mind. He began shouting orders to his assembled warriors in his native tongue, and within a matter of minutes the Shoshones were swinging up onto the backs of their ponies. Cole glanced at the dust in the air. It was even closer now, right on the other side of a gap in the hills to the north. Cole guessed that Sweeney and his men would lead the cavalry through that gap, then swing off to the west, down a narrow canyon and out of sight.

Cole, Casebolt, and the Shoshones had to plug that gap before Sweeney and the others could get there.

With Cole and Two Ponies in the lead, the riders swarmed out of the village, leaving behind the old men and boys to protect the women and children. They wouldn't be able to put up much of a defense, but with any luck, they wouldn't need to.

The slope leading up to the gap in the hills was a gradual one. Cole and the others swept up it, and even over the hoofbeats of their own mounts, the marshal could hear horses approaching at a gallop on the far side of the opening. He reached it first, followed closely by Two Ponies, Casebolt, and the other Shoshone warriors. As Cole hauled Ulysses to a halt he saw the scene spreading out in front of him just as he had thought it would.

Close to the gap, only about a hundred yards away, rode some two dozen men in buckskins similar to those the Indians wore. Clothes didn't make a man a Shoshone, though, and as the riders turned startled faces toward the group waiting for them in the pass, Cole could tell they were all white.

A quarter of a mile behind the renegades came the cavalry, the soldiers yelling and throwing an occasional futile shot toward their quarry. A shallow valley led up to the gap in the hills on this side, funneling both groups toward the opening.

The opening that was blocked by Cole and his friends.

He slid his Winchester '66 from the saddle boot and lifted it to his shoulder, working the lever and jacking a shell into the chamber as he did so. When he pressed the trigger, the rifle boomed and bucked against his shoulder, and the slug plowed up dirt and threw grit in the air some ten yards in front of Sweeney's bunch. The men in the lead reined up desperately as Cole levered the rifle and fired again. Beside him, Casebolt was doing the same thing, peppering the ground in front of the renegades with rifle slugs. Two Ponies and the warriors with him who were armed with rifles added to the fire, although many of the Shoshones' weapons were single-shot carbines. Still, they were able to lay down a barrage effectively enough to make Sweeney and the other hard cases come to a sliding, skidding stop.

"I'll drop the next man who moves!" Cole shouted down at them, and his voice was cold and hard enough to convince them that he meant every word of it. The riders milled around in confusion as the cavalry swept up behind them. Suddenly one man broke away from the pack and raced his mount up the slope toward the ridge that turned into the shoulder of rock protecting the Shoshone village from the north winds. Cole sent a shot after him, but the slug just kicked up dust at the horse's feet.

"Sweeney!" Cole exclaimed. "Got to be! I'm going after him, Billy. Ride down there and tell Burdette what's going on."

"Be careful, Cole!" Casebolt called after him as he sent Ulysses dashing up and along the ridgeline.

Cole threw a glance over his left shoulder and saw the cavalry surrounding the other riders. Two Ponies and his men were staying up in the pass, which was wise until Burdette got straightened out about what was going on, while Casebolt rode hurriedly toward the soldiers to do the necessary explaining. Cole was a little surprised that the troopers hadn't just opened up on the renegades and cut them down when they had the chance, but he was glad reason appeared to be prevailing.

There had been enough killing already.

Sweeney had almost reached the top of the ridge. Cole was close enough now to recognize the broad, florid face of the Irishman as Sweeney cast an angry hate-filled look at him. The man brought up a pistol and blazed away with a couple of shots, but the bullets sailed far wide of Cole. He thought about pulling Ulysses to a halt and blowing Sweeney out of the saddle with the Winchester, but somehow that seemed too quick and impersonal. Sweeney and his boss back in Wind River had made life miserable for Cole, had been responsible for the deaths of over a dozen people, and had come too damned close to starting a conflict that would have killed hundreds, maybe thousands, before grinding to its inevitable end.

No, a rifle bullet was too good for Bert Sweeney, Cole decided. He jammed the Winchester back into the boot and sent Ulysses surging forward along the ridge.

Sweeney fired again, this time when Cole was only ten feet away. Cole ducked as the bullet whipped over his head. Ulysses closed the distance with one long, lunging stride, and the sorrel's shoulder crashed into the flank of the horse Sweeney was riding as both animals came together at the top of the ridge. Cole left the saddle in a dive and slammed into Sweeney. With an incoherent yell, Sweeney was driven off his horse by the impact. Both men fell heavily and rolled down the ridge as they landed.

It was like getting punched all at once by a dozen different fists, Cole thought crazily as he bounced down the slope. He had hold of the buckskin tunic Sweeney wore in his masquerade as a Shoshone, and he didn't let go. They traded positions as they rolled — first Cole was on top, then Sweeney, then Cole again. They finally came to a stop with a numbing crash against one of the boulders that dotted the slope. Cole found himself on the bottom. Sweeney screamed curses at him and tried to smash his clubbed fists into Cole's face.

Cole twisted his head to the side, then arched his back and threw Sweeney off him. He was after Sweeney before the Irishman even hit the ground again. Cole drove a knee into Sweeney's groin, then planted his other knee in the man's stomach. His fist crashed into Sweeney's jaw, rocking his head to the side.

Cole swung again and again, punch after looping punch that jerked Sweeney's head back and forth, battering the man until his features were almost unrecognizable. For a change, though, Cole hadn't lost control during the heat of battle. The red, killing haze that sometimes descended over him at such times was not there now. Instead, the punishment he handed out to Sweeney was brutal but cold, the sort of punishment a man needed who valued money so highly over human pain and suffering, over human life itself. . . .

When he was satisfied that Sweeney was out cold, Cole pushed himself to his feet and stumbled back a couple of steps. He wiped the back of his hand across his mouth and panted for breath.

"My God, did you kill him?"

The question came from Major Burdette, who had ridden up nearby along with Casebolt. The officer was staring at the bloody, battered face of Bert Sweeney.

"He's not dead," Cole said harshly. "Not yet, anyway. He's liable to end up on a gallows when this is all over, but that'll be the law's doing, not mine." He looked up at Burdette. "Did Billy explain everything to you?"

"Yes, Deputy Casebolt told me what you've discovered, Marshal," Burdette said stiffly. "I'm still not certain I believe all of it, but faced with the evidence of my own eyes . . . well, those certainly *aren't* Shoshone my men and I have been pursuing ever since they attacked us. But as you suspected, they're riding unshod horses and wearing moccasins."

"So's this one," Cole said, prodding one of Sweeney's moccasin-shod feet with his boot. "His boss is under arrest back in Wind River. We've got plenty of witnesses to his confession. There never were any Indian raids. Langdon and Sweeney and the men they hired were to blame for all of it."

"Yes, well, I'm sure we'll get it all sorted out." Burdette glanced nervously toward the gap in the hills, where Two Ponies and his warriors still waited patiently. "You're certain those savages represent no threat to us?"

"Not as long as you don't threaten them," Cole said.

Casebolt suggested, "I'll ride back up there and tell Two Ponies that him and his folks can go on back home now. The cavalry won't be botherin' 'em . . . will they, Major?"

"No," Burdette said, a little reluctantly. "Please convey my appreciation for their help to those Indians, will you, Deputy?"

Casebolt grinned. "Sure, Major." He looked at Cole. "Can you get back to town all right, Marshal?"

"Don't worry about me," Cole told him. "I reckon the major's men can handle the prisoners."

"Be seein' you, then," Casebolt said. He

flicked a finger at the brim of his hat as he turned to ride back to the Shoshones.

Still sitting stiffly on his horse, Major Burdette said to Cole, "I suppose all the credit for clearing up this situation will go to you, Marshal Tyler."

Cole gathered up Ulysses's reins. "I don't give a damn about who gets the credit, Major," he said as he stepped up into the saddle. "I just didn't want a bunch of innocent folks, red and white alike, getting killed in a war that didn't make any sense." He jerked a thumb at Sweeney's senseless form. "If you'll bring that bastard along, I'd appreciate it. I'm going home."

He turned the sorrel's head toward Wind River.

20

"A son?" Michael Hatfield repeated in hushed tones as he stared wide-eyed at Dr. Judson Kent. "I have a son?"

"That's right," Kent assured him. "Mother and child are both doing exceedingly well, and you can go in and see them in just a few moments."

Billy Casebolt slapped Michael on the back. "Well, congratulations, boy! You ought to be mighty proud."

"I . . . I am," Michael said, still sounding stunned.

Cole shook Michael's hand, although the young journalist didn't seem to notice. "Congratulations," he said. "I reckon you've got something else to write about in that paper of yours, Michael. Wind River's got a brand-new citizen this morning!"

Two and a half weeks had passed since the catastrophe at the Shoshone camp had been narrowly averted. Since that time,

Abner Langdon, Bert Sweeney, and the men who had been working for them had all been taken to Laramie to stand trial for their activities. Cole suspected that each and every one of them would wind up dangling from a rope, and that was all right with him.

Also during that time, word that the so-called gold strike was a phony had reached the mountains, and men who had already been disappointed by their lack of success had given up entirely and come back to Wind River. Once they heard how Langdon and Sweeney had orchestrated all the trouble, including the rumors about Chinese coolies taking over their jobs on the Union Pacific, the workers were a lot more inclined to listen to the promises of General Grenville Dodge and Jack Casement. The short-lived railroad strike was over, and all the crews were back at work. The Thunder Wagon, as the Shoshones called it, was rolling once again. The new railhead was scheduled to be at Rock Springs, and Cole was ready to see it move along. Things would be a mite more peaceful here in Wind River once the hell-on-wheels had rolled on downtrack.

He and Casebolt had been taking a turn around town this morning when they had seen Michael Hatfield sitting on the front porch of his house along with Jeremiah Newton. Both men had looked sober and concerned, and Cole had naturally paused to ask them what was wrong. Nothing was wrong, it turned out. But Delia Hatfield's time had come, and Dr. Kent was inside the house delivering the baby.

A few minutes earlier they had all heard the thin, wailing cry from inside, and Michael had shot to his feet. Jeremiah had been forced to hang on to him to keep him from rushing inside. "Wait for the doctor," the big blacksmith had advised.

Moments ago Kent had emerged from the house, smiled broadly, and given the proud father the good news. Now the doctor rolled down his sleeves and said to Michael, "I'll just see how they're doing, and then you can come in. Can you wait a few moments longer?"

"I . . . Sure, Doctor. I can wait. But not too long."

"Not too long," Kent promised.

When the doctor had gone back inside, Michael turned to Cole and said, "I liked that, what you said a minute ago. About Wind River having a brand-new citizen, I mean."

"Town's growing," Cole said. "I reckon it's going to be a mighty fine place."

"Are you going to stay here? I remember you said when you took the job you were only doing it temporarily."

Casebolt frowned. "Yeah, that's right. You ain't goin' to leave now that things are startin' to settle down a mite, are you, Marshal?"

Cole looked at Casebolt and Michael and Jeremiah, thought about Simone McKay and Judson Kent and Rose Foster, the Paines and Stan down at the railroad depot, and all the others he had come to know in the months he had spent in this settlement. Good folks, most of 'em. True, there were a few horses' rumps around — Kermit Sawyer and Hank Parker sprang to mind — but there was always a little bad mixed with the good.

He had taken the job reluctantly, Cole remembered, and he had fully intended to ride out of Wind River as soon as he got the chance. But now . . .

He smiled and said, "I reckon I'll be around for a while."

ABOUT THE AUTHOR

James Reasoner lives in Azle, Texas.